Summer's Promise

HARVEST OF HOPE SERIES

HARVEST OF HOPE SERIES

Seeds of Hope
Buried Secrets
Summer's Promise

Summer's Promise

HARVEST OF HOPE SERIES

Barbara Cameron

GILEAD
PUBLISHING
Grand Rapids, Michigan

Summer's Promise: Book #3 in the Harvest of Hope series
Copyright © 2019 by Barbara Cameron

 **GILEAD** PUBLISHING

Published by Gilead Publishing,
Grand Rapids, Michigan
www.gileadpublishing.com

ISBN: 978-1-68370-059-3

Printed in the United States of America
19 20 21 22 23 24 25 / 5 4 3 2 1

*Dedicated to
my readers.
Thank you for your
continued support!*

One

She rose before dawn, donning her favorite workday dress and brushing and pinning her long hair into its usual severe bun. No *kapp* today. Instead she tied a kerchief over her hair and started downstairs.

Pale pink fingers of light crept into the kitchen window as she filled the percolator and set it on the stove. She watched the light as she laid slices of bacon into the cast-iron skillet, turned up the gas flame under it, then went to the breadbox for cinnamon rolls she'd baked the day before. Soon the kitchen was filled with sunlight, the burbling sound of coffee perking, and the scents of sizzling bacon and the cinnamon rolls warming in the oven. Her *dat* and *bruders*, who'd been working out in the barn, would be coming in soon, eager for a hot breakfast.

She set the big wooden table for six and wished that her heart didn't still hurt whenever she looked at the chair her *mudder* had sat in for so many years and would no longer occupy. Filling the little china cream pitcher painted with blue flowers, folding cloth napkins at each place, and cooking her *mudder's* recipes were ways of remembering her *mudder*. The men might not care about such touches, but she did.

She wanted to help in the barn but the men had outvoted her. None of them wanted to eat their own cooking, and with Mamm gone, now she was the only female. But when spring came . . . then they'd want her help doing the planting. She'd be in her element and it wouldn't matter that she was a woman. Although men and women had traditional roles, everyone pitched in as needed whether it was planting, harvesting, or caring for the livestock.

A loud buzzing jarred Summer, waking her from the idyllic dream of her puttering in an Amish farm kitchen. She reached out and slapped the alarm clock, hitting the snooze button without opening her eyes.

Five minutes later the alarm rang again and then Louis Armstrong began singing about what a wonderful world it was in his heartfelt, scratchy baritone.

"Mornings are not wonderful," she muttered.

She blinked and stared up at the skylight in the ceiling of her bedroom. She'd had that dream again—the one where she was Amish and cooking breakfast for the family. She hadn't had it for months now.

Yawning, she sat up but didn't move from her bed. Mornings had to be approached cautiously. Especially when you had to get up as dawn was breaking when you thought work hours should start oh, around noonish.

She chuckled. Well, she seriously didn't have to have work hours starting at noon, but it would be nice if she didn't have to show up at eight in the morning for her part-time job. A hot shower helped her feel more human. She dressed in her usual Oxford cotton shirt, slacks, and linen blazer. As she brushed her blonde, almost waist-length hair, she thought about putting it in a braid. To save time she wrapped a scrunchie around it at her nape and headed downstairs.

The scent of coffee and bacon drifted up the stairs as she descended them. Her mother, Marie, stood at the stove. Mother. She still had one when the poor young woman in her dream didn't . . .

"*Guder mariye, Mamm.*" Then she blinked. "I mean, good morning."

"Had that dream again, hmm?" Her mother patted Summer's cheek. "My little Amish *maedel.* You've been having dreams of being Amish since you were a little girl."

Summer gave a self-deprecating laugh. "Yeah, I know. And as usual I need coffee before I say my first words. I stayed up too late last night studying for a test."

"I always wondered why you had those dreams," her mother mused. "Maybe because your dad worked with the Amish and their life appealed to you."

"Maybe." She kissed her mother's cheek before turning to the automatic coffee maker she'd bought her mother for Christmas last year. For some reason her mother had resisted the new ones, insisting her old-fashioned percolator was just fine. "Why aren't you sleeping in? You're retired."

Marie smiled. "Habit. As I get older I find I need less sleep. And I want you to have a good breakfast to start your day."

"Mom, I'm twenty-four. I can make my own breakfast. I can cook."

"Like I said, I want you to have a good breakfast."

Summer stuck her tongue out at her mother and chuckled as her mother grabbed a dish towel and swatted at her. "Sit your impertinent self down. Breakfast is ready."

Summer inhaled the scent of the bacon, eggs, and toast set before her. Mornings were definitely more bearable with bacon.

Marie joined her at the table with a cup of coffee.

"Aren't you eating?"

"I'll have some toast in a bit. I'm not hungry."

Summer frowned. It seemed her mother ate less these days. Maybe it was time to talk to Doc Turner again.

Pleasantly full, Summer stood and put her plate and mug in the sink. "I won't be home until around ten tonight. Class."

"I know. I packed your lunch. There's enough in there to have something to eat before class too." Marie handed the insulated tote to her.

"Mom, you didn't have to."

Marie kissed her cheek. "I know. I enjoy doing things for you."

"Well, do something fun today." She stopped, then couldn't resist. "Maybe my laundry."

Her mother just chuckled. "No. You have fun today too."

She picked up her purse and walked over to the hook by the door. Her keys weren't there. Frowning, she began rummaging in her purse. Wallet, checkbook, cell phone. No keys.

She dug around in her purse some more. "Have you seen my keys?"

"No. You sure you didn't leave them in your car?"

"Never." The next ten minutes were spent in a fruitless search. Just as she was beginning to think she'd have to call a friend for a ride, her mother gave a cry.

"Look, your keys are in the refrigerator!"

Summer stared. "What on earth are they doing there?"

Marie handed them to her. "You have a lot on your mind with work and school. Better hurry, you don't want to be late. Here, don't forget your lunch."

Mumbling to herself, Summer rushed out to her car. As she put the key in the ignition, she went back over the events of the evening before. Sure, she'd come home overtired from a long day at work and then grocery shopping, but she didn't think she'd have done something like put her keys in the refrigerator.

As she paused at the end of the driveway, Summer saw an electric company truck approaching. She put the car in park, pulled out her cell phone, and checked her bank account. The keys in the refrigerator incident had caused her to doubt her memory. Then she breathed a sigh of relief. She hadn't forgotten to pay the electric bill. Relieved, she tucked her phone back in her purse.

A huge yawn overtook her as she put the car in drive and waited for a break in traffic. Two classes—one on Tuesday and Thursday nights on campus, one online—on top of a job was too much. She couldn't wait for the classes to be over.

Traffic was heavy this morning, a combination of locals driving to work and tourists already out and about ogling the Amish countryside. Paradise in Lancaster County, Pennsylvania, was a popular tourist destination, not just a fertile farming community. She got a break and pulled out. As she passed the fields surrounding their family farmhouse, she waved at Carl, the tenant farmer who continued to work for them, and he waved back.

She reached to turn on the radio for some music on her morning drive before she remembered that it had quit the week before when her battery died. Somewhere she had the security code to make the radio start again, but she hadn't had time to look for it.

Shrugging, she put her hand back on the steering wheel. "Hi ho, hi ho," she sang to kill the silence in the car.

Standing at the edge of his fields, Abram Yoder watched a battered-looking sedan pull up in his drive. A young woman got out and swung a leather bag over her shoulder. She walked over to him. She was tall and her strides were long and easy, her manner purposeful, not short and swaying like so many women calling attention to their womanliness.

"Can I help you?" he asked politely, wondering if she was a tourist looking for directions or some chatter about his community. He'd do what he could to hurry her along. He wasn't part of a tour—would never be if he could help it—and had a long day in the fields ahead of him.

"*Guder mariye.* I'm Summer Carson. We spoke on the phone yesterday." She smiled and held out her hand.

Abram took her hand, shook it, and found it was firm, not limp like that of so many women. *Allrecht*, that wasn't fair. Some men had a limp handshake too—mostly *Englisch* men. Her gaze was direct, her big blue eyes meeting his before scanning the fields.

Then she bent and dug her hand in the soil, feeling its texture, sniffing it. "Good soil."

Something stirred in him, a memory that flitted into his mind and was gone too quickly to identify. Those big blue eyes . . . "Thank you for coming by."

"Happy to do whatever I can to help you," she said briskly.

He led her to the field where the corn crop had been a little disappointing at last harvest. A glance at her boots told him he didn't need to warn her that her shoes would get dirty. She knelt, dug her hands in the soil again, sniffed it, and then set about taking some vials and sample bags from her leather satchel. As she worked, she peppered him with questions. Was he still doing organic farming? How often had he irrigated? Once she'd labeled the soil and water samples, she pulled out a notebook and made some notes in it.

Abram found himself staring at her, watching the way the breeze lifted strands of hair the color of ripening wheat and tossing them around. "I remember you."

She looked up, shielding her eyes against the sun. "Excuse me?"

"As a kid, I mean. You used to come here with your father on days you weren't in school. You wore overalls and always had your hair in pigtails."

"Grubby overalls and lopsided pigtails," she said, chuckling. "My mother despaired of me."

"You always looked like you enjoyed helping your father. Followed in his footsteps, eh?"

She smiled. "Yeah. You did too."

He nodded. "Took over the farm last year when he and *Mamm* went to Pinecraft for winter vacation and they didn't want to come back to the snow."

"I can imagine." She straightened and tucked her notebook back in the big leather tote she carried.

"I'm sorry for your loss."

Pain flashed across her face. "It was so kind of you and the many people from the Amish community to come to his funeral. It meant a lot to my mom and me."

"Howard Carson helped a lot of us through the years. Some of the older Amish weren't so sure an *Englisch* government worker had anything to offer them since they'd been farmers for years. But Howard showed them that he cared about our farms prospering, and he had a way of convincing them."

She beamed, her face glowing at his words, and made him think how apt her name was. "Thank you for saying that. You're very kind."

"It's not being kind to tell the truth." He shifted, uncomfortable with being thanked for doing no more than saying what so many felt. "How is your mother doing?"

"Better, I think."

Abram didn't have to ask if they'd been able to keep their small family farm. He'd often seen Carl, the man who had helped Summer's father before he died, continuing to work the fields.

"You're welcome to step into the kitchen and wash your hands."

"Thanks, but I'm fine." She dug into her bag for the moist towelettes she kept in it and couldn't find them. "Well, it seems I've run out of the wipes I carry. Do you mind if I use the hose there?"

"If you'd rather do so than go into the kitchen."

"No need." She turned on the hose and rinsed off her hands.

He walked with her to the car and watched her blush when the back door screeched loudly when she opened it.

"Needs some oiling when I get a minute," she said as she got into the driver's seat.

"If you can wait, I'd be happy to get some WD-40 from the barn," he told her.

"Thanks, but I need to get into the office. I'll let you know as soon as we get the samples tested."

He nodded and frowned when she turned the ignition key and nothing happened.

"Not now, not now," she muttered as she turned the key again. This time the engine started, and she let out a sigh of relief. "Have a good day!"

"You too." As she drove off, her muffler rattling noisily, Abram reflected that so far her morning had not started off so well.

He knew some Amish who wanted an automobile. Driving a buggy wasn't always ideal. Horses got sick, and they and the buggies weren't suited to long distances. And automobiles were certainly physically more comfortable. But it seemed to him that if you didn't have the money to have a new automobile and had to drive something like Summer's, it wasn't very dependable transportation.

He looked down and saw a piece of muffler lying at his feet. Glancing up, he waved, thinking to call her back for it, but she had driven out of sight.

The rattling of the muffler faded and Abram turned at the sound of a buggy approaching. It pulled into his driveway. He walked over to greet his visitor.

Mark Byler sat there, looking pale, his knuckles white on the reins.

"You *allrecht?*"

"I had no idea. No idea at all," he muttered.

"Pardon?"

"Car after car passed me on the way here," he said, shuddering. "It was harrowing."

"*Kumm*, I'll fix you some coffee."

"I'm not sure my legs are steady enough to walk yet." He got out, tested them, and walked with Abram into the house. "I think learning how to drive a buggy in traffic may well be the hardest part of becoming Amish," he confided. "Well, that and keeping a civil tongue."

"No one expects us to be saints."

"Not even the bishop?"

Abram grinned. "*Nee*, not even him." He opened the door and waved him inside. "What have you done?"

"I yelled a few things at one of the drivers." He sat heavily in a chair at the table. "Thanks—*danki*," he corrected himself when Abram set a cup of coffee before him.

He poured himself a cup of coffee and sat. "You're doing very well, Mark. You need to give yourself credit. It's harder than people think to convert to being Amish."

"I know." He ran a hand over his face and sighed. "I knew it might not be easy. But I'd spent so many summers here, I thought I knew what it would be like. But it's not until you actually do it every day that the reality hits." Mark looked up. "I'm not sorry. I'll never be sorry. But I hope Miriam doesn't feel she made a mistake marrying me."

"I've never seen her so happy. She loves you."

"I'll have to tell her what I said this afternoon in case it gets back to the bishop."

"I'm sure it wasn't as bad as you're making it sound."

Mark chuckled. "I'm not going to sully your ears by repeating what I said."

"Afraid I'll faint?" Abram chuckled. "You think none of us have said something similar in private?"

"If you say so. I've never heard my grandfather curse."

"I'm *schur* he wouldn't say anything in front of you. And I'm not saying he ever said anything we shouldn't in private or public. But circumstances are different, Mark. I'd think it's hard to think and speak one way as an *Englischer* for years and change it completely."

Mark nodded. "It would have been harder if my grandfather hadn't taught me the language when I spent summers here."

"Kids pick it up quick. My visitor just now? She used to come with her father when he visited as an extension agent and she could rattle off Pennsylvania *Deitsch* like an Amish *kind*." She'd greeted him in it when she'd arrived.

"So, you said you had some papers you wanted me to draw up for you." Mark pulled them from the folder and set them before Abram. "These transfer the deed on the farm from your parents to you. All you have to do is send them to your parents in Pinecraft, have them sign before a notary and then return them to you. Once you get the papers back, I'll tell you how to file them with the courthouse. I can go with you if you want. I can't represent you legally since I'm no longer a practicing attorney, but there's no need for that anyway."

"You don't miss your work as an *Englisch* attorney?"

"No, I like taking care of my grandfather's farm."

"It's yours now," Abram reminded him.

"So it is. My grandfather and I signed papers just like this not so long ago. And when someone in the community needs my legal advice I'm happy to help them. Just as they help me with farming matters I don't know."

"Summer was taking some samples of the soil and water in one of my fields. Many of us in the community have used the services of the office."

"I only caught a glimpse of her when she got in her car, but she didn't look old enough for such work."

"She's a couple years younger than me. I hadn't seen her in a few years."

"And?"

"And what?"

Mark grinned. "You were staring off after her when I pulled up. Interested?"

Abram could feel heat rushing up his neck. "*Nee*. She's *Englisch*."

"So was I."

He shuffled the papers in front of him. "Like I said, I haven't seen her in years."

"But you will again when she brings you a report, right?"

"I guess. She may just mail the report."

"Maybe you'll need it explained to you," Mark said with a grin as he rose.

Maybe she would stop by, Abram thought as he walked Mark out to the buggy. He thought he might like seeing her again.

Two

Summer caught herself doing it again. Chicken pecking.

That was what her dad had called it, her sitting there trying to stay awake, nodding off, then snapping her head up.

Embarrassed, she glanced around to see if anyone else noticed. It was gratifying to see that a number of other students appeared to be struggling to stay awake. John, to her left, was propping his chin up and blinking hard. Julie, to her right, was hiding a yawn.

The professor didn't help things by droning in monotone. Finally, finally, it was time for the mid-class break. Students quickly headed out to the vending machines for soft drinks and coffee and a variety of crackers and candy. Professor Tabor was stern about a break being exactly fifteen minutes for the three-hour class—not one minute more. Those who came in late from a break were treated to a lecture in front of the class.

Summer settled down at a table in the student lounge and looked in the lunch tote her mother had packed. She'd eaten the egg salad sandwich for dinner between work and class and now pulled out the apple juice and peanut butter cookies she found.

Julie dropped down into the seat opposite her and blew on her hot coffee to cool it. "You always have the best snacks."

She held out the plastic baggie, offering a cookie before taking one for herself. "My mom is still packing me a lunch."

"Amazing. Mine didn't do that when I was a kid."

"I keep telling her she doesn't have to."

Julie bit into the cookie and sighed. "What, are you nuts? This is delicious. I haven't had a homemade cookie since . . . well, since the last time you brought some."

She laughed. "That was two classes ago." She watched the other woman slump in her seat and sip her coffee.

Zach wandered up to the table gulping down an energy drink.

"That stuff's bad for you," Julie told him.

"Caffeine, same as your coffee." He sat and stretched out his long legs.

"Too much caffeine. It's going to give you the jitters, make you crash an hour from now."

He shrugged and looked over with interest at Summer's cookies. She held out the baggie. "So, we gonna have a study session before the test Thursday? Say four o'clock?"

"I'll try. I have to work," Summer told him.

"Why are you killing yourself taking courses if you already have the job you want?"

"I have to have the degree to be hired full-time." She stuffed the empty baggie in the tote and downed the last of her juice. "We need to get back."

As they walked back to the classroom, Summer glanced at Julie. "You said once you have a full-time job and kids. I don't know how you single parents do it."

"It's not easy. A lot of us take night classes, online classes. My dad babysits my kids when I have night classes."

Summer bit her lip. "Two classes on top of my part-time job with the county and my own little business growing, canning, and selling vegetables and fruit from my kitchen garden are too much. We found my car keys in the refrigerator this morning. I could have sworn I put them on the hook by the door like I always do."

"You think that's bad." Julie slid into her seat in the lecture hall. "Last semester I took six classes. One day I got to class and realized I'd left my book bag at home. I didn't have my book, my notepad to take notes on, even my wallet."

"So I'm not losing my mind?"

Julie laughed. "Nope. Stress just makes us forgetful. "

"Let's hope I can remember what I need to on the test," she muttered as she pulled her notebook out of her book bag and looked at the professor striding back into the classroom. "Promise you'll elbow me if I start to drift off?"

"Deal. Same goes if I do it."

She made it through the class without any more chicken pecking and breathed a sigh of relief as she walked out to the parking lot with Julie. Her long day was nearly over. But when she got inside her car and tried to start it, she heard the same clicking noise it had made earlier in the day.

"Oh, Betsy, don't fail me now," she wailed as she turned the key again. The parking lot was emptying, and she didn't want to sit there by herself and wait for the auto club. They'd recently sent her a notice saying she'd called them often and should think about seeing to some maintenance for her car. What was the good of an auto club if you felt you couldn't call them? Sending up a prayer, she turned the key a third time and the engine coughed to life. Putting the car in gear, she drove home.

She pulled into the drive and saw her mother had left the back porch light on. Home had never looked so good. She shut off the engine and wondered if it would start tomorrow. Oh well. Tomorrow was another day. When she walked into the kitchen of the old farmhouse, she found her mother standing at the stove.

"Heard you drive in. I put the kettle on. Thought you might like a cup of tea before you go to bed."

"Sounds good." She set her book bag and purse down and made certain she put her keys on the hook. As she did, she frowned. She was so sure she'd put them there yesterday. With a shrug, she sat down at the table. "Julie and Zach loved your cookies."

Marie smiled as she set a mug of hot water in front of her. "I'll pack more next time. Hungry? There's some soup I can warm up."

She shook her head and dunked her teabag in the mug. "This is enough. Why aren't you in bed? You didn't wait up for me, did you?"

"Of course not."

"Of course not."

Summer smiled. It was an old argument. Summer always said her mom didn't need to. Her mother always insisted she didn't wait up. Every time Summer came home late from a class night, her mother just happened to be up. Not waiting up, she'd always say. Just up. Summer might have believed her if her mother didn't go to bed at nine sharp on nights she was home and it was nearly ten now.

"Only a few more weeks to go. Then we have a break for the holidays."

"That'll be nice."

"Mmm." Summer yawned and felt herself drifting. "I was chicken pecking in class tonight. I was lucky the professor didn't notice."

"You're doing too much."

"Semester's almost over."

Her mother reached over and grasped her hand. "I'm so sorry you lost time taking care of your father."

Summer shook her head vigorously. "Don't you say that. I don't regret a minute of the time I spent with Dad."

She stood. "Let's go to bed."

They climbed the stairs and hugged before going into their own rooms. Summer got ready for bed, and when she climbed in and pulled her quilt up to her chin, she lay there thinking about Abram and his dark chocolate brown eyes. She thought if she had a dream tonight of being an Amish *maedel* and he was in it, that would be very nice indeed. And maybe she'd be hand-delivering that soil report when it came in.

SSS

Abram didn't expect to find Summer at home, so he was surprised when he pulled into her drive and saw her car parked there.

He got out of his buggy and, with the piece of muffler in his hand, walked up to the house. When he caught a glimpse of a slender woman kneeling in the kitchen garden to the side of the yard, he veered off in that direction. It was Summer, he saw, not her mother.

"Hello!" he called.

Summer looked up as he approached and stood. She wore faded jeans and a long, flowing blue cotton shirt that the breeze molded to her body.

"I have something of yours."

"What?" Then she saw what was in his hand. "Oh my gosh! My muffler!"

"I'm not sure if it can be reattached, but I thought I'd bring it over."

She stood and took the piece of metal from him. "I thought the muffler seemed louder last night. I'm surprised I didn't get a ticket."

"I'd put it on for you if I knew how."

"That's very nice of you," she said as she studied it. "I don't know much about these things, but I have a feeling once it falls off it can't be put on again." She sighed. "It's just one thing after another with that car. But I can't seem to give it up. My dad bought that car for me when I was in high school. It was old back then."

"So it's helped get you around since then."

"Mostly. It didn't want to start again last night after class. I began to wonder if I'd have to push it home."

"You wouldn't—" he began.

"I'm exaggerating. I have the auto club for emergencies." She sighed again. "I'm not sure how much life's left in poor old Betsy."

"You call your car Betsy?"

"Your horse has a name, doesn't it?"

"Point taken," he said with a chuckle.

She used the back of her hand to wipe at her forehead. "I was about to stop for something to drink. Can I get you some lemonade?"

He'd been on his way to town for supplies, but looking into those big blue eyes of hers, he decided it was a fine idea to sit for a spell with her on the porch.

She handed him a tall glass of lemonade when she walked back onto the porch and sat in the rocking chair next to his.

"You said you were in class last night."

"I'm working on a degree in agricultural science."

"Takes a long time to get this degree, eh? I seem to remember your father talking about you being in college."

Her smile faded and he frowned. He must have said something wrong.

"It's taking me longer than it should. I dropped out for a while. Mom needed help when Dad got sick."

"Of course. I wasn't thinking."

She shrugged. "It's okay. You couldn't know. I might not have known just how sick he was. I have to admit I was quite caught up in classes, but I happened to come home early one day and saw my mother looking so exhausted after driving my dad to chemo. I stopped taking classes for a while, and when I returned I decided to go part-time because I got the job at the extension office." Part of the reason was finances but that wasn't something you talked about with a stranger.

He nodded. "You are a good daughter. Was there no family to help?"

She shook her head. "Dad was an only child and Mom's sister lives in California." She sipped her lemonade. "It's not like your community where family tends to stay close and help each other."

"Your father was respected in our community," he told her. "If we'd known how sick he was, there would have been offers of help."

"Dad was so proud, he didn't want anyone to know," she said simply. "And I don't think any of us really believed he wouldn't recover. Dad was just so . . . strong, so full of life. His illness took us all by surprise."

He looked out at the fields and considered her words. "Life is a mystery for sure. I know God has a plan for all of us, but it's hard to see it. Maybe we do at the very end."

A pickup truck pulled into the drive. Carl, the man Abram knew helped take care of the Carsons' farm, got out and stepped up onto the porch carrying a bushel of apples. He looked surprised to see Abram but held out a hand and shook it when Abram stood.

"Abram brought my muffler that fell off in his driveway yesterday," Summer explained. "Is it possible to put it back on?"

Carl set the bushel of apples down, picked up the part, and studied it. He was a tall, lanky *Englisch* man with a weathered face and unassuming air. He squinted at the part with faded blue eyes and seemed to consider her question seriously, but Abram watched the man's mouth twitch. "Nope. Gotta get a new one. But I keep telling you, there's no point in spending more money on that heap. Time to give it a decent burial, Sunshine."

Sunshine?

"You know I can't do that, Carl. How much is a new muffler?"

He set the part down and lifted the bushel. "I'll call the parts store and find out. I can go pick it up this afternoon. Don't drive the car until I install it or you'll get a ticket."

"I'm going into town now. I can go get it," Abram offered.

"That'd be nice of you," Carl said. He picked up the bushel and walked over to the kitchen door.

As he opened it an apple fell out of the bushel and rolled toward Abram. He stopped it with his foot then reached down to get it.

"You don't have to pick up the part," Summer told him. "I can go get it. Today's my day off."

"Carl said not to drive the car until he fixes it," he reminded her. "I wouldn't want you to get a ticket. I have no idea what that costs, but why waste money on a ticket?"

He glanced at the kitchen garden. "And it'd be a shame to interrupt your gardening."

She brushed at the dirt on the knees of her jeans. "It's my favorite thing."

Abram drained his glass and set it on the small table between their chairs. "Well, I'd best be on the road. Tell Carl to let the store know I'll pick the part up for you. Then I'll drop it off on my way home."

"Thanks again for stopping by."

"It was good to see you again."

"I'll let you know when we get the test results," she told him as she walked with him to his buggy.

"Appreciate it." He realized he had the apple in his hand and held it out to her.

"Take it with you," she told him. "Carl brought us a lot of apples.

There's just Mom and me. It's not going to take all of them to make him a pie."

His horse, Joe, turned his head and neighed when he scented the apple. Summer laughed. "I guess someone's hinting he'd like it."

Abram twisted the apple into halves and offered Joe one piece and watched him chew it.

"May I?" Summer asked him, holding out her hand.

Abram handed the other section to her and watched her feed it to Joe, then stroke his nose. "I love horses. I had one for a long time. She died two years ago. I miss her."

He frowned. "I'm afraid Roy, my other buggy horse, isn't doing well. The vet was out to see him earlier today and the news wasn't good."

"I'm so sorry. It's so hard to lose a friend and helpmate."

"Thanks." He took a deep breath. "Maybe you'd like to go for a drive with Joe and me one afternoon," he blurted out before he knew what he was saying. He found himself holding his breath while he waited for her to turn him down.

"That'd be nice. Can I call you and let you know after I check on how the paper I have due in class is going?"

"That'd be fine." He climbed into the buggy and as he did, he saw Carl standing on the porch watching him. "See you later."

As he headed toward town Abram shook his head and asked himself what he thought he was doing. The Amish and *Englischers* mixed more than they did in some other communities because so much business here in Lancaster County involved mutual cooperation and enterprise. But that didn't mean singles of either community dated each other.

It's just a drive, he told himself.

But he knew he was attracted to her and the suggestion had been more than a friendly gesture.

He rubbed the bridge of his nose and caught the scent of the apple. He couldn't let Summer tempt him.

Three

Summer walked into the kitchen, hot and tired from gardening, and found her mother rolling out piecrust. "So what are you going to do with all those apples?"

Her mother looked up and smiled at Summer. "Carl got a little carried away. But I'll make use of them. He wants an apple pie. So I'll make him one—"

"I want one too!"

Marie chuckled. "Big surprise. So I'm making three today. I'll do more tomorrow, put them in the freezer. Make applesauce, apple spice cake. None of them will go to waste."

"And there's always apple turnovers, apple and cinnamon muffins. I remember how many ways we ate zucchini this summer," she said with a sigh. "Still are." She opened the refrigerator and scanned its contents. "Want a sandwich? There's some egg salad left over from yesterday."

"Is it lunchtime already?" Marie glanced at the kitchen clock. "I'll take a half sandwich." She fit the piecrust in the pan, poured in the apple filling, and topped it with another crust. After sliding both pies into the oven, she set the timer, then put bowls she'd used in the sink.

Summer made the sandwiches—a whole one for each of them—then added a pile of potato chips to her plate, and set them on the table.

"Mom, sit. You need to eat."

"Who's the mom here?" Marie asked with a smile.

"You've been going since early this morning and haven't stopped."

Marie sat, picked up her sandwich, and took a bite. "Happy now?"

"If you eat all your lunch," Summer told her with a straight face.

"That was nice of Abram to bring your muffler by."

"Both of us thought maybe it could be put back on. Carl informed us that isn't the case."

"I wouldn't have known that either. What's that on the counter behind you? A bug?"

Summer turned without thinking, didn't see anything, and when she glanced back, her mother looked at her with an innocent expression. But Summer heard a loud crunching noise when her mother chewed.

"If you want potato chips, why don't you let me put them on your plate?" she asked, laughing and shaking her head.

"It's more fun to steal one of yours."

The chip stealing was an old game Marie had started when Summer was a little girl, distracting her and stealing a French fry from her plate. At some point Summer had learned to cover her plate with her hands.

There was a knock on the back door, and Carl stuck his head in the doorway. "Abram just dropped off the part."

Summer stood, but Carl shook his head.

"Said he had to head home."

She sat again. "Okay."

"I'll put the muffler on."

"Pie will be done soon," Marie told him.

"Sounds good." He shut the door.

"I hope he was nice to Abram."

"Why wouldn't he be?"

Summer popped a potato chip in her mouth and crunched. "I think he thought it was . . . inappropriate for Abram to visit me today."

"I think Carl was just being protective."

"Abram wasn't here on a date."

"Too bad."

Summer gaped. "What?"

"Nice young man. Might be nice to go out on a date. All you do is work and go to classes."

"Mom, have you forgotten he's Amish?"

"Oh, that's right."

Shaking her head, Summer stood and took her plate to the sink. She decided she wouldn't tell her mother about Abram asking her if she'd like to go for a ride in his buggy. It didn't mean anything anyway. Just a casual thing. A friendly thing.

"I thought when you went back to college you might meet someone nice."

"That's not why I went back."

"No, but there *are* young men there, aren't there?"

"Most of them are younger than me now." That's why she liked her evening classes. More of what the college called "non-traditional age" students attended classes then. Summer had even seen students her mother's age there.

"Speaking of classes, I'm going to go study. I have a test tomorrow night."

The oven timer went off as she started for the stairs.

"Come down for a slice of pie when you need a break," her mother called after her.

"I will." Summer pulled off her kerchief when she walked into her room. Flopping onto her bed, she opened her textbook and began to read.

Lying on the bed was a mistake. The warmth of the sun and the manual labor of working in the garden—combined with a long week—had her yawning and the print blurring. She blinked hard, shook her head, but it didn't help. It wouldn't hurt to close her eyes for just a moment . . .

She leaned back in her buggy seat and enjoyed rolling along, listening to the clip-clop of the horse's hooves on the road. It had been a long, hard day at the farmer's market, but it had paid off handsomely. She'd sold all the jars of jams and jellies, and the chow chow she'd made with the special recipe her grandmother had passed down to her.

A summer's bounty meant hours and hours of picking and cleaning the vegetables and fruit she'd toiled over in the blazing heat outside. Then it meant more hours in a hot kitchen cooled only by a battery-operated fan as she canned. Some days she'd fallen into bed so exhausted she fell asleep the moment her head hit the pillow.

But each Saturday, when she could drive home and hand her dat all the dollars and cents she'd been paid by her customers, she was grateful she could contribute to the family funds. She might wish sometimes that she could work more in the fields as her bruders did, but she'd learned to enjoy her kitchen garden, her role as the woman of the family who cared for her men, and looking forward to the time she'd be the woman of her own home.

Tomorrow she'd attend church and after . . . she had a date.

She hadn't had much time for a date since her mudder died. But one special man had understood and waited for the times she could spend a Sunday afternoon with him taking a drive in his buggy, having a picnic somewhere quiet, and talking with her.

Summer woke, blinked, and stared up at her ceiling for a long moment.

She glanced at the alarm clock on her bedside table and saw she'd slept for an hour. Weird. She never napped. And at the fringes of her memory, she realized she'd had another of those dreams of being a young Amish woman.

Yawning, she got up and padded downstairs. Carl and her mother were talking quietly and huddled at one corner of the table when she walked into the kitchen. Was it her imagination that Carl jerked back when he saw her?

It must have been. Feeling a little groggy, she sank into a chair and rubbed her eyes. "I fell asleep studying." A pie sat in the middle of the table. It smelled amazing.

"Time for some tea and pie," her mother announced, bouncing up from the table.

"I can do it."

"No, you sit there and wake up."

Summer glanced at Carl, bent over his plate.

"Good?" she asked him.

He nodded, chewed, and swallowed. "No one makes better."

"Got a little sun today," she told him. "Fell asleep studying."

He shrugged and pushed his empty plate aside.

She started to push the pie toward him, then realized it had three pieces cut from it. Her mother's plate held the remnants of one piece. She figured she knew where the other two pieces had gone when her mother cut one for her and didn't offer Carl another.

Marie set a cup of tea before her and then brought a plastic pie carrier to the table and set a pie inside it. "There you go," she told Carl. "One apple pie as promised."

He grinned. "Just one?"

"I'll bake you another when you've eaten that one."

He stood. "Then I'll be back for it tomorrow."

Marie laughed.

Carl turned to Summer. "Your muffler's all put on."

"Thank you. I don't know what I'd do without you, Carl."

"Probably buy a new car like you should."

"Not likely," she said, laughing and shaking her head.

He left and her mother brought another carrier to the table and set the second pie inside. She snapped the top onto it and pushed it toward Summer. "There you go. All ready to take to Abram."

"Abram?"

Marie sat at the table. "I think you owe him a thank you for picking up that muffler for you, don't you?"

Summer gave her a long, thoughtful look. "I guess that would be the right thing to do, wouldn't it?

Her mother smiled.

SSS

Abram heard a car pull up into the gravel driveway and walked to the barn door to see who was visiting. He felt his spirits lift as he saw it was Summer.

Carl must have installed the muffler already because Abram didn't hear the racket he had heard the day she'd driven off, leaving a part of the muffler behind.

He had to be grateful that had happened. Of course he couldn't tell her that. It had cost her money to replace that part—a lot of money as he well knew since the bag had a copy of the receipt stapled to it.

But it had given him an opportunity to stop by her house and talk with her. And he'd enjoyed the visit enough to actually ask her to go for a buggy ride with him.

It wasn't a date. Couldn't be a date. That would imply that they could have a future, but the Amish and the *Englisch* didn't marry.

Except for rare cases like Mark and Miriam Byler, he thought as he walked to meet her.

"*Guder mariye*," she said, smiling as she approached.

"Good morning." He wondered if he was grinning too much. If he looked too happy to see her.

She wore a nice jacket and slacks with her hair neatly braided in the back so he supposed she must be working today. He liked the way she'd been dressed the day before—in a casual shirt and jeans with her hair flowing—better.

"I don't have your test results yet," she told him. "I was sorry I missed you when you dropped the muffler off. I was upstairs in my room studying. I brought you something to thank you for what you did yesterday." She handed him a plastic pie carrier.

"I did little."

"You saved me a trip into town to pick up the part. I would have done it to keep Carl from taking the time, and who knows, I might have gotten a ticket. So I brought you an apple pie."

"Is this from the bushel of apples Carl got?"

She nodded. "I have to tell you my mom baked it. So I can guarantee it's good. Much better than if I made it, I'm sure. Even when I use her recipe, it never comes out as good as hers."

"Then I'm sure I'm going to enjoy it."

"Carl ate two pieces and took his home."

He hesitated. "Do you have time for a cup of coffee?"

She looked regretful. "I wish I did, but I should get going. You never know what traffic will be like, and I like to be on time. Maybe some other time."

"Sure."

"Maybe this weekend? We could go for that buggy ride you mentioned."

"If you still want to."

"I do. Can I call you when I see if I get a paper that's due done?"

"Sure."

Abram walked to the car with her and managed to open the door before she could reach for the handle.

She rewarded him with a big smile. "See you then."

"Drive careful. You know how the tourists can be."

"How well I do." She got in, shut the door, and grimaced when the engine coughed but finally turned over.

"Déjà vu all over again," she muttered and gave him a rueful grin. "Betsy better behave or she'll make me think what Carl said about her." She put the car in reverse and backed down the drive.

Abram wondered if Carl wasn't right. Well, he knew what it was like to want to hold onto something that had special meaning.

He took the pie carrier into the house and set it down on the kitchen counter. A plastic container of brownies rested there—a gift from Sarah Bontrager earlier in the week. Single men in the community never lacked for baked goods or the occasional casserole from Amish *maedels*. They always wanted to show off their cooking and baking skills and flirt a little.

Summer had been different. She'd freely admitted that her *mudder* had baked the pie. And she'd been the one to bring up the buggy ride. Not that Amish *maedels* were shy and retiring. Not with the single men in their community. He'd been asked for a ride home from a singing more than once.

Abram popped open the carrier and took a sniff of the pie. Now that smelled as good as his *mudder's*, and she was the best baker in the community. He had eaten many a slice of pie at church functions and work frolics, and he'd had a lot of fine baking to compare hers to.

He'd just finished his chores in the barn and hadn't had breakfast yet. He thought bacon and eggs and a slice of pie with some coffee sounded pretty good.

Soon he had bacon sizzling in the cast-iron skillet. He wasn't a great cook, but he'd learned how to make simple meals after his *mudder* and *dat* left to winter in Pinecraft. It was that or starve. Or marry, one married male friend had joked. But that wasn't an option. Marriages were for life here. Best not to get married just to have someone to cook and care for the house.

If a marriage wasn't made in love, it *schur* would prove to be a very long, lonely prison.

Shaking off such a depressing thought, he lifted the browned slices to a plate covered with a paper towel to drain, then fried several eggs. As he ate he found himself looking at the container of brownies on the counter. There had been a heavier-than-usual stream of *maedels* stopping by with baked goods the past few months as the time for weddings grew closer.

Abram didn't think of himself as cynical, but he didn't think of himself as good-looking. While he had dated for a time, he felt he became someone of more interest after it got around on the Amish grapevine that he'd taken over the farm.

He chided himself for such thoughts and pushed aside his empty plate. After cutting a good-sized piece of pie, he rose and poured a mug of coffee. Summer hadn't oversold her mother's pie. It was excellent—the filling made of large chunks of apple that hadn't been over-sugared, with just the right amount of cinnamon. The piecrust was light as a cloud and melted on his tongue. He ate two pieces and then forced himself to cover the remainder and save it for dessert after supper.

Summer had said she wasn't as good a baker as her mother but claimed to be a fairly good cook. He'd heard *Englisch* women didn't have much time to cook these days because they worked so many hours. So often they had to rely on takeout—something almost unheard of in his community.

He put his dishes and mug in the sink and headed outside. His *mudder* would be horrified at dirty dishes in the sink, but he didn't see any point in doing them until he had more at the end of supper.

Thinking of her, he decided to check the answering machine in the phone shanty. No voicemail, but there was a postcard in the mailbox. It showed a scene of the beach near the community of Pinecraft and a message written in his *mudder's* script: "You must come visit. Your *dat* says the fishing is *wunderbaar*, and I must admit having fresh fish for supper is a nice treat. I'm enjoying visits to the nearby ocean. No swimming for me, but it's nice to walk barefoot in the sand."

He missed them, but he was glad they were having some time to relax after working so hard for so many years. Farming was a hard job—one that was twenty-four hours a day, seven days a week. But he didn't know any farmer who didn't love it and worked until he often dropped to the very ground he'd tended most of his life.

Now it was his turn. He said a prayer of thanks and headed out to his fields.

Four

Summer turned in her test and, feeling cheerful, walked out of the classroom. Her long hours of studying had paid off. She felt she'd done well on it.

When she dug her hand in her purse for her car keys, she came up with her fingers streaked with ink. Her pen was leaking. Disgusted, she found the pen and threw it in the nearby trash can and headed into the women's restroom to wash the ink off her fingers. Loud weeping came from behind one of the stall doors and echoed in the tiled room. She squirted liquid soap onto her hands and held them under the automatic faucet. Scrubbing them was doing little to wash away the ink. Sighing, she rinsed and reached for a paper towel.

The weeping continued. Whoever was crying sounded like her heart was breaking.

Frowning, she walked over and rapped her knuckles on the metal door. "Are you okay in there?"

The weeping stopped and loud nose blowing ensued. The toilet flushed, then the door was unbolted and a young woman with auburn hair stepped out. Her eyes were puffy from crying. Summer recognized her from the class she'd just left. The woman sat in the back and didn't say much in class.

"Sorry, I didn't know anyone else was in here." She walked over to the sink and splashed water on her face then dried it with a paper towel.

She looked at Summer in the mirror. "I'm fine," she said dully.

"You're not." Summer touched her shoulder and gave her a sympathetic smile. "What's wrong?"

The woman's eyes welled with tears. "Nothing. Everything."

Summer walked back to the stall and grabbed a length of bathroom tissue and handed it to her.

"Thanks." She mopped at her eyes. "It's just a test, right? Not the end of the world."

"No, it's not. But it's important. I know that." She held out her hand. "I'm Summer."

"I know. We're in the same class. I sit in the back. My name's Kim. I'm just so stressed. I knew college was going to be hard, but I didn't know it was going to be this hard."

"First semester?"

Kim nodded.

"How are you doing in your other classes?"

"Good. I guess I should feel a little relieved about that." She bit her lip. "Do you know what Professor Tabor said when I turned in my test tonight?"

"No, I was too busy double-checking some of my answers."

Kim made a sound that was half laugh, half sob. "When I double-check my answers I second-guess myself. Then later I find out my original answer I changed was correct."

"So what did Professor Tabor say?" Summer asked, curious. He wasn't one of her favorites. Students complained that he didn't seem like he liked teaching anymore.

"He glanced over the test as I handed it to him and said, 'Well, Ms. Sanders, at least you're consistent.'"

Now it was Summer's turn to frown. "That's bad?"

"Since I've flunked every test in this class so far, yeah." And she burst into tears again.

Summer grabbed more tissue and held it out to her. "I'm so sorry. He didn't have to be sarcastic. Have you gone to see him in his office?"

Kim nodded. "I did. I asked him if he could help me. He said college wasn't for everyone."

Summer felt her temper rising. "That's just plain mean. None of us are good in everything."

"He said to go to the tutoring lab. But they're closed by the time I get off work."

"Maybe I could help you. The only thing is I get here just before class. I work too. But maybe we could figure something out."

Kim took a breath that came out shaky. "We should go. It's getting late."

"Yeah, my mom always worries if I'm late because I've had so much trouble with my car."

"My mom is babysitting my kid so I'm keeping her up. Well, not exactly keeping her up," Kim corrected as she grabbed her backpack. "We live with her to save money. I'm trying to take out as few student loans as I can, you know?"

"My mom and I live together too. I had my own place when I went out of state to college, but then Dad got sick and I came back."

"Gee, I'm sorry. My dad took off when I was a kid. Just like my ex." They walked downstairs and out of the building. The parking lot was brightly lit, but a security guard was driving around slowly in a golf cart. He stopped and picked them up.

"That's my car there, the dirty old Kia," Summer told the guard. She tore a sheet of paper from her notebook, jotted down her name and phone number, and handed it to Kim. "It's my day off tomorrow. Call me and we'll set up some time to study soon, okay?"

Kim took the slip of paper and smiled. "Thanks. See you."

Summer unlocked her car and got in. The engine coughed but started up. She stopped by Kim's car and saw it was an older model too. Once she saw it was moving, she drove out of the lot and started home.

Her mother had left the porch light on like she always did. Summer let herself in and dumped her backpack on the bench near the door. She'd forgotten to bring in her lunch tote, but she wasn't going back out to her car for it now.

Seeing Kim so upset had rattled her. She wished she'd been able to do more to make the poor woman feel better. She'd have suggested going somewhere for coffee or something, but it had been too late. Hopefully the offer of some tutoring would help. She just didn't know where they'd find the time for it. She put the kettle on for tea, and her glance fell on the recipe box sitting on the counter. She picked it up and took it to the table to flip through recipes while the water heated. Thinking about how she'd enjoyed so many of the things her grandmother Waneta had made from the handwritten cards soothed her. It was interesting how the recipes were a mixture of Amish and *Englisch* favorites, she mused.

"So how did your test go?"

Summer looked up as her mother walked into the room. "I think I did pretty good."

Marie bent to kiss her cheek. "You always do. Are you hungry? I put a plate in the refrigerator. It'd just take a minute to warm up."

"Sounds good." She started to get up, but her mother beat her to it. "I met a student I'm going to try to tutor."

"That's kind of you but you're so busy."

"We'll do it when we can. She's really struggling."

Summer propped her elbow on the table, rested her chin on her hand, and studied the index cards. "Mom, I had this dream about recipes. I couldn't get it out of my head. I want to plant some different vegetables in the spring, try using some different recipes."

Marie slid into the chair next to her. "Some of these are your paternal grandmother's."

"I know. I'd like to revamp my label. Call the new products Grandma's Recipe. I think the stores that already carry my canned fruit and vegetables would take them. I'll be checking with them first, of course."

Her mother hugged her. "I think it's a great idea. You know I'll continue to help you."

"Thanks. I couldn't do what I do without you." She sighed. "The things the Amish produce sell better in this area of course, but there's still room for my products. People like homemade, and many have good memories of the food their grandmothers made."

"I'm sorry both your grandmothers died when you were little."

She shrugged. "That's life. It's not always fair. I'm sorrier Dad left us too soon." She pushed away the memory of coming home to find her mother draped over her father lying on their bed. For a long moment she thought she'd lost both of them. Her mother had exhausted herself taking care of him at the end . . .

The microwave beeped, bringing Summer back to the present. Marie brought the plate of food to the table and after fixing herself a cup of chamomile tea settled at the table to keep Summer company while she ate.

The kitchen clock chirped as she ate. Summer glanced up as bird-song filled the room.

Her mother smiled. "Your dad was so silly. But it was my favorite anniversary present from him." Her expression became far away. "I saw the blue jay in the yard again today."

A frequent visitor in the backyard. They'd talked about it a couple of times.

Summer swallowed before speaking. "An Amish friend of mine said a cardinal was in her yard a lot after her husband died."

"Blue jays were your dad's favorite bird."

Summer reached over and took her mother's hand and squeezed it. "I know." She yawned.

"Time for my chick to get to bed."

Summer laughed, stood, put the empty plate in the sink, and linked her arm in her mother's. "Time for both of us to go to bed."

They climbed the stairs and went to their rooms.

$$\mathcal{SSS}$$

Abram was standing at the stove pouring a cup of coffee when he heard a knock at the back door, then Wayne strode into the kitchen with the ease of an old friend.

"*Guder mariye.*"

"*Guder mariye.*" Abram held up the percolator. "Want some coffee?"

"*Ya, danki.*" Wayne took a seat at the table and eyed the casserole sitting by Abram's plate. "You made this?"

"Hey, I can cook."

"Uh-huh. You made this? C'mon, I've known you for years and you don't cook."

"I haven't had to. You haven't either." Abram got a plate and fork and set it before Wayne. He sat at the table and used a big spoon to scoop a large serving of the casserole onto his friend's plate, then his own.

Wayne forked up a bite and rolled his eyes. "Mmm, *gut*." He looked at Abram. "You didn't make this."

"*Nee*. But I could have. It can't be that hard. Sausage, eggs, potatoes."

"You go on believing that," Wayne said with a grin.

Ignoring him, Abram ate. "Hannah dropped it off yesterday." Along with a not-so-subtle hint that it was something she wouldn't mind sharing with him sometime even though she well knew an Amish *maedel* didn't eat breakfast with a single Amish man in his kitchen . . .

But Abram wasn't sharing what Hannah had said with his friend. A decent man didn't ever do anything that would cast a shadow on a *maedel's* reputation. Even if some got a little . . . assertive as the time for weddings got closer.

He and Hannah had gone to *schul* together and he'd given her a ride home from a singing or two. That was the extent of their relationship. She'd continued to act interested in him even as he tried to gently let her know it wasn't mutual.

"Mind if I have more?" Wayne asked as he quickly polished off his serving.

"Go ahead." He grinned. "Maybe you should let Hannah know how much you like the casserole. You're single."

"And liking it right now, *danki* very much. I'm in no hurry to get married." He finished the second serving and leaned back in his chair, looking satisfied.

"I was kind of surprised when you joined the church after *rumschpringe*," Abram told him.

"*Ya*? Why?"

"You're enjoying bachelorhood a little more than you should, don't you think? Our community's all about marriage and family life."

"Well, I don't see you hurrying to get married."

"*Nee*. But I want to be. I just haven't found the right woman yet." As he said that, his thought went to a certain *Englisch* woman with hair the color of sunshine and an unusual name.

"I want that. But with marriage lasting forever, I'm not going to be in any hurry." Wayne shook his head at the offer of another cup of coffee. "So, are you ready to go buy a horse?"

Abram sighed. "Not ready but the vet says Roy isn't going to last much longer."

"I'm sorry to hear that. I know how hard it is to say goodbye to a horse who's served you well."

"Joe's great, but there will never be another Roy." Abram stood. "There will, however, have to be another horse. Let's get on the road or all the good ones are going to be sold before we even get to the auction."

They took Wayne's buggy. Wayne had tricked it out with a battery-operated stereo system he had carefully hidden from view. The minute they were clear of the community, he set it to blast hard rock.

"Ouch!" Abram protested.

"Are you gonna be an old man?" Wayne shouted over the noise.

"Take it down some or I won't have any hearing left."

Wayne rolled his eyes but lowered the volume.

"Guess the bishop hasn't seen this little feature."

"Nope. And I'm doing my best to make sure he doesn't. I miss the music, movies, television." He fell silent. "*Rumschpringe* was fun. Maybe too much fun. But I came to realize that stuff was entertainment. Family, friends—they're everything."

Abram nodded slowly, so glad his friend had come to that conclusion. He'd been worried about him for a while. Prayed for him. Some young people left the community for the *Englisch* world but most stayed and joined the church. They'd found they missed the connection, the closeness, of family and friends. The bonds. The security of ties they'd formed in the community. Like Wayne said: family and friends were everything.

The auction was packed as usual. They spent some time looking over the available horses and, after buying a cup of coffee, found a seat and prepared to bid. Wayne bid aggressively for a horse he wanted but stopped when another man topped the maximum bid he'd told Abram he was prepared to spend.

"You're not going to bid on the horse you liked?" he asked Abram. "I thought you said the vet told you Roy didn't have much longer."

Abram sighed. "He did. But I don't know. It doesn't seem right to bring another one home yet. And none of the horses I looked at . . ." He paused, searching for words.

"None of them were Roy."

He shook his head. "None will ever be."

"Why don't we go, then?"

They headed home, stopping in town for something to eat first. Wayne dropped Abram off at his farm and headed home. The minute Abram walked into the barn to check on Roy and do evening chores his heart sank. Roy put his head over the top of the stall and his eyes were filled with misery. His breathing seemed labored.

Abram pulled out his cell phone and called the vet. Then he let himself into the stall and pressed his cheek against Roy's. "It's *allrecht*, old *freind*. I know you're tired and hurting."

He sat on the straw and wasn't surprised when Roy knelt, then lay with his head on Abram's lap. "I remember when *Daed* brought you home," he said, stroking Roy's nose. "I was just a boy and I thought you were the most beautiful horse I'd ever seen. And so fast! We've had a lot of years together, haven't we?"

He stared off into the distance, remembering. "You took me so many places and always got us home safely. Even a couple of times when I drank beer with my friends and couldn't have found my own way home you got us here. You've been such a good horse. Such a good *freind*."

Roy closed his eyes and his breathing evened out and came slower. And then with a sigh he was gone.

Abram kissed his friend's cheek and then sat there and bawled like a *boppli*.

Five

Summer saw the test results. She was getting quite a crick in her shoulder today. The phone hadn't stopped ringing from the minute she'd walked into the office this morning. And maybe it was because she was tired from being swamped with coursework as the semester was ending soon.

Today, it seemed like she was the only one who was picking up the phone. She felt so . . . jangled, her nerves on edge.

It was tempting to run the report over during her lunch hour and get out in the fresh air, talk with someone who didn't want her to type something while she was answering a phone.

Finally the day that seemed never-ending was over. She grabbed her things and headed out, grabbing the report on her way. She'd stop and talk to Abram in the morning before work.

But his farm was on her way home, and when she glanced over she saw him in his front yard standing next to a buggy. Another Amish man was putting a shovel into the back of it. She slowed, debating whether to stop. The man got inside and pulled out onto the road and headed in the opposite direction.

Summer found herself pulling into the drive. It would take just a minute to give Abram the report. She put the car in park and rolled down the window. Abram walked over and smiled at her. The smile didn't reach his eyes—and if she wasn't mistaken they looked damp, as if he'd been crying.

"What's wrong?" she asked quickly.

He shrugged. "Wasn't the best day."

"For me either. But I have the feeling yours was worse than mine." She paused. They weren't friends and the Amish were private people. But it looked like he needed a friend. "I'm sorry, I'm being nosy. I—"

"My horse Roy died. My friends came over to help me bury him. Wayne was the last to leave."

"I'm sorry! It's so hard to lose one."

"Thank you."

"You had him a long time?"

"*Daed* brought Roy home when I was a boy." He swallowed hard. "You probably think I'm being silly. He was just a horse."

"No, he wasn't!" she said indignantly. "I had a horse myself. Missy was my best friend."

"Was? What happened to her?"

"She got sick not long before Dad died. The vet couldn't save her."

"That's rough. A double blow."

She nodded and found her hands were clenching the steering wheel. She let go of it and flexed her fingers. "She was my rock when he was going through chemo. I spent a lot of hours in the barn crying into her mane. Mom and I tried so hard to stay positive around Dad. Missy let me grieve." She took a deep breath. "Sorry. That's enough about me. Tell me about Roy."

"He was old when we got him. You probably know we—the Amish—sometimes buy retired racehorses. Roy sulked when arthritis made pulling the buggy hard for him and I had to use Joe. It was a point of pride to Roy to work."

"Would you like to go for coffee?"

"Coffee?"

She felt her cheeks warm. "Never mind. You probably have a lot to do."

"No, actually. My friends helped with chores after we buried Roy." He glanced back at the barn. "I'll go hitch Joe to the buggy."

"I can drive us. Unless you're afraid of women drivers?" she teased.

"No, no, of course not. I wasn't thinking." He looked down at his pants. "I need to change."

"You don't have to. We can get some takeout and drive around. I've been cooped up in an office all day, so I'd just as soon not go inside somewhere."

"But your seats."

"The finest genuine fake leather. Nothing can hurt them." She picked up the report she'd been dropping off and handed it to him. "I brought this for you. We can talk about it here if you want or during the drive. It's up to you."

"Okay. A drive does sound good." He rounded the hood and got into the passenger side.

She was relieved when he put on the seat belt without her having to show him how. *Silly me*, she thought. *He's probably been in a car many times before, getting rides when a buggy wouldn't do.*

"So the car has been running okay for you?"

"Yes. And it's certainly quieter since it got a new muffler." She backed out carefully and found herself relaxing as they drove through the countryside.

Abram opened the manila envelope and scanned the contents as she gave him an overview. Then, nodding, he slid the report back in the envelope. "Thanks. I think it's time to try a different crop in that section of the land." He glanced at her. "Enough farm talk. Tell me about your day."

She gave him a rueful glance and then turned her attention to the road. "You don't want to hear about it."

"Sure I do."

Summer sighed. "The job hasn't been what I expected. I know I don't have much experience yet, but I mostly answer phones and do secretarial stuff. There's another part-timer in the office—a guy—but he doesn't do secretarial like I'm assigned."

"It doesn't sound like the job your father had. Wasn't he mostly out in the field?"

"Yes." She found her fingers clenching the steering wheel and tried to relax them. "I've been told that will happen after I get my degree." She shrugged. "It's my own fault. I dropped out of college while Dad was sick and a degree is required for the job. Let's face it. I was probably hired because of his history there, not my qualifications."

"I doubt that. Look at all you learned from the years you followed him around. The fact that you grew up on a farm and still live and work on one. And I've seen your canned goods at local stores."

"You have?"

"Sure. I go into stores, you know. I don't grow everything I need on my farm. Oatmeal doesn't grow in my fields. Thank goodness. Otherwise my mother would have made me eat it even more when I was a kid."

She grinned at the dry tone in his voice.

"I'm thinking of some new things to grow and preserve. If I can find the time." She found herself talking about the scene with Kim earlier in the week.

"It's kind of you to offer her help."

"Other students have helped me in the past. I really struggled with algebra."

"I never had that in school."

"There is no earthly reason for anyone to take algebra," she said with meaning. "Ever."

He chuckled. "You sound very decisive about that."

"Unfortunately I said it to my professor. He wasn't very happy with me. There's a McDonald's up ahead. We can get some coffee from the drive-through. Unless you'd prefer something fancier."

"McDonald's is fine. I've seen the prices at those fancy places. I can't believe people pay that for coffee."

"Me either." She put on her turn signal and pulled in. "How do you take yours?"

"Black. And it's my treat." Now it was his turn to sound firm.

She placed their order and didn't argue with him. After they got the coffee they set it in the cup holders between the seats to cool. Summer pulled back onto the road.

"So tell me what the professor said," Abram said.

"Professor?"

"The one you told algebra had no earthly reason to exist."

She made a face. "I got a lecture. I'll spare you the details. It went on for more than ten minutes. I didn't believe any of it but he said even if I thought we didn't use it, that it trained our brain to look at things differently."

"And has it?"

"Maybe. About six months after I took it, I had this problem come up in my life, and I realized that I didn't react the same way I'd always done. I was calmer about figuring out what to do. I'll concede his point when I figure out my life a little better."

He picked up his coffee and took a careful sip. "Let me know if you decide it helps. I might consider taking algebra then."

She gave him a dubious glance. "What do you suppose your bishop would have to say about that?"

"I think that might have to be something I don't tell him," he said with a mischievous wink.

She lifted her cup and sipped. "Kind of like going for a drive with an *Englisch* woman?" she found herself asking.

"Kind of like," he said and their gazes met. "Careful," he warned, pointing at the road.

Summer looked back at the road and saw she'd drifted over the yellow line. "Sorry. Didn't mean to scare you."

"That's the advantage of driving a buggy. The horse keeps his eyes on the road and you can even fall asleep and still make it home in one piece."

Summer didn't have to see his face to know how he was feeling . . . who he was remembering. She heard it in his voice.

SSS

Abram stared out the window and fell silent.

"I'm sorry," Summer said quickly. "It made you think of Roy, didn't it?"

"Yeah." Abram sipped his coffee. "But it's okay."

"Have you ever fallen asleep in the buggy?"

"More than once. When I . . . stayed out late."

"Oh?"

He watched her mouth curve in a smile. And chuckled.

"Just because you were tired. Of course."

"Of course."

"Those stories of wild times during *rumschpringe* are fake, then?" she asked.

"Just like the stories of wild college parties, I'm sure."

Now it was her turn to chuckle. "Most of us college students work either part-time or full-time jobs. We're in bed or studying at night, not out drinking lots of beer. At least most of the students I know." She finished her coffee and set it in the cup holder. "We're just trying to stay awake at work and in class. Some days it takes a lot of caffeine."

"Sounds hard. Guess I'm lucky I wasn't expected to go to college." He wondered if she thought less of him because he hadn't. The Amish often were looked down on by the *Englisch* for stopping their education at the eighth grade.

"Actually there's talk of bringing back vocational education," she told him. "Not everyone needs college if they're going into farming or the trades. Apprenticeships are coming back. At least that's what I hear from a friend who's an education major."

Abram studied her. "Are you happy with your decision?"

She jerked her head to look at him, then stared back at the road. When she was silent for a long moment he wondered if he'd offended her.

"Funny you should ask," she said at last. "Sometimes I am. I tell myself that it's like any big decision. Any big goal. You're bound to question yourself." She drummed her fingers on the steering wheel. "But yes, I am."

"Maybe you just need a break."

"I've already lost time because I cut back on classes to help Mom with Dad. At this rate I feel like I'll be sixty by the time I graduate."

"I think you might be exaggerating."

She laughed. "Maybe." She slowed the car. "Do you mind if I stop for gas?"

"Of course not."

He watched her pull into a gas station, turn off the car, and get out to insert a credit card before pumping the gas. It didn't take long before she was back in the car.

"I would have offered to help, but I've never pumped gas."

"No problem. I can even change my own tire if I get a flat. Dad insisted a woman needed to know how to do such things so she didn't get stranded."

She buckled her seat belt and turned to him before she started the car. "Guess I ought to start back. Mom's expecting me for dinner since it's not a class night. This has been fun. I'm glad you could go for a drive with me."

"I'm glad you asked me."

"You probably think I'm a forward *Englisch* woman."

He watched the color rise in her cheeks as she turned the key. "I think you're a woman who cared about someone who looked sad," he said honestly.

She turned to him and gave him a smile. "I know what it's like to feel sad."

Something stretched between them, a tenuous thread of awareness in the small confines of the car.

A car honked behind them.

"Oops, sorry!" she said, waving at the other vehicle and pulling out of the gas station.

"Everyone's always in such a hurry."

"Well, it's nicer to be home, isn't it, than being on the road. Especially at the end of the day." She sighed. "But we live in such a pretty part of the country. I never get tired of driving on these country roads."

Abram wasn't looking forward to going home, but he wasn't going to tell her that. Then she might feel compelled to drive around with him some more when she needed to get home. Too soon she was pulling up before the farmhouse, and he was thanking her for the drive and the coffee.

"It was fun talking to you."

"Would you like to go to church with me on Sunday, take that drive we talked about, and have lunch after? I remember your father brought you once."

"You remember that?" she asked, surprised. "It was years ago."

"Well, it's not like a lot of visitors come to our services. You may remember how long they are."

"I remember how nice the family was who hosted the services that day." She stared out the window. "They made us feel welcome. Everyone did. The service was long, but I thought it was nice that it wasn't in some big, impersonal church like ours was. Everyone stayed for a snack afterward and didn't go rushing off to a restaurant."

"So think about it and let me know. You can meet me here and we'll drive there together."

Summer turned in her seat to look at him. "I don't have to think about it. I'd love to."

"Good."

"Thanks for going with me today." She traced a finger around the rim of her coffee cup, then looked at him. "It's funny. I thought you looked like you needed a friend. But I think I needed one too. You're good at listening, Abram Yoder."

"So are you, Summer Carson. I'll see you Sunday."

Six

"You're home early!"

Summer closed the door behind her and stared at her mother. She was sitting at the kitchen table with a cup of tea in front of her. "It's not a class night."

"It isn't?"

She tried to remember if she'd told her mother that before she left that morning. But it had been a very long day . . . maybe she hadn't. Dropping her purse and lunch tote on the bench by the door, she went to the refrigerator and got the pitcher of iced tea.

"I'll fix you something to eat. There's ham left over from last night's dinner. And salad."

"No, I'm not really hungry. I just want something to drink right now." She got a glass from the cupboard, filled it with ice, and poured the tea. Then she sat at the table.

"You look tired."

"It was busy today. Then again it's always busy."

Marie sipped her tea.

"Have you eaten?" There were no pans on the stove, no aromas of food in the air.

Her mother shrugged. "I'm not hungry."

Summer was tired, but her mother looked pale and fragile. "So what did you do today?" she asked as she sipped her tea.

"Did some gardening. Finally packed up your father's clothes and donated them."

So it wasn't so much tiredness as maybe sadness. "I told you I'd help you pack them."

"I know." Marie sighed. "But I wasn't ready." She traced the grain in the wood with her finger. "I saved his favorite cardigan for you. The one you gave him. He loved that sweater."

"What did you save for yourself?"

"Many things. Probably too many. Every card he ever gave me. All the big and little things he gave me. The silly ones like the bird clock there. When I'm gone you'll have to deal with all of it." She smiled ruefully. "Sorry."

"Don't talk like that." Losing her father had been devastating. Losing her mother . . . well, she couldn't think about it. Wouldn't. She and Abram had talked of loss enough that day. Summer got up and rummaged in the refrigerator. "How about a ham and cheese sandwich, maybe some of this leftover tomato soup you made?"

"That's fine. You should let me fix it. You worked all day."

"I mostly sat and answered the phone. You know that new girl they hired? Every time someone called she'd tell them she had to find a pencil to write things down. She'd put them on hold and look all over her desk for it. I swear, I'm going to tie one on a string and hang it around her neck."

Marie chuckled. "Like the way they used to sell soap on a rope. Don't know why they don't do that anymore. Soap is always slipping out of your hands and you have to bend down and grab it."

Summer put the kettle of soup on the stove and turned the flame up under it. Soon the rich scent of late summer tomatoes they'd canned and her mother had made into soup filled the kitchen.

"Here, you carve the ham," she told her mother, setting it before her. "I always make a mess of it."

Marie sliced the ham, and when she had enough to make two sandwiches she sliced the loaf of homemade bread Summer set before her.

It was a simple meal but a satisfying one, a calming one at the end of a day that had jangled her nerves. They washed the dishes afterward. Marie had resisted the idea of modernizing the kitchen with a dishwasher, laughing and shaking her head when her husband had suggested it.

"Just wants to tie me to the kitchen sink with her, drying the dishes," he'd pretended to grumble to Summer.

But she'd seen them standing at the sink together after dinner so many evenings and envied their easy closeness. One night she'd wandered into the kitchen and seen her father lean down to kiss the nape of her mother's neck. She'd blushed and tiptoed back out of the room.

She sighed. They'd set the standard for what she wanted when she got married one day.

Her thoughts went back to the easy way she and Abram had talked in the car . . .

"I think I'll go watch a little television," her mother said. "Do you want to join me?"

"I need to do some work on a paper for class."

Marie kissed her cheek. "Don't stay up too late."

"I won't." She settled down at the kitchen table to do the assigned reading. But it wasn't long before she found her eyes drawn to the recipe box on the counter.

Summer got the box and spread the recipe cards on the table. She'd always felt such a connection to her grandmothers through these yellowed cards with the directions so carefully jotted down in flowing handwriting.

She realized that the stack of cards had more recipes for zucchini than any other ingredient and found herself smiling. Zucchini was a known over-producer in a kitchen garden. What gardener hadn't thought she'd have more than enough zucchini seeds planted . . . then found herself with several times more than she needed. So there were cards for stuffed baked zucchini, zoodles—zucchini cut into long, thin strips and cooked like noodles—zucchini lasagna, pickled zucchini.

And then cooks got sneaky and made chocolate cake with zucchini hidden inside. And zucchini chopped up and hidden under cheese on pizza and casseroles.

So, she mused, what if you deliberately planted a lot of zucchini and found many ways to use it? Wouldn't that make it less expensive to make your products . . . and make more money?

It was a thought.

Summer leaned an elbow on the table and cupped her chin in her hand. Well, she couldn't make *all* her products with the vegetable. But certainly making as many products with it as possible without going overboard could pay off.

A birdcall trilled out. Glancing at the clock she smiled. When she'd been a girl, the cardinal calling out meant bedtime. She was older now and didn't go to bed so early, but it had been a long day. Sighing, she rose and put the kettle on for tea. Some caffeine might help. She still had twenty pages to read before she could go to bed.

While she waited for the water to boil, Summer rummaged in a cupboard for tea bags. She'd have sworn there was a box of her favorite black tea in there—she'd bought it just last week when she did the grocery shopping. When she didn't locate it, she went through other cupboards and finally found it tucked in with the boxes and jars of spices near the stove.

Weird. Had she put it in here last time she'd fixed tea? Her mother didn't like this brand so Summer couldn't imagine she'd have put it there.

Frowning, she filled a mug with boiling water and dunked a tea bag in it. She set it near her textbook, then gathered up the recipe cards and tucked them into the box. No distractions. She was going to finish the paper and go to bed.

The tea revived her and she sped through the draft of her paper. With a satisfied sigh she closed the laptop and got up. She went into the living room and found her mother had nodded off sitting in the recliner. Her father's favorite chair.

Summer shook her mother's shoulder gently. "Mom?"

Marie woke and stared at her blankly for a moment. "I must have fallen asleep."

"Let's go up to bed."

They went their separate ways at the top of the stairs. Summer still slept in the room she'd had since birth. She'd missed it when she'd gone off to college. Maybe that said something about her, but it was comforting to climb into the wrought iron bed her parents had let her pick out when she was a teen. She'd painted the walls a creamy yellow that caught the morning light and reminded her of buttercups. The quilt that covered the bed was one she'd made with the help of Rebecca, one of her Amish friends.

She tried to read five more pages in her textbook, but she couldn't concentrate. She looked out at the full moon shining on the tree outside her window and found her thoughts drifting back to the drive with Abram that afternoon.

Was he finding it hard to sleep after such a sad day? She hoped not. So she said a prayer for him, one that asked God to help him find peace, and slept.

$$\mathscr{SSS}$$

Living on a farm meant nothing was predictable about your day.

Abram had barely started his day when he heard a commotion outside the barn. Picking up his flashlight, he walked outside. A loud squawking came from the chicken coop. He shone his flashlight at the coop and a blur of dark fur raced past, its eyes glowing red in the beam. It held a limp hen in its jaws. He watched it run down the driveway as he walked to the coop. The hens were squawking as he entered and fastened the door behind him. Bessie, a honey-colored bird, lay still on the ground. Abram crouched down and ran the light over her and saw the dark stain of blood on her feathers.

"Aw, Bessie, I'm sorry." He rose and checked the other hens, while they stomped around the enclosure letting him know how upset they were at the fright they'd endured. A quick scan revealed where the fox had gotten in. Fixing it had to be his first chore of the day after he finished in the barn.

He picked the dead hen up, carried her into the house, and placed her in the sink. Then he returned to the barn to take the horses outside while he cleaned their stalls. That done, he led them back into the barn for food and water. Then he set about repairing the hole in the chicken coop. The chickens were still letting him know they were upset and sure enough, after the repair was finished, they didn't make it easy for him to find the eggs. Hettie, the oldest hen, pecked at his hands until he shooed her aside and put the egg she'd laid in a pail.

He carried the eggs inside the house, washed them in the sink, and set three aside for his breakfast. Couldn't get any fresher than just laid . . . he put the other eggs in the refrigerator and got a package of sausage out while he was there. By the time he sat down to breakfast he'd already put in several hours of hard work. At least this time of year, he didn't have to jump up and rush outside to work in the fields. So he enjoyed a second cup of coffee before washing up his dishes and mentally preparing to clean the hen.

Life and death on the farm, he thought. It was best not to get attached to farm animals—especially ones that might end up on the dinner table. His *mudder* had loved caring for the chickens, but Abram hadn't much liked doing it since she'd left. He liked the fresh eggs but he *schur* didn't like how bad tempered some of the chickens were or the details of preparing one for the pot.

Well, since his *mudder* wasn't here, it was up to him to take care of the hen. He got out a big kettle, filled it with water, and set it on the stove to heat. Rummaging in a drawer he found a pair of pliers and set them on the counter. Every Amish child who lived on a farm learned how to plant and harvest, how to care for the stock, how to butcher and clean a hen or a pig or whatever. It was part of farm life.

So he went through the steps, scalding the bird in the big kettle to loosen the feathers, letting it cool, then plucking the feathers with the pliers. As he worked, Abram asked himself how long it had been since he'd done this. And what was he going to do with it after he cleaned it? He hadn't done a lot of cooking since his parents had left. His *mudder* had left casseroles in the refrigerator freezer, but they had run out at some point. So he'd eaten a lot of soup and sandwich suppers and enjoyed what the *maedels* he knew brought by. And he was always welcome at Wayne's house so that helped.

He set the clean bird in a big bowl, washed his hands, then covered the bowl with plastic wrap and set it in the refrigerator. As he cleaned the blood and feathers from the sink and the surrounding counter—the job had been messy—he ran through the list of chicken dishes he could prepare. His glance fell on the recipe box. He fixed himself a cup of coffee and sat at the table to look through it.

That's where Wayne found him a while later.

"What's up?"

"Fox got in the chicken coop early this morning. Killed one of the hens and took another off with him. I'm looking through *Mamm's* recipes."

"You're gonna cook?" Wayne gave him a disbelieving look as he set some papers down on the table, poured himself a cup of coffee, and sat down.

Abram shrugged. "Horse dies you bury it. Chicken dies, you clean it and cook it, right?"

"Right."

"Besides, I cook."

"As little as possible."

He shrugged. "You don't do much either."

"That's what's nice about having the *eldres* still around." He sat in the chair and watched Abram flip through the cards.

"Don't rub it in."

"Sorry. But it must be nice to have the place to yourself."

Abram looked up from a card. "It was nice at first. Now it feels a little lonely sometimes, rattling around in this place."

Wayne glanced at the counter. "No baked goods. No *maedels* been around to drop any off?"

"I expect that'll trail off for a while now that wedding season is almost over."

"Yeah. Too bad. I was enjoying stopping by to help you eat them."

"What's your favorite chicken dish?"

"Fried. Baked. Barbecue chicken. Chicken noodle casserole. Chicken potpie. Wings and beer. Don't tell *Mamm* about the beer," he said with a grin. "That was back during my *rumschpringe*."

"And you haven't touched beer since."

"No comment." He picked up a recipe card, studied it, then set it down. "Seems to me I remember my *mudder* saying the older the hen, the longer it takes to cook it and make it tender. My *mudder* makes chicken and dumplings with the older birds when they stop laying." He set his cup down. "You know what I'm thinking?"

Abram chuckled. "I don't even try."

"We could drop the bird off for *Mamm* to cook for you."

Abram considered it. "*Nee.* I eat at your house often enough as it is. Time for me to start cooking more. Even if my *eldres* come back someday and stay in the *dawdi haus*, it wouldn't be right to act like my *mudder* or yours should cook for me."

He scanned the recipe for chicken and dumplings and figured it was simple enough. His *mudder* had always said that recipes were just directions used to cook. So he got up and filled a big pot he'd seen her use to make the dish. He put the bird in the pot, added some salt, and turned the gas flame up under the pot. Then, after consulting the recipe, he set the timer and sat down.

"So what are we going to do now? Watch water boil?"

"Well, that's what I'm going to do. Do you have something more interesting to do?"

"I thought we could look over this information I got on horse auctions coming up." He pushed them over to Abram.

So they sat in the kitchen poring over the auction information while the chicken simmered in the pot and gradually made the kitchen smell great like it had back when his *mudder* cooked.

And long after they discussed the auctions, the timer went off, and the chicken was cooked, Wayne stuck around to see—as he said—what the final result would be. Abram consulted the recipe again, mixed the ingredients for the dumplings, and dropped the mixture by the tablespoonful on top of the bubbling liquid and covered the pot.

Abram set the timer again but stood by the stove to make sure the dumplings didn't boil over.

"You gonna invite me to lunch?"

"You sure you're not afraid to try it?"

"I've eaten Barbie Troyer's cooking. I think I can survive yours."

"Maybe I'll tell Barbie you said that." Abram got plates from the cupboard and set them on the counter. When the timer went off again he lifted the lid and found fluffy dumplings that looked just as good as those his *mudder* made. He shut off the flame, spooned up a serving on a plate, turned to hand it to Wayne, and found him standing right behind him.

"*Gut* job."

Abram served himself and sat at the table. They thanked God for the meal and looked at each other as if to say, "Who tries it first?"

So Abram tasted it cautiously and nodded. "Not bad. Not what I'd have wished for Bessie, but she had a *gut* life."

"So if a guy can learn to cook that good, why get married?"

Abram just shook his head. "If you need me to answer that, you're worse off than I thought."

Seven

Summer pulled up in front of Abram's house early Sunday morning, turned off the ignition, and checked her appearance in her rearview mirror. She'd pulled her hair back in a big braid and worn a soft gray blouse and long flowing skirt in deference to the church service and hoped it was okay. She took a deep breath. It had been a long time since she'd gone to a church service—any kind of church service. Part of her was still angry at God for taking her father home. If that was wrong, well, that's how she felt. Watching a strong, wonderful, loving man fight cancer for two years had been the worst time of her life.

She took a deep breath, reached for the picnic basket she'd brought, and got out of the car. Abram was hitching his horse to the buggy out by the barn so she walked there to meet him.

"What's this?" he asked, spying the basket. "I told you we'd go to lunch."

"I thought you might like to have a picnic."

He took the basket from her and they walked to his buggy. "That'll be fun, but weren't you busy enough with all you do?"

She shrugged. "I enjoyed it. My mom does most of the cooking during the week." She watched him take a peek as he put the basket in the back seat, then got into the buggy. "Fried chicken, potato salad, baked beans. Isn't a picnic without them. Hope you like all that."

"Who doesn't? Service is at the Fisher home today."

"Barbie and Levi Fisher?"

"*Ya.* You know them?"

"I came here with my dad once." She smoothed her long skirt as he got into the buggy. "They were so nice to me."

Abram nodded. "They're nice people."

They chatted about their week as they rode to the service.

"This is so much more relaxing than being in a car," she told him. "I can see how easy it would be to fall asleep."

"Tired?"

"A bit. I stayed up to put the finishing touches on my paper."

He pulled up in the Fishers' drive and let her out and then drove the buggy back to the barn to unhitch his horse. As Summer stood on the porch and waited for him, members of the church began arriving.

"Summer! How nice to see you again!" John Byler said as he climbed the stairs. He leaned heavily on his cane and smiled at her. "It's been a long time."

"It has. How have you been, John?" He looked older and a little frail.

"Good. How is your mother?"

"She's doing well. We appreciated you coming to Dad's funeral."

"He was a good man." He turned as a young woman stepped up beside him. "You remember my daughter-in-law, Miriam?"

"I do. I was sorry I couldn't come to your wedding. I was away at college." She smiled as she saw the chubby-faced toddler Miriam carried. "But I haven't met this little one."

"This is Johnny," Miriam told her. She shifted him on her hip. "Mark will be happy to see you. Who did you come with?"

"Abram invited me."

She smiled. "That's nice. *Kumm*, let's go inside and find a seat."

They went into the house and others greeted her: the Troyers, the Zook family, some of the people she knew from following her father on his work visiting their farms. Some she knew from the visits she made to collect soil and water samples. They greeted her warmly and made her glad she'd come.

Summer sat in the women's side with Miriam, who she'd met on a visit to the Byler farm with her father. Miriam quickly introduced her to other women. Summer nodded and hoped she'd remember their names.

Memories from her visit with her father came rushing back. She'd sat on a bench just like this one with the women and babies on one side, the men and boys on the other. Abram entered the room and she flashed back to seeing him as a lanky young teen. He was taller now and had filled out, a handsome man in his Sunday best white shirt and dark coat. When he saw her, he grinned at her before sitting on the bench next to Miriam's *mann*, Mark.

Although the room was full and many children were with their parents, everyone was quiet as the lay minister strode to the front and began the service.

Summer's church—the one she used to attend with her parents—was large and elaborate. The service always began with ponderous organ music and a choir dressed in satin robes.

Here the congregation held simple songbooks and sang a cappella. Their voices rose in reverent notes that seemed to enter her soul and soothe her. She felt herself relaxing, singing along, the words and notes familiar somehow. When the lay minister began his lesson, she liked the way he seemed to be sharing the truth he'd found in a passage from the Bible instead of preaching at the congregation and having greater knowledge than them.

Several times she felt as if someone were staring at her, and when she looked surreptitiously over in Abram's direction she found him gazing at her, looking thoughtful. She smiled shyly and looked away.

Summer felt someone lean against her and smiled at Miriam's little boy who'd fallen asleep. She shook her head when Miriam started to move him. "He's fine," she whispered.

If she were a member of this community she might be married and have children of her own by now, she thought, and then shook her head as if to banish the thought. Her life was different and she liked it, didn't she?

The service was long, but it seemed to pass quickly with the gentle lesson and the many songs that all resonated deeply within her. Still, it felt good to have Johnny stir, for them all to stand and stretch. She was invited to help the women prepare and serve the simple meal of bread and church spread—she remembered eating a slice of bread with the peanut butter and marshmallow church spread with the same glee as Johnny when she was younger.

She was serving coffee with Rose Miller when Rose paled and swayed. Quickly she set down the coffee pot and grasped Rose's arm.

"Are you all right?"

"I'm fine," Rose said. "I think I'll go out on the porch and get some fresh air. The smell of the coffee just caught me there for a moment."

Only then did she realize that beneath the white apron the woman wore was an obvious baby bump.

"Shall I get your husband?"

"No, he'll just worry."

"I think I'd like some fresh air too, if you don't mind."

"That would be nice. We can catch up."

They walked outside and took seats in the rocking chairs most Amish porches seemed to have.

"I heard you moved back and took over your family's farm." She studied Rose. "Are you sure you're all right? I can get you some water."

"I'm fine. Mornings are still a little rough, but I'm told it passes after the fourth or fifth month." She grinned. "I don't mind. We're all thrilled. Especially my son, Daniel."

Summer smiled. "Congratulations on the marriage and the baby. I'm glad you moved back. I guess Lillian is too."

Rose nodded. "It's so nice for all the cousins to be together."

A little boy raced out onto the porch. "*Mamm! Daed* was looking for you."

"Daniel, this is Summer."

He looked at her. "Summer? Your name is Summer?"

"It is."

"Why?"

She chuckled. "My mom said she loves summer best." She looked at Rose. "It was a very long winter that year. Thinking about summer helped her get through it. If you know what I mean."

Rose chuckled. "I do."

"I like summer," Daniel spoke up. "We don't have *schul* then. I like *schul* but summer's fun. We play *all* day."

"I like *schul* too, but I like it when I don't go and I get all day to play too."

He giggled. "Big people don't play."

"I guess we don't the way kids do. But I work in my garden more in the summer and it feels like playing to me."

"*Mamm* and I garden, don't we, *Mamm?*"

"We *schur* do."

Rose's twin sister, Lillian, walked out carrying a toddler, followed by Lillian's husband who held another. Two older children followed them, elbowing each other in the way of brothers and sisters.

"*Aenti* Lillian has *zwillingbopplin!*" Daniel told Summer.

"I—see." She smiled at Lillian. "They're adorable."

"I want *zwillingbopplin*," Daniel told his mother earnestly.

"I know, *Lieb*. But God's sending us one *boppli* this time, and we're all very happy about that, aren't we?" She stood and smiled at a second man who joined them on the porch. "Summer, this is my *mann*, Luke Miller. I don't think you've met."

✐✐✐

Abram saw Summer go outside with Rose Miller, and he excused himself from talking to the bishop as soon as he could. He was looking forward to leaving as soon as possible and going on that picnic she'd mentioned. Outside he found her admiring Lillian's *zwillingbopplin*.

He blinked. She seemed so much a part of his friends sitting there, chatting so easily, it took him aback for a moment. She looked so relaxed, so different from the day she'd asked him if he wanted to go for a drive with her.

"Abram! I'm just catching up with everyone," she said when she saw him standing there.

"Well, we're going to get home and get everyone down for a nap," Lillian said. "Wave bye-bye to Summer!"

The toddlers waved their chubby little hands as they were carried off. Summer watched the older children follow their parents. When they reached the bottom of the stairs, their mother called, "Stop the elbowing!" without turning her head. They stopped after a glare at each other.

"Mothers have eyes in the back of their heads," Summer said.

"They do. Did you enjoy the service?" he asked.

She nodded. "I'm so glad I came," she told him. "It was a wonderful service. And what fun to see everyone."

"I'll go get the buggy."

Wayne caught up with him as he walked to the barn. "Saw you invited Summer this morning."

Abram led Joe out of the barn, began to hitch him to his buggy, and waited for the inevitable questions.

"She's pretty," Wayne said.

"Ya."

"I remember when she came to church years ago with her family."

"Ya."

"She's *Englisch*."

"She is?" Abram pretended surprise.

Wayne frowned. "I've never known you to bring an *Englisch* woman to church."

"First time for everything, I guess." Abram climbed into the buggy and tried to ignore Wayne peering into the back seat.

"Looks like a picnic basket."

Abram glanced back then grinned. "It does." He watched his friend put his hands on his hips. "Gotta go. Have a nice afternoon."

Summer waited at the bottom of the porch steps and climbed inside. "Beautiful day for a picnic."

He drove to a small park maintained by the city. It had picnic tables set near the small pond where ducks swam. A family with children tossed breadcrumbs to the ducks.

Summer spread a checked cloth on the table and then began setting out plastic containers of food. "I hope you like fried chicken."

Abram grinned. "Love it. Haven't had it since my parents left. Unless you count picking it up at KFC once or twice." He put a leg and a wing on his plate. "I thought about trying to make it recently."

He told her the story of the fox and the chicken coop, leaving out the details of cleaning the bird before he cooked it.

She grimaced. "I watched my mom kill and clean a chicken once. I grew up on a farm, remember? I was about ten and I cried and wouldn't eat it. As I remember it, I refused to eat chicken for months. I finally caved. I'm glad I can go to the grocery store and buy a package of it all ready to cook." She chose a breast and opened the containers of potato salad and baked beans. "So you cook?"

"I wanted to eat after the parents left so, yeah, I learned." He helped himself to a large serving of potato salad and beans, then took a bite of chicken. "Mmm, good."

"Thank you."

"I made chicken and dumplings for the first time. My friend Wayne stopped by and we looked through recipes like a couple of housewives." He listed all the options they'd scanned and she laughed.

"Sounds like Bubba in *Forrest Gump*."

He frowned. "What?"

"Oh, sorry, sometimes I forget not everyone knows every movie made. Especially the older ones. Bubba was a character in *Forrest Gump*. It was a favorite of Dad's. There's this character who lists all the ways to cook shrimp. You know . . . fried shrimp and boiled shrimp and shrimp gumbo and . . . well, the character goes on and on."

"I don't think Wayne has seen that movie. But he sure went on and on about every way you could cook a chicken. Wayne told me his mother once said older birds needed slower cooking so we went with that." Abram finished the two pieces and debated taking another.

Summer pushed the container toward him.

"Read my mind," he said with a chuckle as he took a third piece.

"So how did the chicken and dumplings turn out?"

"Pretty good. If I do say so myself. We each had a couple of servings."

"I bet you don't have to cook often. I happen to know Amish single ladies drop off casseroles and baked goods."

"Who's been talking?"

She laughed. "I did it myself, bringing you an apple pie that day."

"I thought about proposing to your mom."

"Oh really?" She arched an eyebrow at him.

"Just kidding."

"I know. But you noticed Carl brought her a bushel of apples. He figured he'd get some pies from her for doing it."

He wiped his lips on a paper napkin. "Wayne is glad the marriage season is over. He likes being a bachelor and doesn't want to settle down yet."

"What about you?"

"What about me?"

"Are you ready to settle down?"

Eight

"I'm sorry, that's nosy," Summer said quickly, a little embarrassed that the question had slipped out.

Abram grinned. "It's okay. I don't mind. I'd like to think we're becoming friends and you can ask me things like that." He pushed aside his empty plate. "Yes, I think I am."

"I know my Amish friends have told me that they believe God sets aside someone for them. Do you believe that?"

"I do. How about you?"

"I believe God has a plan for us so I guess that means He has someone chosen for us. I'm not sure why people sometimes end up with the wrong person, but God gives us freedom of choice and it's all a learning lesson. Sometimes a hard one."

"Are you ready to settle down?"

She laughed and shook her head. "No. I have college, a career to get started." She sighed. "I do hope one day I'll have the kind of marriage my parents had."

He nodded. "Mine have that." Thoughtful, she reached into the basket and pulled out a container. "Do you want dessert?"

"I'm a man. What do you think?"

Summer laughed. "Dumb question." She opened the container and saw his eyes light up. "Mom baked another pie yesterday."

"Apple?"

She nodded and served him a slice.

"I see why Carl brings her apples." He waited until she'd served herself and then he took a bite. "So good."

"She makes the best." She took a bite and then frowned. "I'm lucky I still live at home and have most of my meals cooked for me. I was talking to another student one day who was going home to a can of SpaghettiOs. My mom had packed my lunch and had dinner for me when I got home from class."

"The student doesn't know how to cook?"

"Money's so tight that's all she had. She's a single parent putting herself through college." Just the thought made Summer feel guilty that she had the meal they'd just eaten. She'd made sure when she tutored Kim that she always brought an extra sandwich and a bag of cookies after she realized her situation.

"That's awful." He finished his pie with a satisfied sigh. "I have to say my mother often said I have a hollow leg, but I've never gone hungry."

"I can't say I have either. I'll have to invite her to dinner some night." She sighed. "But that's just a solution for one meal." She saw him eye her unfinished slice of pie and pushed it toward him.

"You sure?" he asked politely, but her "yes" had barely slipped from her lips when he had her plate in front of him.

She propped her elbow on the table, rested her chin in her hand, and watched him eat. "If the single women in your community hear that you're ready to settle down, they're going to be bringing you all sorts of casseroles and desserts." She tilted her head and studied him. Was he trying to hold back a smile? "They're doing it already, aren't they?"

"Were. Now that the marriage season is over, it'll slack off for a while."

She could see it. Abram was a handsome man with his dark brown hair, brown eyes, and strong features. And he had a successful farm. He probably had Amish *maedels* falling all over him.

"Why did you invite me to church today?" she asked him as she pulled a thermos of coffee from the basket and poured them each a cup.

He shrugged. "Worship always comforts me. You seemed so stressed the other day." He sipped his coffee. "Did you enjoy it?"

"I did." She smiled. "Do I look less stressed?"

"You do."

"I hope it lasts for a while. The trouble is, while I'm in classes there's always a hundred or so pages of textbook to read for the next class, another quiz to study for, a paper hanging over my head I haven't started yet." She sighed. "Speaking of, I should be thinking about heading home."

"The *Englisch* run run run," he said quietly. "They always have a thing to do. A project. A goal that must be met right away. Yet you have an expression, 'Stop and smell the roses.' Summer, remember, 'You will find rest for your soul.'"

"From Matthew. In the Bible," she remembered. "My favorite book in the Bible."

"I'm glad you came today."

Their gazes met.

"Me too," she said. She told herself she was imagining there was a deeper meaning beneath his words. She looked down and picked up the thermos and the empty cups and packed them into the basket. He helped her fold the tablecloth, and when their fingers touched she tried not to turn her hand up against his and hold it. Flustered, she finished packing the basket.

They got into the buggy and started the drive back to Abram's.

"Maybe we can do this again."

Summer looked at him. "Maybe."

"Maybe I'll bring the picnic next time. I don't think I'll try making fried chicken."

"It's not hard."

"We'll see. I'm cooking more since my parents are away. Thank you for coming today and for the picnic." He pulled into the drive and they got out. "And thank you for giving me part of your pie. I'm afraid I was shameless in asking for it."

"You didn't ask. I offered."

"Sure," he said, trying to hold back a grin.

She drove home, feeling relaxed, pleasantly full from her lunch, and ready for a Sunday afternoon nap before hitting the books again.

The house was quiet when she stepped into the kitchen. Her mother was probably upstairs taking a nap. Summer unpacked the basket and put the containers in the sink. She'd wash them later. Nap first. When she went upstairs she saw her mother's door stood ajar. She peeked in. Her mother's bed was empty. And she wasn't in the bathroom.

Summer went back downstairs and walked through the living room. Her mother wasn't there either. She didn't see her car, but her mother usually parked in the garage behind the house. She didn't remember her mother saying she was going anywhere today when she'd left to go to church with Abram. Nothing was written on the calendar in the kitchen. Her mother always wrote down appointments and lunch dates with friends. There was nothing written on today's date.

Well, maybe something had come up. Maybe a friend had stopped by and invited her out. Carl might have driven her into town. She looked out the window and saw his truck parked in front of his cottage.

Well, she was sure she didn't need to worry. Her mother wasn't a child.

Summer climbed the stairs, went into her room, and kicked off her shoes. She'd take her nap and when she woke up, her mother would probably be home and starting their Sunday dinner of soup and sandwiches.

Bed felt so good after getting up early for church. Summer snuggled under her quilt and slept. She woke an hour later, yawned, and made herself get up. When she walked past her mother's room, it was still empty. The kitchen was empty too. She glanced at the clock. It was after five.

Something didn't feel right. She went to the phone and called Carl.

"I haven't seen her today," he told her. "She probably went out with a friend."

"Maybe. She didn't say anything this morning."

"I'm sure there's no need to worry."

She agreed and hung up. With a sigh she washed up the plastic containers from the picnic, then heated the soup her mother had

71

made and left in the refrigerator. The homemade vegetable soup and a grilled cheese sandwich were the perfect simple Sunday supper after the picnic earlier in the day. That done, she settled down at the table with her books and tried not to worry about where her mother was.

An hour later her mother walked in. Her face looked pale and there were tears drying on her cheeks. She took off her jacket and dropped it and her purse onto the bench by the door.

"I was worried about you. Where were you?"

"Driving around." Marie started for the stairs.

"Mom, wait! What's wrong?"

"I went to church and afterward, some of us went to lunch. Mona Fitzpatrick asked how long Howard had been gone and when I told her, she said I should be over him by now."

"What a horrible thing to say!" She jumped up and hugged her mother. "I'm sorry."

"I know I've been dragging around feeling sorry for myself. Look, I just want to go to bed."

Feeling helpless, Summer let her go.

$$\mathscr{SSS}$$

"Welcome to your new home," Abram told Samson as he led his new horse into the barn. He went slowly, knowing Samson was a bit skittish, giving him time to get comfortable. The other horses stuck their heads over their stalls, so Abram introduced them.

"This here's Joe. He's one of the horses that pulls the buggy and the spring wagon. He's a Standardbred like you. And here's Jim and Jake, the draft horses. They help me out in the fields. And that's Lucy, the barn cat. She likes mice."

Samson eyed Lucy warily. Abram suspected he might not have been around a lot of barn cats. The whip marks on Samson's back also told him his last owner had ill-used him and he'd need some careful handling for a time.

Abram glanced over his shoulder as he made the introductions. His friend Wayne would probably laugh at him. He knew some people thought talking to their horses or cows or whatever was silly. They were animals—helpers but not companions, after all. But when you worked alone for so many hours outdoors with your horses, they became partners in the work, didn't they? And gave their all to you.

Roy had been with him for so many years. He'd become a friend as well as helpmate, and Abram had confided in him so often and felt not just companionship but a deeper connection.

Wasn't that why God had put them on this earth? To be helpful to man?

Summer had looked embarrassed admitting she named her car Betsy. That was just a machine. But until recently her car had been a trusted device that had gotten her safely and dependably to where she needed to go, so in an odd way, he supposed it made sense. They both spoke to what helped them. Their worlds were different but underneath it all, were they?

They both loved the land. He saw it that day she came here to test the water and soil, but more, he saw it in the way she worked in her garden when he stopped by and found her there. How at home she looked, how happy and relaxed.

He was sorry that she was stressing herself out so much with school and work. He hadn't been the best of students and had been glad when he graduated. Working and learning beside his father on the farm had been where he wanted to be. Not that he'd stopped trying to improve himself. Like many of his friends and family he read a lot; he had a subscription to *The Budget* and read a lot of books—and not all of them on farming techniques. After all, learning didn't stop in the classroom, and he enjoyed reading.

With the new horse settled in nicely and his morning chores done, Abram headed inside for lunch. As he ate a thick ham and cheese sandwich and glanced through his mail, he wondered what Summer was doing. If he remembered her schedule at her part-time job, it was a workday today. He hoped she hadn't eaten a sandwich at her desk so she could leave work early as she'd said that day she stopped by. That sounded too stressful.

There was a knock at the kitchen door and then his brother, Eli, walked in.

"Abram, my *fraa* made you a casserole." He set the casserole dish on the table and snatched a potato chip from Abram's plate before plopping down in a chair.

"What took you so long?"

"What do you mean?"

"I know why you're here."

"Delivering a casserole my sweet *fraa* made for my *bruder?*"

"*Schur.* Are you going to try to pretend she didn't send you over to ask me about Summer?"

"I don't have to pretend. She's capable of asking her own questions."

"But she's not here."

The door opened and Mary walked in carrying their two-year-old *dochder.* "Linda, say hello to *Onkel* Abram."

He pushed his plate aside and held out his arms for her. "There's my favorite girl!"

Mary plucked a potato chip from his plate and sat beside her *mann.* "Your favorite girl isn't the one you brought to church?"

Ignoring her, he gave a potato chip to Linda. She grinned at him and crunched it.

"Didn't know you were here."

"We were admiring Linda's shadow. She just discovered it on the way inside."

"Ah, wish I'd seen that," he told her. "Everything's a discovery at this age, isn't it?"

"Like Summer?"

Abram turned to Mary. "You know her."

"*Schur.* So why did you bring her to church?"

"I thought she'd enjoy it."

"Are you seeing her?"

"She's a friend," he said firmly. "Linda, would you like to see my new horsie?"

"Horsie!" she cried and clapped her pudgy hands.

He held her hand as they walked outside. As they stepped off the porch steps, Linda pointed at her shadow. "Look! Look! Shadow!"

Abram nodded. "Shadow." Hers was so small next to his. He saw her comparing them, her eyes huge.

"Horsie," he reminded her, and hauled her up into his arms for safety as they walked into the dim barn.

"Samson's a little nervous," he cautioned. "It'll take some time for him to get adjusted to his new home."

"Whip marks on his back," Mary murmured, frowning.

Abram nodded.

"You always were one for the mistreated," his *bruder* said.

Samson put his head over the stall and his nostrils flared as he scented the newcomers.

"Be careful," Mary said, moving closer.

"Sh, it's *allrecht*," he assured her as Linda reached out and touched the horse's nose.

"Soft," she said. "Shadow," she said, looking at Abram.

"Yes, he is like a shadow, isn't he? Big and black. Maybe I'll call him Shadow." He glanced at Eli and Mary "Seems like Samson deserves a new name for his new life."

"Shadow," Linda repeated firmly.

And that was that. Samson became Shadow.

Nine

Summer sat in the snack bar waiting for Kim and scanning her notes on her laptop.

A woman came in and pushed a dollar into the coffee machine. It spit it out. She tried again. It spit it out again. She turned and saw Summer watching her. "I guess it would be unseemly to kick the machine, wouldn't it?" she asked ruefully.

"Yes, Professor Allen." Summer bit back a smile.

The woman sighed. "I really need some coffee before class." She tilted her head and studied Summer, frowning as if she were trying to remember. "You took my Psychology of Adjustment last semester. I don't always remember names, but I remember your essay about losing your father. You got an A."

"I did. I enjoyed the class. I'm Summer Carson. Would you like some coffee I brought from home? I can guarantee it's better than the machine."

"You're sure I'm not disturbing your studying?"

Summer shook her head and unscrewed the cap on the thermos. "I'm waiting for a study partner. She's probably been held up in traffic." She poured the coffee into one of the extra cups she'd packed, then pushed the baggie of oatmeal raisin cookies she'd brought toward the professor as she sat down.

"You came well prepared." The professor chose a cookie and smiled. She bit into the cookie. "Mmm, this is good. Can't remember the last time I had a homemade cookie. They certainly don't get made at our house very often. Great coffee too."

"My mother loves to bake. I still live at home. She made the coffee too." Summer paused. "Could I ask you a question?"

The woman grinned. "You just did."

Summer tried to smile. "I'm worried about my mom. She came

home from church Sunday and was upset. Someone told her she should be over my dad's death."

"Oh my. How insensitive." She sipped her coffee. "I wonder if that person has ever truly suffered a loss. There are no time limits on grief."

"Do we ever get over a loss?"

The professor dug in her briefcase and pulled out a pad of paper and a pencil. "You remember the unit we did on loss." She drew a circle on the paper and then filled it in with the pencil. "When we have a loss it consumes all of our being, everything in our life, like this, doesn't it?"

Summer nodded. "I woke up thinking Dad was gone, and I went to bed thinking of him."

"As did your mother. Perhaps even more if that's possible since she knew him longer than you did. And so while, over time, life doesn't feel as dark and things fade a bit, it doesn't go away. It doesn't disappear."

She sat back. "Then anniversaries, birthdays, all sorts of things happen and remind us again of our loss. Even if it's not as painful as in the beginning, it's there."

"So what can we do?"

"We learn to go on. To live with it," she said simply. "How long has it been?"

"Two years."

"If grief is still consuming—if it's debilitating—it's time to get some help. Has your mother been in a grief group? Seen a psychologist?"

"She was in a group at church for a while but stopped going."

The professor tucked her pad and pencil back in her briefcase, drained her coffee, and glanced at the clock on the nearby wall.

"See if you can talk your mother into getting back into the group or talking to someone professional." She leaned back in her chair and regarded Summer with kind eyes. "And how are *you* doing?"

Summer blinked, taken aback at the question. "I'm fine. The course helped me a lot, I think. I had a chance to really think about my feelings, read about what people go through. Talk to other students who had lost their parents and grandparents."

"I'm glad it helped you." She patted Summer's hand and then stood. "Come see me during office hours if you'd like to talk again."

"Thank you so much, Professor Allen."

"And thank you for the coffee and cookie. I enjoyed the break."

Summer sat there thinking about their conversation. When Kim rushed in a few minutes later apologizing for being late, it took Summer a moment to gather her scattered thoughts and say hello. She pulled out a cup and poured Kim some coffee. When she pulled out the ham and cheese sandwich her mother had packed and handed it to Kim, the younger woman shook her head.

"No, I couldn't. That's your sandwich," she demurred.

Summer pulled out a second. "Mom packed two. She's always been this way. She'd tuck an extra sandwich in my lunch bag when I was in school in case some kid forgot his lunch." She pushed the plastic bag of cookies over. "She loves baking cookies too. Says she's a throwback to Donna Reed."

Kim stared at her blankly.

"Reed played a housewife on a TV show back in the fifties." Summer bit into her sandwich.

They ate quickly and then dived into their study session. Zach came in a half hour later and joined them. He eyed the half sandwich that sat untouched in front of Summer. She pushed it toward him, and after a token refusal he scarfed it down.

"The cookies are gone," Summer told him. "You'll need to come earlier next time. But I have apples."

"Cool." He crunched into one. "I have a friend who took the test earlier. He said if we took good notes in class we'll do fine."

"I don't take good notes," Kim complained. "I can't write fast enough. And I never know what's important."

So they compared their notes.

Zach's cell phone alarm went off. "Time to go. Let's kill it."

"If it doesn't kill us," Kim moaned.

"You'll survive," Summer assured her.

And she couldn't wait until they walked out to the parking lot afterward. She'd told her mother about Kim the other day and her mother had done more than pack an extra sandwich and cookies for her. A lot more.

✐✐✐

Abram led Shadow out of the barn and began hitching him to the buggy. He'd given the horse a couple of days to settle in and get used to him and the farm routine. Now it was time to get down to the reason he'd bought Shadow. "Let's go explore your new neighborhood."

Shadow waited with a typical Standardbred's patience while he was hitched to the buggy. Abram had gotten him at a good price as a retired harness racer, but his skittishness, the welts on his back, meant he might need some time adapting to his new life.

Abram climbed into the buggy and had a moment's flashback to the last ride with Roy. He felt a lump in his throat at the memories and sent up a silent prayer of thanks to God for all the hours of safe travel, pleasure, and friendship with him. And then he picked up the reins, called "giddyap," and Shadow set off down the drive.

"Let's take a drive down some back roads today, shall we? Work up to a drive into town maybe tomorrow." He talked as Shadow pulled the buggy, giving him a kind of guided tour. If it was silly to do so, well, he didn't mind looking or sounding silly. Abram figured that it might ease Shadow's transition to his new area and besides, who could hear him other than the horse?

He remembered the last time he'd taken a drive—taken the time to do so. It had been with Summer, the day Roy had died and his friends had come by to help him bury him. Summer had stopped by and they'd taken a drive in her car. He wondered what she was doing today. It was her day off. Maybe she was home. Maybe he and Shadow should stop by. Maybe.

The weather couldn't have been more perfect. Blue sky with no hint of clouds, a slight nip in the air. They passed farm stands where his fellow Amish were selling pumpkins, squash, jars and jars of jams and jellies. Abram waved and received waves and nods from friends and church members.

Business appeared good. *Englisch* cars were parked in front of many of the stands and tourists were buying, it seemed. He stopped at Sarah Bontrager's stand and bought two loaves of bread. The bread his *mudder* had baked and left in the freezer was long gone, and he didn't fancy store-bought. She asked him about his *eldres*, and he told her about the latest postcard reporting on his *mudder's* amazement at picking oranges from a tree in her front yard and his *dat's* success in fishing.

"Sounds *wunderbaar*," she told him as she handed him the bag with the bread and took his money. "But I like home too much to go off to Florida even to escape our winters." She tucked in a jar of pear preserves. "I seem to remember these are your favorite."

"They are indeed. *Danki*."

"Fine new horse there. How's he doing?"

"*Gut* so far."

An *Englisch* man approached and looked over the baked goods. "Everything smells *wunderbaar*," he said jovially, mispronouncing the Pennsylvania *Deitsch*. "I'll take three loaves of bread and a dozen of those pumpkin whoopie pies." He turned to Abram. "Mind if I take a photo of your horse and buggy?"

Because he was so polite and didn't ask to take one of him—and because he was being such a generous customer of Sarah's baked goods—Abram nodded.

"The original horsepower, eh?" the man asked, snapping some photos with his cell phone.

"Only kind we use," Abram said, not really knowing what else to say. He pulled a carrot from his pocket, fed it to Shadow, and spoke quietly to him as the man walked to the other side of him. "He's new and a bit shy still so if you don't mind—"

"No problem." The man walked slowly back to where Sarah stood with his purchases. "Thanks for letting me take the photos."

"You're *wilkumm*."

"I tucked in a jar of apple butter for you to try," Sarah told him. "You'll have to let me know if you liked it next time you stop."

"Will do, will do," he said, handing over his money. "You keep the change and have a nice day."

"A regular?" Abram asked as he watched the man drive away.

Sarah nodded. "Stops every couple weeks. Sometimes he visits me out at the farmer's market."

Abram saw another car approach full of noisy *kinner*. "Time for me to be getting along," he said. "Have a *gut-n-owed*."

"You too."

They resumed their ride, and Abram waved at friends as they passed in their own buggies. Shadow took commands well so Abram decided to go a little farther. He found himself wondering again what Summer was doing. It was her day off . . . maybe he'd take them by her place.

Abram pulled into the drive and saw her working in her garden. She stood, shielded her eyes against the sun, and waved. He waved back and got out to stand by Shadow and watched her walk gracefully toward him.

"Hello," she said with a smile. She glanced at Shadow. "I see you have a new horse. How are you, fella?" Keeping her voice low, she reached out slowly and stroked his nose.

"This is Shadow."

"Nice to meet you, Shadow. I'm Summer."

Shadow made a low snuffling noise and took one step closer.

"He likes you."

She grinned. "I like him. Maybe we have an apple in the kitchen for him."

"I brought one with me you can give him. We're on our first trip out."

"And you came by to see me? How nice."

"I should have called first."

She shook her head and stroked Shadow's nose. "It's my day off. I'm just gardening, relaxing."

"Maybe you'd like to go for a ride?"

"Maybe I would. If you two wouldn't mind waiting while I wash up."

"We're not in a hurry."

Abram was glad he'd thought to stop by, take a chance to see her. He couldn't remember a time when he thought about a woman so much.

When she returned she'd washed her hands and changed her shirt. And she had a carrot in her hand for Shadow.

"Trying to make friends with him, are you?"

"I love horses." She fed Shadow the carrot, and he rewarded her with a nuzzle on her shoulder. "I miss mine."

She climbed into the buggy. "I saw the scars on his back. He's had some rough treatment."

Abram nodded and set the buggy in motion. "He's been a bit skittish, but he warmed right up to you."

She favored him with a grin. "Well, I'm a likeable kind of person."

Ya, he thought. Too likeable. *What am I doing spending time with you when I should be looking at a woman in my own community?*

But he wanted to be with Summer Carson.

Ten

Summer leaned back in the front seat of the buggy and sighed. "I love riding in a buggy." When a car zoomed around them, she frowned and sat up straight. "Well, when someone isn't being an idiot. I'm proud of Shadow. It didn't faze him at all."

Abram muttered under his breath.

"What is it?"

"Maybe it wasn't a good idea to ask you along on our first trip. What if Shadow had bolted?"

"Then you'd have handled it," she told him.

"I don't know. Maybe I should take you home."

"Absolutely not. I trust both of you."

"Okay. But if you feel uncomfortable at all, I want you to let me know."

"Deal."

"I'm just getting him used to the neighborhood. We went down some back roads, bought some bread from Sarah, then found ourselves going down your road."

"I'm glad you did. I worked in the garden all morning and it was time for a break."

"You really love it."

"I do. I don't know how much longer we'll have before it gets cold so I'm enjoying it."

"My mother loved her kitchen garden, but after all the canning at the end of summer I think she was ready for a little rest."

"Is she getting it in Florida?"

"Well it seems like they're awfully busy having fun. Not sure how restful their vacation really is."

"I can't even remember what a vacation is," Summer murmured.

"Maybe you should take one."

"That's not going to happen anytime soon. I haven't built up enough

time at work yet for vacation. And I lost too much time from college."
She stopped, looked horrified. "I didn't mean that the way I said it. I
took time off when Dad was sick. He didn't want me to but—"

Abram touched her hand. "Don't. I know you didn't mean that."

Summer stared at his hand and he pulled it back.

"Mom's enjoying bicycling around with her friends, playing shuffle-
board, eating a meal out now and then instead of cooking them. And
Dad's fishing every day."

"I wonder if my mom had a little vacation if it wouldn't do her
some good." She hesitated then told him about how her mother had
come home upset after church on Sunday. "I talked about it with one
of my professors but . . ."

"But you're still worried."

"Yeah."

"My parents would love to have her. They rented a two-bedroom
bungalow. Do you want me to ask if she can visit?"

She bit her lip. "That's so generous of you to offer. I'll ask Mom if
she'd like to get away for a few days. She and Dad rarely left the farm
when he was alive. But I'm not sure she'd go by herself, and I can't
leave right now."

"If the time is right it will happen." He glanced at her. "I hate to
see you so worried. It seems you have so much on your shoulders. I
wish I could ease some of the burden."

Summer turned in her seat to look at him, really look at him. He
seemed so calm, so steady. "You do. You are. By being a friend. You're
a good man, Abram."

He shook his head. "I've done nothing."

"I'm sorry. I've embarrassed you." She looked out her window and
tried to think what to say. "You listen, Abram. Really listen."

"Anytime, Summer. I mean that."

"Thanks."

"Shadow's doing so well maybe we should take him through a
drive-through. What do you think? Would you like something to
drink?"

"That would be great. An iced tea?"

Abram guided Shadow into the lane for the fast food restaurant and ordered a tea for her and a coffee for him. The young woman at the window didn't bat an eye when she saw their vehicle, no more than Summer did when she saw one on the road or at a store. Buggies were a fact of life in Lancaster County and businesses accommodated them.

Summer sipped her drink while they resumed their drive. Abram held the reins in one hand and drank his coffee. A comfortable silence stretched between them. Summer knew some people thought buggies were an anachronism in modern times. But she was enjoying it today. Of course, buggies weren't so comfortable in the middle of a Lancaster County winter, but that was some time away. The fact was that the heater didn't work very well in her aging sedan either.

"You had a test last night, didn't you? How do you think you did on it?" he asked her.

"Pretty good, I think. I had a study session with two classmates and that always helps."

Another buggy approached from the opposite side of the road. The driver waved at Abram and then glanced over to see who his passenger was. He continued to stare as their buggies passed each other.

Summer chuckled. "Nothing like being curious. I didn't recognize the man. Who was he?"

"Vernon Stoltzfus. The bishop."

Her smile faded. "Oh. Is that a problem?"

Abram glanced over curiously. "Why would it be?"

"He looked . . . shocked."

He shrugged. "Curious, maybe. I don't think shocked."

"You're sure? I wouldn't want you to have any problem with him."

"We're taking a drive. Doesn't seem controversial to me."

They were two friends taking an innocent drive in a buggy in the middle of the afternoon. But buggy rides were often a part of the courting ritual for Amish couples. What if the bishop got the wrong idea?

Seeming unconcerned, Abram talked about the auction he'd gone to with his friend and how he'd come to choose Shadow. It was obvious he was happy with his choice of Shadow and she agreed with him.

He must have seen her surreptitious glance at her watch. "Need to get back?"

"I should. I don't want to. I'm having fun."

When he pulled into her drive a little later and the buggy came to a halt, he turned to her. "Are you busy Saturday? Would you like to have dinner?"

The invitation took her by surprise. Choosing her words carefully, she looked at him. "Abram, where is this going?"

"Going? We're in your driveway," Abram said.

"You know what I mean."

"Maybe you should explain," he told her patiently.

"The bishop gave us that look because he saw an Amish man taking an *Englisch* woman for a ride in his buggy." When Abram continued to look at her, she rolled her eyes. "He looked at us as if we were doing something inappropriate."

"We aren't."

"You know it doesn't take someone actually doing something wrong for people to think they are."

"We're friends," he said quietly. "If the bishop has a problem with that, I'll be happy to tell him so."

"I don't want to cause you any trouble."

"You won't. Summer, you worry too much about too many things."

She sighed. "Maybe."

He grinned. "Maybe?"

"I don't think I worry more than any other woman. Any other *Englisch* woman. I think maybe it's just that you haven't been around so many of us."

"If you say so." When he saw movement out of the corner of his eye, he glanced over at the back door of her home. "Your mother is waving at us."

They watched as she walked toward them. "Hello, Abram. Would you like to stay for dinner? I made a nice pot roast and there's plenty."

Pot roast—or his own still mediocre efforts at cooking. And more time with Summer. "If you're sure it's no trouble."

"No trouble at all. I've asked Carl to come too."

"Then yes, thank you."

"I'll be right in to help, Mom."

"Everything's done," Marie told her. "We'll eat in fifteen minutes." She left them and returned to the house.

"Mom likes to feed people."

"Mine too. I guess it's a mom thing."

"Why don't you pull down the drive more, unhitch Shadow, and give him some water? I'll go in and set the table. You come in when you're ready."

"Okay."

She got out of the buggy, and he drove down and parked near the house.

"You back again?"

Abram looked up from unhitching Shadow to see Carl walking toward him. "Yes. Marie just invited me for supper."

"Seems like you're spending a lot of time with Summer." Carl regarded him from under bushy black eyebrows.

He couldn't help feeling like he was getting the kind of suspicious look Summer had felt she'd gotten from the bishop a few minutes before.

"We're friends."

"Friends?"

Abram nodded.

"Some people say you can't be friends with the opposite sex. Or with someone from a totally different background."

Abram gave him a brief glance. "They'd be wrong," he said calmly.

But how many times in his life had he heard that warning from Corinthians: "Be ye not unequally yoked together with unbelievers: for what fellowship hath righteousness with unrighteousness?" Here in Lancaster County, the Amish and *Englisch* often dealt with each other more than they did in other Amish communities because of the tourism business, but still, it wasn't a casual thing for an Amish man to be friends with an *Englisch* woman . . . and marriage to someone not of the Amish faith just wasn't done. And few *Englisch* converted. They just felt the Amish way of life was too different. Too hard.

He tied Shadow to a fence post, got a bucket from the back seat of the buggy, and poured water from a jug into it.

"Good job today, Shadow."

"Shadow? Different kind of name for an Amish horse, isn't it?"

"My niece named him. It's his first time out with the buggy."

Carl stiffened. "Was it wise to have a passenger the first time you hitched him to a buggy?"

Abram had had that thought shortly after he'd stopped and picked Summer up. Before he could speak Shadow raised his head and looked at Carl. His ears twitched as if he knew what the man was saying about him. Then he went back to drinking water.

"He's been well trained. I wouldn't have bought him otherwise."

Carl grunted. "Summer means a lot to me. I've kinda looked after her and her ma since her pa died."

He looked at the man and nodded. "I know. I wouldn't let anything happen to her."

"Just so we understand each other." Carl turned his gaze to the horse. "Maybe Shadow here would like to explore the pasture while we eat." He opened the gate and Shadow lifted his head. Water dribbled from his mouth. He looked at Carl, then Abram.

"You can go," Abram said, gesturing at the pasture.

Shadow entered the enclosure at a sedate walk and then once inside, took off at a gallop, clearly enjoying the freedom.

"Beautiful animal," Carl said, closing the gate and leaning on the fence. "Been a long time since we had a horse in there. Sure do miss having a horse on the property. But Summer won't consider having another. It hurt her bad when Missy died. And I've got the tractor so we don't need horses to farm the way you Amish do."

"Time to eat!" Summer called from the back porch. "Unless you two aren't hungry."

"Girl don't know men if she thinks we're not hungry," Carl said.

Before he turned to walk into the house Abram thought he saw the man grin.

They sat at the table near each other, and although Abram was still conscious that Carl watched him as carefully as he had that other time he'd eaten here, Abram didn't feel the man was as suspicious as he'd been before.

The pot roast melted on his tongue. Abram couldn't remember when he'd enjoyed a meal more. Marie urged a second helping on him and smiled at his praise. Summer had told him she was worried about her mother, but the woman seemed cheerful as they enjoyed her cooking.

The only sour note came when she served the dessert.

Carl got the first serving of the mixed berry pie and his mouth puckered as if he'd eaten a lemon. Then as the others tasted it, they did the same.

"What—?" Marie said and looked puzzled. "My goodness, this doesn't taste as if I put any sugar in it." She put her fork down and frowned.

Getting up, she walked to the kitchen counter. "Sugar," she said, picking up a measuring cup full of it. "I forgot to sugar the berries. Nobody has to eat it," she told them quickly, and she tried to take Carl's plate from him.

"Tastes fine," he said. "You just forgot the ice cream." He rose to get it, then went to a kitchen drawer with the ease of someone used to being in the kitchen and found an ice cream scoop. He set the carton before Marie, sat, and patted her hand. "Scoop me up some, please."

Marie did as he asked and gave him a tremulous smile. Then she turned to Abram. "Ice cream?"

"I never turn down ice cream," he told her.

"Me either," Summer chimed in. After Marie was finished serving all of them she rose and put the carton back in the freezer.

But then she sat staring at her dessert, blinking hard, and didn't pick up her spoon.

Summer looked distressed as her gaze met Abram's.

"Fine meal, Marie," he said quickly. "It makes me miss my mother even more than usual."

"How—how's she doing?" she asked him, struggling for composure.

He launched into the latest story his mother had written him, and as Marie seemed to relax, Summer gave him a grateful look. She mouthed *thank you* and he nodded.

But he saw her continue to watch her mother and look worried.

Eleven

Summer walked with Abram to the pasture. Dusk was falling and the air was turning cool. "That was nice of you to distract Mom at dinner."

He shrugged. "It was nothing." He turned to her. "Really, nothing. She got too upset about a minor thing. The pie was fine."

She leaned her arms on the pasture fence and watched Shadow running. "It's not just about forgetting to put sugar in a pie. You know I've been concerned about things lately. Episodes where I wondered if *I* was having a problem with my memory. But I think it's Mom, not me."

"Everyone makes a mistake in cooking, if they do it for any length of time," he told her. "Nobody's perfect. My mom even makes a mistake now and then." He slanted a glance at her. "And if you ever say that to her, I'll deny it."

Summer laughed. "Oh, you're such a good friend, Abram." She leaned her head on his arm and sighed. "It wasn't just this one thing. It's been a lot of things." She went over the list.

"If you're really worried maybe it's time to talk to her doctor."

She turned to him, her eyes wide. "You're right."

"Try not to worry so. A woman in our church always says it's arrogant to worry. God knows what He's doing."

"I know." She sighed again. "You need to go. People don't look out for buggies at night." She glanced up at the sky. "It's supposed to rain tonight."

"We can use it." Abram called for Shadow and the horse galloped up to the fence. "Let's go home, fella."

Summer watched him hitch the horse to the buggy then climb inside. She handed him the plastic container of leftovers her mother had insisted Abram take home with him. "I had a good time today. Thank you for stopping by and asking me."

"Thank you for going with us. And tell your mother thanks again for supper and for the leftovers."

She smiled. "Be grateful she cooked, not me."

"You're a good cook. I've tasted your fried chicken, remember?"

"That might be the only thing I know how to cook."

"I doubt it." He paused. "Talk to your mother about visiting my parents."

"I will."

"Good night, Summer. Sleep well."

"You too. And Abram?"

"Yes?"

"We need to have that talk."

He met her gaze and something passed between them. "We will. Soon."

She nodded. "Good night. Be safe."

The buggy rolled down the drive, the safety triangle on the back gleaming in the darkening light until it was out of sight.

Summer walked back into the house and found her mother and Carl drinking coffee at the table. She began clearing the dishes.

"Leave them," her mother said. "I'll take care of them in a minute."

"You cooked, I clean up. And it'll just take a minute."

She washed the dishes, gave the counters a quick swipe with a damp sponge, and then went upstairs.

Her mother tapped on her door a little while later. "You didn't have to rush upstairs."

Summer looked up from her book. "No?" she said with a smile, remembering the time she'd come downstairs unexpectedly and found them sitting close, talking intimately over coffee.

"No. Carl and I were just talking."

"Okay."

Marie walked into the room and sat at the end of Summer's bed. "Carl is just a friend. A good one. I think he feels he needs to look after us now that your father is gone."

"I think he wants more than that."

Color rushed into Marie's cheeks. "Oh now, I doubt he's interested in me." She hesitated. "Carl thinks Abram wants to be more than a friend."

Summer nodded. "I think he's right."

"How do you feel about that?"

"I like him more than I've ever liked a guy before."

"He seems very nice."

"But?"

"No buts." Marie stroked the quilt on the bed and looked thoughtful. "You've had dreams of being an Amish girl for years. It's a hard life, Summer. I wouldn't want you to romanticize it."

"I don't. But there are a lot of positives to their religion, their way of life. That's why so many people come here to see how they live."

"And then talk about how they couldn't do without electricity and so on."

Summer laughed. "Yes. While they drive around in their air-conditioned cars."

"Well, it's been a long day. I'm ready for bed." Marie leaned over, kissed Summer's cheek, and rose. "Don't stay up too late studying."

"I won't."

But she lay awake worrying, long after her mother left the room.

$$\mathcal{SSS}$$

"Let's go home, Shadow."

The horse took them there without any direction from him. Abram found his thoughts traveling back to that moment when he and Summer had looked at each other and something passed between them. He'd never had that happen with a woman before, and he'd *schur* looked for it for a long time now. After all, while he and other Amish were marrying later these days, just like the *Englisch*, his *bruders* and most of his friends had married and even had *kinner*.

Abram had been taught from an early age that God had a plan for him, that He had someone special set aside for each of His children.

Someone to love and cherish. To marry and have *kinner* with. To serve God's purpose.

Well, Abram had always thought of himself as a pretty patient sort of a man, but he had come to realize that while being alone didn't mean lonely, he was lonely. And he'd been drawn to one woman . . . and an unlikely woman at that.

Summer said they needed to talk. She was right. From the moment that she had come to his farm to take water and soil samples and he'd had the chance to see her as an adult—not the pretty little *Englisch* girl who'd followed her father into the fields—he'd found himself drawn to her. Thinking about her. Finding ways to be with her, like today.

Shadow pulled into the drive of the farmhouse. He stood patiently while Abram unhitched him and then moved toward his stall without being led.

"I think you like it here," Abram said, following the horse. He made sure there was water and grain in the stall, then took care of the other horses, apologizing for being late with their supper and making amends by treating them to a carrot each.

As he walked into the house, the rain that had been predicted for that night began pelting down. He sent up a silent prayer of thanks for the safe journey home. Too often automobile drivers didn't slow down in the rain or see a buggy at night.

The house was too quiet, as it had been since his parents left. He poured himself a glass of water and went into the living room, settled into the recliner to read. As an Amish man he might not have pursued higher education like Summer and many of the *Englisch*, but he loved to read, just like his family and friends did. His *eldres* had moved some of their books to a bookcase in the *dawdi haus* before they left for Pinecraft, but many still filled the bookcases lining the walls. He hadn't read all of them, but they were there for when he wanted to.

But his thoughts kept wandering back to Summer, and he wondered what she was doing. Probably studying. It seemed to take an immense amount of time studying to get through her classes—not just the time spent sitting in them for lectures. He wondered how often she got to relax and read a book for pleasure. Just relax, period. It didn't sound like it was often.

Restless, he got up, took the empty glass, and walked into the kitchen to put it into the sink. His gaze went to the door of the *dawdi haus*. He'd helped his *eldres* move their things into the *dawdi haus* and declared the house and farm his own. They'd tried to get him to take over their old master bedroom that day. He'd refused, saying he'd do it later. But it had been months now and he still hadn't done so. He wondered what they'd think if they returned from their extended vacation in Pinecraft and found he was still sleeping in his old room.

He climbed the stairs and walked past his room and stood in the doorway of the now empty master bedroom. He'd been in it a few times as a child, of course, when he'd woken from a nightmare and wanted his *mudder*. She'd take him back to bed and that would be the end of it. Now he stepped inside and looked around. They'd moved the furniture to the *dawdi haus* so the room was bare. He supposed he could move his single bed into the room and sleep here, but it didn't seem right.

The room should be occupied by a man and his *fraa*. And he didn't have a *fraa*.

It stood empty. Waiting.

Abram walked out of the room, shut the door, then went into his smaller one and got ready for bed. As he lay in his bed listening to the rain patter against the window, he thought about how the colder weather was coming and with it came the time to do repairs and turn his attention to building some furniture for that master bedroom—and maybe some to sell for extra money.

He reached for the pad of paper and pencil he kept on the bedside table and began sketching an idea for a headboard. Maybe tomorrow he'd take Shadow into town and get some supplies, look at what kind of wood he'd like to work with. Something that wasn't too heavy or dark. He was *gut* at building furniture, although he didn't have as much skill or experience as his *dat*. But he had been building furniture since his teens and had sold a number of pieces to the Graber furniture store in town.

When he yawned for the third time, he set the pad and pencil back on the table, turned off the battery-operated lamp, and closed his eyes. Mornings came early on a farm.

It seemed the sun would never poke through the clouds the next morning. The rain had stopped, but the wind was a bitter slap when Abram left the warm barn after chores. He decided to wait until afternoon to go into town.

A buggy pulled into the drive. Abram saw who his visitor was and he sighed inwardly.

The bishop.

"*Guder mariye,*" he called as the bishop stepped from his buggy and glanced up at the gray sky.

"*Guder mariye.* Had a good soaker last night. We needed it."

"*Ya,* we did."

The bishop grabbed at his black felt hat as the wind threatened to carry it away. "Cold front moving in."

Abram's *mudder* had taught him courtesy and respect. "Let's get inside, out of it. I made some coffee before I did morning chores."

He held the back door open for the older man, helped him take off his jacket, and hung it along with his hat on a peg. As he walked past him to fix the coffee, he spotted the pile of mail he'd brought in yesterday and tossed on the kitchen table. The bright red lettering on the postcard read "What happens in Pinecraft stays in Pinecraft." He picked up the pile, moved it to the counter, and hoped the bishop hadn't seen it. The man was a fairly tolerant sort, unlike the last bishop who was no longer with the living, but Abram wasn't *schur* that he'd think the postcard was humorous.

Vernon settled at the table while Abram opened the top of the percolator, sniffed at the coffee, and found it stale. He dumped the contents in the sink, rinsed out the pot, and started a fresh one. It just wasn't neighborly to serve a guest—especially the bishop—less than the best.

But this meant they'd be sitting there while it perked. Well, he told himself, having coffee ready might not have made for a shorter visit either. He knew what was coming, and whether it be short or long, what the man had to say wasn't what he wanted to hear.

He put some cookies on a plate and set it on the table before the older man. They were store-bought. The delivery of baked goods by the *maedels* of the community had dried up since the wedding season was over. Vernon chose one and eyed it dubiously. Since the man's *fraa* was one of the community's finest bakers, Abram doubted he'd ever tasted an Oreo. He watched him eat it in two bites and then leave the rest of the cookies untouched.

The only sound in the room was the burbling of the percolator. Abram willed it to perk faster and then finally sat down at the table.

"Saw you yesterday on my way home," Vernon began.

"*Ya*, I saw you too. I waved hello."

"Thought I must be mistaken. You had a young woman in your buggy."

"I did."

"Not an Amish *maedel*."

"*Nee*. It was an *Englisch* friend."

"A female *Englisch* friend."

"*Ya*. Her name is Summer Carson. Her *dat* was Howard Carson, one of the county extension agents."

"I remember him. He died a couple years ago?"

The coffee had stopped perking. Abram got up to pour them each a mug and set them on the table.

"This young woman. She came to church with you last week."

"That's right. Her *dat* brought her a number of times years ago."

Vernon put two spoons of sugar in his coffee and stirred it. "That he did. Howard Carson was a *gut* man." He stirred his coffee some more. Then he looked at Abram and his eyes were direct behind his silver rimmed glasses. "A *gut Englisch* man."

The kitchen clock ticked off the time.

"We here in Lancaster County mix with the *Englisch* more than they do in other Amish communities," Vernon said. "But it's important to remember something."

Here it comes, thought Abram.

"Be ye not unequally yoked together with unbelievers: for what fellowship hath righteousness with unrighteousness?"

Abram repeated it with him in his head.

"I see you remember those words."

For one horrible moment Abram feared he'd said the words. "I do. But Summer is a friend. A *gut* one." Guilt stabbed him for a moment and, fearful the man would read his expression, he rose and got the coffee pot to freshen the man's mug.

"Now that you've inherited the farm, it's time you should be thinking about finding a *fraa*," Vernon said. "I wouldn't want to see you looking in her direction."

Well, that was blunt. Abram hadn't felt the need for *rumschpringe* as Wayne had, hadn't spent much time exploring the *Englisch* world. He felt comfortable, secure, as an Amish man.

But something rose up in him, the smallest seed of rebellion. He didn't like someone telling him what he couldn't have. Summer was a *gut* woman, one who had shown him compassion and friendship. He didn't see her as a corrupter, and he didn't like someone implying that.

Then his glance fell on the postcard lying on the kitchen counter, and he remembered his *eldres* and what they'd always taught him about respecting the authority and wisdom of the church. "I appreciate your concern," he said carefully, and he looked directly at Vernon. "And I will keep it under consideration."

Vernon nodded. "You've always been a stable, responsible young man. I trust that you'll remain that way." He glanced at the kitchen clock, drained his coffee, and stood. "I have other calls to make. *Danki* for the coffee and the cookies." He slanted Abram a look as he pulled on his jacket and set his hat on his head. "You went to *schul* with Rebecca as I recall."

"*Ya.*" Here it comes, thought Abram. Rebecca was the bishop's *grossdochder.*

"She makes delicious snickerdoodles."

With that he nodded and walked out the door.

Abram looked at the Oreos the bishop had spurned. He put one in his mouth and crunched it. He would not be dating Rebecca Yoder to get some home-baked snickerdoodles.

He didn't care how *gut* they were.

Twelve

Summer walked the fields with her father.

The sun beat down on her back, and she felt perspiration trickle down her spine. But there was nothing better than trudging through the fields and absorbing all he told her about his work. He was just the smartest dad in the whole world.

"So you think you want to follow in my footsteps, little girl?" he asked, his voice warm, his blue eyes sparkling in his wide, ruddy face. He grinned down at her as she stepped into the footprints his boots left in the soft earth, and the skin around his eyes crinkled.

Summer's pigtails swung as she marched along. "Yes, sir!"

"You'll have to work hard. Study hard and do well in school. Your mom and I have tried to save for your college, but you'll need a scholarship with prices being what they are these days."

"I get good grades."

"Don't let the boys distract you. I see them hovering around you like bees on that flower there."

She laughed. "Silly Daddy. I don't like boys."

"You say that now, but when you get in high school you'll sing a different tune."

He stopped so suddenly she ran into him. "Snake, Summer."

She peered at it. "Eastern worm snake. Got the name 'cause he looks like a big worm. He's a good guy. Not poisonous." She reached down, picked it up, and showed it to him. "See? You taught me how to tell, how to look at the shape of their head. Bad guys have large, triangular heads. Vertical elliptical eyes. There are only three venomous snakes in Pennsylvania: copperhead, eastern massasauga rattlesnake, and the timber rattlesnake."

"That's right."

She put the snake back on the ground and watched it slither away. "Most snakes get out of our way before we see them."

100

"But we keep an eye out so we're not on top of them before we see them."

"Right."

"And we don't tell Mom that Dad let us pick one up."

She laughed. "What happens in the field stays in the field."

"You got it."

Dad was the best. He never acted like he was sorry she was a girl, and it wasn't because she was a tomboy. He loved her.

They stopped and sat on a log beside the creek at the back of their property and watched sunlight glisten on the water.

"I love you, Dad."

He looked down at her. "I love you, Summer. Promise me you'll always be my little girl."

He loved to say that.

"I promise."

"Promise me you'll always do what makes you happy."

"I promise."

"Promise me you'll always do the right thing."

"I promise."

"Promise me you'll keep God first in your life."

"I promise."

"And promise me you'll always look after your mother if I'm not there to do it."

"Aw, Dad, you'll always be here."

She woke and blinked back tears as she realized she wasn't still in the dream, walking and talking with her dad. It had been so vivid.

Promise me you'll always look after your mother if I'm not there to do it.

She'd told him then he'd always be here with all the childish innocence and belief that parents lived forever. She sighed. Oh, to be a ten-year-old again.

"Miss you, Dad," she whispered. "And I promise to look after Mom." She rose and dressed then went downstairs.

Her mother stood looking into the refrigerator . . .

"Good morning!"

"Good morning." She turned. "We're out of eggs. I thought I brought in eggs yesterday."

Something was burning. Summer glanced at the stove and saw smoke rising from the cast-iron skillet on the stove and hurried over to it. Strips of bacon were turning black. She turned off the gas, grabbed a potholder, and moved the skillet to the back range. A moment later the smoke alarm began screaming.

"What on earth?" her mother exclaimed.

Summer frowned. "You don't smell the bacon burning?"

Marie came over to stare into the skillet. "No. That's strange."

Summer got a broom, used the end to turn off the alarm, then returned it to the kitchen closet.

"No bacon and no eggs." Marie sighed. "I'll make you some oatmeal."

"Don't worry about it. I'll have cornflakes. I need to leave early." Summer got the box of cereal from a cupboard and went to the refrigerator for milk. "Why do you get up so early when you could sleep in?" she asked her mother.

"Don't seem to need as much sleep as I did when I was younger. And after so many years living on a farm and getting up early it's a habit, I suppose." Marie poured a glass of orange juice and set it before Summer and then sat at the table with a cup of coffee.

Summer filled the bowl with cereal and poured on some milk. She ate a spoonful and chose her words carefully. "Mom, I'm worried about you. I think we need to see the doctor."

"I'm fine."

She reached for her mother's hand and squeezed it. "Mom, you're not sleeping enough and you've lost weight."

"It's called getting older."

Summer shook her head. "You're depressed and forgetful."

"I'm fine," Marie insisted. But she stared down at her coffee and wouldn't meet Summer's gaze.

"I'm really worried, Mom. Do it for me?"

102

Marie's lips trembled as she raised her eyes to Summer's. "What if something's wrong? What if it's Alzheimer's? My grandmother had it."

"Whatever it is we'll handle it together, Mom."

"We'll go together?"

"Of course."

She sighed. "All right. Make the appointment."

It was a step, thought Summer. She ate another spoonful of cornflakes. "I had a dream about Daddy last night."

Her mother's smile was tremulous. "Tell me about your dream."

SSS

Two days of steady rain had kept Abram at the farm. When the sun peeked through the clouds, Abram led Joe out to the buggy and hitched him up.

"Time to take a trip into town," he told the horse. "It's your turn today. I'm ready to get outside and get some sunshine, aren't you?"

Joe shook his head as if in agreement. Abram had been using Shadow more often, getting him used to the area, and Joe had sulked a bit—just like a child who felt a sibling got more attention.

They stopped first at the mailbox. Abram reached into the roomy black box and found the latest edition of the *Budget*, sales circulars, and a bill or two. And another postcard from his *eldres*. Well, his *mudder*. He knew if it was up to his *dat*, he'd be lucky to get a postcard once a month.

The postcard she'd sent today bore a photo of a huge alligator. She wrote on the back that she and his *dat* had eaten alligator at a local restaurant and it hadn't tasted like chicken. Abram shuddered. He couldn't imagine eating something that came from an animal that was so ugly.

He then turned Joe's head toward Wayne's farm. Wayne was sitting on his front porch when the buggy pulled up in front. He got into the buggy and spotted the postcard sitting atop the pile of mail.

"Alligator, huh?"

"*Ya.*"

"Quite the adventure the *eldres* are having down there in Florida." He leaned back in his seat. "Maybe we should visit. I've heard some Amish wear swimsuits and go to the beach."

"I doubt my *eldres* have done that." Abram paused. "Although you should have seen the postcard they sent the other day. It said, 'What happens in Pinecraft stays in Pinecraft.'" He glanced at Wayne. "I'm pretty sure the bishop saw it the other day when he visited."

"Ouch."

"I can't wait to tell *Mamm*."

Wayne laughed. "I'd like to be there when you do. Well, at least Vernon isn't stiff-necked like our last bishop." When Abram didn't agree he turned in his seat. "What?"

"He stopped by after he saw me taking Summer for a ride."

"He had a problem with that?"

Abram nodded. "I got the lecture. You know the one."

"The unyoked one?"

"*Ya.*"

"I see. My *mudder* did that one a few times when I was on my *rumschpringe*. She was really worried I'd fall for an *Englisch* girl." He sighed and stretched out his legs. "She could make that lecture last for ten minutes. More if she caught me rolling my eyes. So what did you say to him?"

"I told him Summer was a friend."

"And then what did he say?"

"He thinks it's time I looked for a *fraa*."

"An Amish one of course."

"That goes without saying. He even had a suggestion. Rebecca, his *grossdochder*. Says she makes *gut* snickerdoodles."

"That's a *gut* quality in a *fraa*?"

"I had a plate of Oreos on the table at the time. He looked appalled."

"Hey, I like them. So, what are you going to do?"

"I'm not marrying Rebecca to get home-baked cookies."

Abram turned into the parking lot for the furniture store. Mervin, the owner, came out from the back and greeted them as they went inside.

"Got orders for both of you."

"*Danki*, glad to have them," Abram told him.

"Me too," Wayne said.

Mervin handed them the orders. Abram looked over the paperwork. Two chests of drawers, a spice rack, and a storage bench. He nodded. "I can do these and have them for you by the requested deadlines."

"Wayne?"

He nodded. "No problem, Mervin. *Danki* for the work."

"I'd like to look at your catalog book, if you don't mind," Abram said.

Mervin waved a hand at it on the nearby sales counter. "Looking for another project? You know I'll take whatever you want to make after you complete the orders."

"Just getting some ideas." He wasn't going to tell Mervin—even Wayne—that he'd decided to start a bedroom set and invite speculation.

Abram said hello to Mervin's *fraa* as he walked over to the counter to look at the catalog. He flipped through the bedroom furniture section of the catalog while the two men talked. He wanted something lighter in color, more modern than the bed his *eldres* had. A light oak, maybe, with a curved back like the one he found after several minutes of looking.

Wayne wandered over. Abram gave him a warning look when Wayne opened his mouth.

He closed the catalog and said goodbye to Mervin before they exited the store.

"So why'd I get the look?"

"I didn't want you announcing I was looking at bedroom sets." Abram climbed into the buggy.

"Is it a secret?" Wayne got into the passenger side.

"*Nee.* Just my business. Mervin's *fraa* was sitting at her desk behind the counter. She'd have had the news on the Amish grapevine in minutes."

"Ah, true." Wayne folded up the orders in his hand and tucked them into his jacket pocket. "Is there some reason you're building it now?"

He shrugged. "We have a lot of time to work on furniture and such during the winter. I'm still sleeping in my bed in my old room. If I make a new bed—a bigger one—I can move it into the master bedroom. I figure it isn't going to get built in spring planting season or harvest."

"And it'll be ready for when you bring a *fraa* home." Wayne chuckled when Abram shot him a withering look. "Hey, if the looks my *mudder* used to aim at me didn't kill me, yours won't."

"She ever make you walk home?" Abram asked mildly.

"*Ya.* But you won't. You're too nice."

"Don't count on it."

Of course he didn't put Wayne out of the buggy. They stopped at a favorite restaurant and had lunch, then visited the lumberyard and chose some wood.

"Wonder why we're taking this way home?" Wayne said casually.

"You're a smart man. I bet you can figure it out."

"You never said what you're going to do about what the bishop said, about looking for a *fraa.*"

"I told you I wasn't going to date his *grossdochder.*"

"So are you still going to see Summer?"

Abram frowned. "Of course. She's a friend."

"You know what I'd have done if he'd talked to me about not seeing someone?"

"Let me guess. You'd have done it even if you didn't want to."

Wayne chuckled. "You bet. My *mudder* once said she learned not to tell me not to do something because that just made me want to do it."

"You were a trial to that poor woman."

"I was. She said I was worse than two *sohns*." He leaned out the window. "Why, look at that, Abram my friend. I believe that's Summer sitting on her front porch with an attractive young woman. A redhead. Surely you must have some reason we should stop by and say hello."

Abram turned into the drive. "I'll leave that up to you. Seeing as how you're such a smart fellow."

The buggy had barely stopped when Wayne jumped out. "Just follow me, my friend. Just follow me."

Thirteen

Summer was surprised to see Abram's buggy pull into her driveway. His friend Wayne jumped out almost the second the buggy stopped. Abram followed him, frowning.

"Afternoon, Summer. Abram and I were just on our way home and spotted you two lovely ladies enjoying the nice weather. I haven't met your friend."

Summer glanced at Abram and smiled before turning to the woman beside her. "This is my friend, Kim. Kim, this is Wayne."

"I'm sorry, it seems we've interrupted your studying," Abram said quickly.

"No problem," Kim said, smiling up at Wayne. "I could use a break."

Summer set her book on a nearby table and stood. "My mother promised us some cookies."

Wayne looked at her. "Is she making snickerdoodles by any chance?"

"I'm not sure. I'll see." She glanced at Kim, then at Wayne. "Abram, maybe you'd like to help me."

"*Schur.*" He noticed Wayne quickly took the rocking chair Summer had vacated.

"I'm sorry," Abram said as he followed her inside. "I didn't realize the two of you were studying until it was too late."

She smiled at him. "It's okay. It really *is* time for a break." They walked through the house back to the kitchen. There, Summer came to an abrupt halt. Her mother sat at the table, her head on her folded arms. She was sound asleep.

The oven timer went off and Marie started awake. "What?"

Summer moved quickly to turn off the timer. She picked up mitts and removed a tray of cookies from the oven and set them on top of the stove.

"I'm sorry, I'm just so tired lately," Marie apologized. "Hello, Abram."

"Hello, Marie."

"Maybe some coffee will help you wake up, Mom." Summer poured her a mug and set it before her. "Abram? Coffee?"

"I'd love some."

Summer poured him a mug, handed it to him, and then turned to use a spatula to lift the cookies from the baking tray and transfer them to a plate.

"I can do that," her mother said.

"Enjoy your coffee, Mom." Summer paused and looked at Marie closely. "On second thought, you look really tired. Why don't you take a nap instead and let me finish these?"

Her mother sighed and pushed her hair back from her face. "I think I'll take you up on that." She rose, leaving her coffee on the table, and walked over to kiss Summer's cheek. "Nice to see you, Abram."

"You too. Hope you feel better."

"Thanks."

Summer frowned as she watched her mother climb the stairs to her room.

"You okay?"

She turned and looked at Abram. "I took Mom to the doctor. He seems to think she's depressed and run-down." She picked up the bowl of batter and carried it to the refrigerator, then turned off the oven. Getting down four mugs, she poured coffee into them and set them on a tray, then added the plate of cookies.

"Not snickerdoodles," she said. "Maybe next time you and Wayne stop by."

"Don't say that to him. He'll be over tomorrow."

She smiled and picked up the tray and frowned when the dishes on it rattled.

He took the tray from her. "Still worried about your mother?" he asked quietly.

"Yes. Something still doesn't feel right." She found herself twisting her hands and shoved them into the pockets of her jeans.

"Listen, I wasn't thinking when I stopped. We'll clear out so you two can go back to studying. Then maybe *you* should think about a nap."

"It's really okay."

They walked back out to the porch and found their friends engrossed in conversation. Wayne jumped up and pulled over other chairs so he and Abram could sit. Summer noticed that he pulled his chair close to Kim. Hmm, she thought.

"Kim's going to be a teacher," Wayne told Abram as he chose a cookie and took a bite.

"I hope you didn't scare her off by telling her the kind of pranks you used to pull on our teacher," Abram said as he chose a cookie.

"I thought Amish children were well-behaved," Kim said.

Wayne began laughing and then began choking on the bite of cookie. Abram leaned over and thumped him on the back.

"*Danki*," Wayne gasped. He took a sip of his coffee.

"Kids are kids," Abram observed.

"My aunt used to be a teacher, so I have a pretty good idea what I'm getting into," Kim told them. She bit into a cookie and sighed. "Summer, your mom's cookies are so good."

"Thanks. You can take some home for you and your daughter."

"You have a daughter?" Wayne said. "You're married?"

Was it her imagination that he looked disappointed?

"No. Divorced."

He definitely looked relieved, thought Summer.

"So how often do the two of you get together to study?" Wayne asked casually.

"Every week."

"We need to be going so that they can study," Abram reminded Wayne.

Wayne stood. "It was nice to meet you, Kim. Summer, maybe you'd like to bring Kim to church sometime."

Summer smiled. "Maybe."

"Thank you for the coffee and cookies," Abram told her. "See you Saturday?"

She bit her lip. "Saturday?"

"Supper?" he murmured quietly as Wayne said goodbye—again—to Kim.

"Oh, I'm sorry. I forgot. Sure. Around six?"

He nodded and grabbed Wayne's sleeve to get him moving.

"Well, that was interesting," Kim murmured as they watched the men walk to the buggy. "I didn't know you were dating an Amish man."

"I'm not. Abram is a friend."

"Okay. Um, Summer, I think Wayne was flirting with me."

"He was."

"But I thought Amish men weren't supposed to look at *Englisch* women that way."

"They're not." Summer put the coffee mugs back on the tray.

"But Abram . . ." Kim trailed off. "He was looking at you like he was interested in you too."

"We're friends," Summer repeated. "I'll be right back."

But she wondered if she were lying to herself and Kim.

SSS

"You were flirting with Kim."

"*Ya,*" Wayne said, smiling as he leaned back in his seat. "She's cute. What, you have a problem with that? You're seeing Summer."

"She's a friend."

"So Kim and I can be friends."

"You were flirting with Kim."

Wayne looked at him. "Abram, you're more than friends with Summer."

"You don't believe a man and woman can be friends?"

"Maybe some can, but you and Summer are more than friends. I watched you."

111

"You never took your eyes off Kim."

"Hey, I can do more than one thing at once."

Abram pulled into his drive and they unloaded his wood. Then they set off for Wayne's house. But when they got there he sat, staring ahead. If Wayne—not the most observant of people—could see how he felt about Summer . . . well, he had to think about that.

"Hey, you okay?"

"Hmm? *Ya.* Let's get your lumber unloaded."

They worked silently, carrying what Wayne had bought into the barn. He walked with him back to the buggy.

"So what are you going to do? About Summer?"

"I'm going to stay friends with her."

Wayne laid a hand on his shoulder. "Look, I don't want to see you get hurt."

Surprised, Abram stared at him. Wayne. They were lifelong friends, and Wayne was the guy who was always goofing off, joking around, flirting with every attractive young *maedel* in sight. The one who knew how to get beer underage during *rumschpringe.* Abram had been afraid he'd leave the Amish community because he'd enjoyed so many aspects of *Englisch* life. Even the bishop had appeared a bit surprised when Wayne joined the church.

Yet here he was, worried that Abram's heart would be hurt.

"*Danki,* but I'll be fine. Had a *gut* afternoon. I'm heading home for chores."

Wayne gave him another clap on the back and nodded. "*Gut-n-owed.*"

Joe took them home. Abram did his chores without thinking and enjoyed the company of his horses before heading into the house. He stood peering into the refrigerator without much enthusiasm. A sandwich seemed the best option. He assembled one and ate it at the kitchen table.

Silence seemed to echo around him.

Abram found himself remembering how it had been to visit Wayne at the apartment he'd rented in town during his *rumschpringe* and watching television for hours. He could use some mindless entertainment right now.

Well, there was no television, no distractions. He could sit here and think about what he didn't have now, or he could do something with his time. It was a sad thing when he wanted to "tune out" as Wayne called it and be a couch potato.

And his *mudder* would tell him wasting time was a sin, wasn't it?

So Abram pulled out the orders he'd gotten from Melvin and spread them on the table. The order for a kitchen spice rack would be first on the list. It was for a birthday present a few weeks in the distance. Spice racks were a popular item—something used often in Amish and *Englisch* kitchens.

He glanced over at the empty spot near the stove where his *mudder* had hung the one he'd made her the first year his *dat* had started teaching him how to build furniture. He hadn't done the best job on it, but his *mudder* had cried over it when he gave it to her for Christmas. She'd refused to let him build another when his skills improved and took it off the wall and carried it into the *dawdi haus* and hung it near the stove there. With as little cooking as he'd done since his *eldres* had left he hadn't missed a spice rack. His idea of spices ran to salt and pepper.

The second order would be a bedroom dresser and then a storage bench. After that he'd see how Christmas orders did. There'd still be a lot of cold weather after Christmas to work on his own master bedroom furniture.

He was grateful for the woodworking skill. A man had to find ways to pay the bills, keep a farm running. Many Amish farmers had a second job during the long winter months when the land slept under the blanket of snow and the wind blew bitter cold. Some built furniture, some worked factory jobs. Some found temporary jobs in the tourism industry that had boomed as *Englischers* wanted to know more about them.

He found himself glancing at the notebook where he'd sketched his ideas for his own master bedroom furniture. Looking through the catalog in Melvin's store had made him rethink the headboard. He'd share that bedroom, that bed, one day with a *fraa*. It wouldn't do to make it too heavy, too masculine, or she wouldn't feel it was hers . . . that he'd had her in mind.

He sighed and then gathered up the orders, tucked them into the notebook, and headed upstairs to bed.

Starting the first of the orders after he did chores kept him busy the next day. He enjoyed the work, and being inside the warmth of the barn as a cold front moved in wasn't a hardship. Shadow seemed to be more interested in sticking his head over his stall door and watching him work than Joe did. So he found himself talking to him, explaining what he was doing. You found company with animals when a human wasn't available, he told himself ruefully.

Yet almost hourly he thought about Summer and wondered what she was doing. He hoped she was enjoying her day and not stressing too much over work or school.

They hadn't discussed where they'd go for dinner. He ran over a list of restaurants and pictured them sitting in one, talking about the time since they'd last seen each other. He'd let her choose. He didn't care what food they ate. It was about having her company, hearing her voice, listening to her laugh, seeing how her expression changed as she talked.

He wondered if she was looking forward to it as much as he was. Saturday couldn't come soon enough for him.

Fourteen

Sunlight beamed into Summer's room.

She groaned and pulled the pillow over her head. It was the one day of the week she didn't have to set the alarm to wake up early, and she was going to stay in bed and be a slug. But she found it impossible to fall back asleep. She pulled the pillow off her head and lay there staring at the ceiling. Habit, she thought, frowning. She threw the quilt back and sat up. Somewhere she'd read that it wasn't a good idea to sleep in on weekends—that it threw off your schedule if you did.

So okay, fine. She was up.

Yawning, she got up and started downstairs and then returned to her bedroom for her robe and slippers. The house was chilly.

When she walked into the kitchen she frowned. It was already eight o'clock and her mother hadn't started coffee and wasn't making breakfast. Strange. She was always the first one up.

Summer started the coffee and decided to surprise her mother and make her favorite—French toast. She got milk and eggs from the refrigerator and bread from the breadbox. After melting some butter in a skillet, she whisked the eggs and milk and she added a touch of vanilla like her mother always did. She dipped the bread in the mixture and then laid the slices in the skillet. Soon the kitchen was filled with the delicious scents of coffee and browning French toast. She drank her first cup of coffee and flipped the toast.

Surprised her mother still wasn't up, she walked over to the stairs. "Hey, Lazybones! Breakfast is ready!" she called.

Returning to the stove, Summer plated the French toast and set it in the oven to keep warm. She climbed the stairs, peeked into her mother's room, and found her sound asleep. She debated waking her and then decided to let her sleep. It didn't feel right to wake her. Maybe she'd had trouble sleeping . . .

Frowning, she walked back downstairs and got her plate from

the oven. Her mother seemed so tired lately. She ate her breakfast—alone for the first time in a very long time—and drank a second cup of coffee.

A half hour later her mother walked into the kitchen yawning hugely. "'Morning," she said, bending to kiss Summer's cheek. "I overslept."

"Sit. I made breakfast."

"Mmm. My favorite," she said as Summer set her plate in front of her. "Is it Mother's Day? Did I sleep like Rip van Winkle?"

Summer chuckled. "No. Moms should get breakfast made for them more than once a year. You can go eat it in bed if you want." She poured a mug of coffee, added cream and sugar, and set it on the table near her mother's plate. She joined her at the table with a third cup of coffee and tried not to notice that while her mother exclaimed enthusiastically over her breakfast, she ate it in tiny bites and consumed only one of the two slices Summer had placed on it.

"So good," she said, wiping her lips on a paper napkin. "What is that you put into it? Something special."

Summer set her cup down slowly. "You can't taste it?"

"It tastes good."

"You can't smell it?"

Marie frowned and shook her head.

"It's vanilla, Mom. You always put a little vanilla in the eggs and milk."

"I do?" With a shrug, Marie sipped her coffee.

She was slipping away. Her mother was slipping away before her eyes. A lump rose in Summer's throat and she swallowed hard. Fighting tears, she rose and took her plate to the sink. She stood there staring out the window. "Oh, Daddy, what should I do?" she whispered.

"Did you say something?"

Blinking furiously, she turned. "Just talking to myself. Thinking about all I have to do today."

"You have to go to work? What day is it?" She looked at the calendar. "Sometimes I lose track of what day it is. Comes from being retired, I guess."

Summer picked up the coffeepot and filled her mother's cup. "It's Saturday, Mom. I just have to work on my online class today. Why don't you try to eat a little more? The doctor said he didn't want you losing any more weight."

Marie shook her head. "I'm full. Put it in the fridge and I'll eat it tomorrow." She looked up at Summer and smiled. "So what are you planning to do today?"

"Go over my last paper for the online class and study for the final in the on-campus one. Later Abram and I are going to dinner."

"That's nice. Leave those dishes, Summer. I'll do them."

"I'll take you up on that," she decided when she glanced at the kitchen clock.

An hour later she sat at her desk in her room staring at the screen of her laptop. She'd only managed to proof a page so far. She rubbed at her temple. With a sigh she saved her paper and clicked on the browser. She went onto a medical information website and typed in the name of the medication the doctor had given her mother for depression. Drowsiness and lack of appetite were listed as side effects. Typically these were supposed to get better after a patient was on them for a couple of weeks. She sighed. Maybe they just had to give it some time.

She browsed the site until the alarm on her cell phone went off. Where had the time gone? She hadn't left her room for lunch or checked on her mother. Shutting the computer down, she poked in her closet for something to wear. Abram hadn't said where they were going but she really didn't have much dressy anyway. She pulled out a long-sleeved white man-style shirt and a pair of black slacks and added a gray suede blazer. That should be appropriate for just about any place around here.

Her spirits rose as she brushed her hair in front of the mirror. Thinking about getting out for dinner and talking with Abram had helped her get through a busy week. He was always fun to be with—and so thoughtful and kind. She didn't remember ever being with a man who listened—actually listened and cared about what she was saying. Well, sometimes other men had listened but it was only until they realized she wasn't interested in doing more.

She was fastening some silver studs to her ears when she heard the teakettle whistling madly downstairs. The sound went on and on. She frowned. Funny, her mother wasn't taking it off the stove. Flipping her hair over her shoulders, she grabbed her purse and went downstairs.

The teakettle on the stove clattered on the burner. It had boiled dry. She rushed over to turn off the gas under it.

And saw her mother lying unconscious on the floor.

Abram knocked on the back door of Summer's house. Then, when there was no answer, he knocked again.

"Come in!" he heard her call and wondered at the frantic note in her voice.

He opened the door and saw Summer kneeling beside her mother lying on the floor. Marie moved slowly, drowsily, peering up at Summer.

"What happened?" he asked, rushing over to kneel beside her.

"I just found her when I came downstairs."

"I'm fine," Marie said, looking up at them. "I just felt faint when I got up from my chair. Stop fussing so, Summer, and help me up."

"Wait," Abram cautioned. "Don't move her, Summer. Do you hurt anywhere, Marie?"

"No, I'm fine," she repeated. "I want to get up."

"I'm calling 911," Summer said as she rose. "Abram, don't let her get up." She crossed the room to use the phone.

"I don't need to go," Marie told him. "I'll be just fine if you help me up." She smiled at him persuasively.

"I can't do it." He patted her hand. "It's best if you get checked out."

Summer returned to her mother's side. "They'll be here in a few minutes. The dispatcher said to stay where you are."

"Such a fuss."

"Why don't you get a blanket?" he told Summer. "I'll stay with her." He didn't like how pale Marie looked. And her hand was cold when he'd touched it.

When she returned and tucked the blanket around her mother Abram got to his feet. "I'll go outside and wait for them."

It wasn't long before they heard the siren, and Abram directed the paramedics to Marie and then stood outside so that he was out of the way. A few minutes later the paramedics rolled Marie out on a gurney to the ambulance, and Summer locked the kitchen door behind her.

"I'm sorry about tonight," she told him. "I'm going with her."

"Of course you should. I'm sorry your mother isn't well."

One of the paramedics called to her and she rushed away. Abram watched her climb into the back of the ambulance. One of them shut the door behind her. Abram watched the vehicle roll down the drive and head down the road to town.

A pickup truck pulled into the drive, stopped, and Carl hopped out. "What happened? I just saw an ambulance."

Abram briefly explained what had happened to Marie. "I'm going to follow them to the hospital."

"Drop your horse and buggy off at your farm and I'll drive us both in," Carl told him and he got back into his truck.

"Thanks." Abram drove to his farm with Carl following him. He quickly unhitched Shadow, put him in his stall, and got into Carl's truck.

"Something's just not been right with Marie for some time," Carl told him. "It's more than losing Howard."

"Summer's been worried."

"Me too." Carl frowned as he drove. "Something's been off for some time."

Carl pulled into the hospital parking lot and found a parking spot.

They walked into the emergency room and took seats. Abram pulled out his cell phone and texted Summer as Carl looked on.

"My son keeps telling me I need to learn how to text," Carl said. "Don't see why. Easier to just call someone."

"This way I can let Summer know we're here while she's in the room with Marie."

"Good idea." He watched Summer's answering text flash across the screen of Abram's cell phone. "Maybe I'll learn one of these days."

They waited for an hour before Summer came out looking pale and worried. "They're running tests. They did a CAT scan to make sure she didn't hurt her head when she fell."

Carl patted the seat beside him. "Sit, little girl. You look worn out."

"That's all I've been doing," she said.

Abram stood. "Let's take a walk, get some coffee. Carl? Shall we bring some back for you?"

"That'd be great. Black."

Summer glanced back. "I'm not sure I should leave."

"Carl will call us if the doctor comes out." Abram gave Carl his number, then they walked to the cafeteria. Abram knew the way well. He'd been in the hospital often with the usual broken bones and childhood misadventures.

Hospital staff sat at tables eating a late dinner. One intern looked like he was eating in his sleep. A man herded two small children along the line and set cartons of chocolate milk on a tray. The kids jumped up and down when they saw the macaroni and cheese among the selections in the warming trays.

"Can we get some for Sissy?" one asked his father as the cafeteria worker scooped up servings and put them in small bowls.

"Could I get some in a to-go box?" he asked the worker, and she nodded and made it up. "My wife has our youngest in the ER getting stitches. She'll have a fit if she doesn't get what the others do when we head home."

The little family settled at a table in the far corner of the nearly empty cafeteria.

Abram picked up a tray and chose two chicken salad sandwiches while Summer filled three to-go cups with coffee. He pulled out his wallet and paid over her objections.

"Let's sit here," he said, choosing a table. "I want you to eat a sandwich before we go back."

"Carl's coffee will get cold."

"It's got a lid on it. It'll be fine. You didn't have dinner."

She sat and sighed. "Neither did you."

"That's why I bought two. Unless you want both of them."

That tugged a small smile out of her. "No. I've never eaten two sandwiches at the same sitting in my life."

"I once ate three. What can I say, I was a teenage boy and we'd been working in the fields all morning." He sat and pulled the wrapping from his sandwich and bit in. "Not bad," he said.

"I'm sorry about tonight."

"Me too. But only because you're worried about your mom."

"I'm glad you were there," she said. "It helped me stay calm."

"You'd have stayed calm because she needed you to." He finished the first half of his sandwich and started on the second. "I've had some experience with women fainting. My sister did a lot of it with her first child."

"I don't think that's what made Mom faint."

He grinned. "No." He reached across and took her hand. "It could have been something as simple as she hadn't eaten enough today."

She nodded. "Mom admitted that she hadn't eaten lunch when the doctor asked her. I told him she only had one slice of French toast for breakfast."

"You see?" He pushed her sandwich toward her. "You need to eat so you don't fall on your face too."

"I don't think we need to worry about the Carson women having a fainting spree," she told him. But she picked up her sandwich and resumed eating.

When they walked back, Carl looked up from the magazine he was reading as Abram handed him his coffee. "No one's come out looking for you," he told Summer.

"I'm going to ask if I can go back and sit with her." She turned back. "The two of you don't need to stay."

"I got no place more important to be," Carl said. He looked at Abram. "You?"

"Absolutely not."

Summer smiled. "Thanks, guys." She hurried back to the exam rooms.

When she emerged an hour later, her shoulders were slumped and she blinked away tears. Abram stood with Carl.

"They want to keep Mom overnight for observation and run some more tests. They told me to go home and come back in the morning. I wanted to stay, but Mom is insisting I go home."

"Nothing you can do here," Carl told her. "She'll have a fit if she finds out you stayed in a chair here."

Abram nodded. "It's a good hospital. My family's used it a lot over the years. Let Carl drive you home, get some rest, and come back first thing in the morning."

She sighed and nodded slowly. "I know you're right."

Carl dropped Abram off first on the way home. He got out and turned back to look at Summer. "Is this the first time you've been by yourself in the house?"

She nodded. "Except for one night when Mom stayed with Dad at the hospital near—near the end."

"Try to get some rest. Call me no matter how late it is if you want to talk." He paused and met her gaze. He knew what it was like to be alone in a big farmhouse, and that wasn't because he had a parent in the hospital. "I mean it. Call me."

"I will. Thank you, Abram."

He saw her turn and look at him as Carl's truck drove away. She waved and he waved back as the truck turned onto the road before he went into his house. It was hard not being able to do more to help her. He didn't like feeling powerless.

And then he remembered that he wasn't powerless. He could pray for her and her mother. God was in charge and He knew what He was doing.

Fifteen

Summer found her mother dressed and impatiently waiting for her to take her home when she arrived at the hospital the next morning.

They spent the next two hours waiting for the doctor to discharge her.

The good news was they couldn't find any reason for Marie to faint. Summer didn't want to be negative, but she sure wanted to know the reason for it. When she said so, the doctor handed her a thick sheaf of printed information to read about fainting and its causes.

So in the end she followed her mother as Marie was escorted in a wheelchair to the entrance, and Summer went to get her car and drove her home. Marie didn't argue about going to bed with a cup of tea.

"That's only the second time I've been in a hospital—the first being when I delivered you—but you sure don't get any sleep in one," she said as she lay down on her bed. "Especially since they did hourly checks on me because I fell." She smiled. "Put my tea there on my bedside table, and I'll drink it in a minute."

Summer found her sound asleep and the tea cold and untouched when she checked a few minutes later. Closing Marie's door, Summer went downstairs and settled at the kitchen table with her textbooks and laptop.

There was a knock on the door. Summer jumped up and opened it to find Kim standing there with a pizza box and her textbooks.

"You don't look like you were expecting me."

"I wasn't. I'm sorry, I forgot."

"We can skip it if it's a bad time for you."

She shook her head. "Don't be silly. I have to study. But you didn't have to bring food."

"It's frozen from the grocery store. Found it on sale and we can pop it in the oven whenever we're ready for it." She set the pizza on the counter.

"Sounds great. I was just going to make some coffee."

Kim pulled off her gloves and stuck them in the pockets of her jacket before she shrugged out of it. "Love some."

Summer started the coffee maker and heard another knock on the door. This time it was Abram. He thrust a bouquet of mums into her hands when she opened the door.

"I'm not staying," he told her quickly. "I got your text. Glad you were able to bring your mother home from the hospital this morning."

Wayne appeared at his side. "Hi," he said, glancing over Summer's shoulder to smile and wave at Kim. His gaze flicked back to Summer. "Hi. We brought these for your mother. They're from Abram and me. Hope your mother is better."

"She was in the hospital?" Kim asked. "Why didn't you tell me?"

"Didn't have a chance to yet. You just got here. Come in and have some coffee, guys."

Abram grabbed Wayne's arm as he started in. "No," Abram said firmly. "I told you they're studying for an important test." He looked at Summer. "Do you need anything picked up? Groceries, that kind of stuff."

"We're good but thanks."

"Nice to see you again, Kim."

What am I—chopped liver? Summer wanted to ask. Chuckling, she closed the door.

"So, tell me about your mom."

She filled her in while they sipped their coffee.

Kim sighed and shook her head. "I'm so sorry. You must have been so scared."

"I have to take her for a follow-up visit to her primary care doctor tomorrow. I have a lot of questions for him." She stood. "Let me check on Mom real quick and then we'll study."

She ran upstairs and found her mother still asleep. When she went downstairs she found Kim with her nose in her notes.

"She okay?"

"Still sleeping. She said she didn't get much sleep at the hospital last night."

"I sure didn't the night I had Gabby."

"So, let's review the notes we took the other night. The professor always sticks pretty close to his reviews for his tests."

Two hours later Summer heard footsteps over their heads. The sound moved to the stairs. Summer jumped up and stood by the stairs while her mother descended them.

"I'm fine," she insisted when she saw Summer. "Don't fuss." Her color was better and she looked rested.

"How are you feeling?"

"Good." She yawned. "I slept like a log. Hi, Kim. What would you two like for lunch?"

"Kim brought a pizza. Sit, I was about to put it into the oven."

"Haven't had pizza in ages. I'm hungry. They served biscuits and gravy for breakfast." She wrinkled her nose. "I hate biscuits and gravy."

"Want some coffee?"

"Let me get it."

Summer frowned at her. "Sit." She poured her mother a cup and refreshed Kim's cup before turning on the oven to preheat and getting out a sheet pan for the pizza.

She and Kim gathered their notes and set them aside.

"Guess you girls are looking forward to Christmas break," Marie said as she sipped her coffee. "Don't know how you manage classes on top of jobs and such."

"We have great moms," Kim told her with a smile. "Mom says thanks for the basket you sent with Summer."

"Summer and I enjoy sharing the things we grow in our garden, don't we?"

She nodded. "I'm sorry to see it over for the season." She went to the refrigerator. "Kim, we have Coke and Diet Coke."

"Diet Coke, thanks."

"Where did the flowers come from?" Marie asked, suddenly noticing them on the kitchen counter.

"Abram and Wayne brought them by."

"Such nice young men."

When the oven timer dinged Summer pulled on oven mitts and pulled the pan out and set it on top of the stove. She cut slices, set them on plates, then served them. To her surprise her mother ate two whole slices.

There was a knock on the door and Carl walked in.

"Perfect timing like usual," Marie teased.

"I didn't see anyone deliver pizza."

"It's grocery store pizza," Kim informed him. "You're welcome to some."

"Maybe a slice," he said and got down a plate. "Nice flowers. You bring those too?" he asked her.

"Abram and Wayne brought them," Marie told him.

Summer watched color sweep over Carl's face. "That was nice," he mumbled.

"Aren't you going to have another slice?" Summer asked when he took his plate to the sink.

"Got things to do. Need anything from town?"

"No, thanks."

He thanked them for the pizza and grabbed his jacket as he left.

"That was odd," Marie remarked. She shrugged. "Men love to eat and run sometimes."

❦❦❦

"I don't see how having a cup of coffee would have taken so much time," Wayne complained as Abram drove into town on Monday.

Abram just shot him a look.

"Really, what are we talking about? Five minutes?"

"They need to focus on their studies, not have you wasting their time flirting with Kim."

"Now, you see, that's the problem with you," Wayne told him with a grin. "Time spent flirting is never wasted." Wayne stretched out his long legs.

"Summer had a lot of stress yesterday with her mother. She looked exhausted."

"So when's their big test?"

"Tomorrow."

"Then when is their Christmas break?"

"Starts end of this week, I think."

"So then you'll get to spend more time with Summer. Maybe we could double date."

Abram rolled his eyes. "Told you I'm not dating her."

"Whatever you say."

"Wayne."

"*Allrecht. Allrecht.*" He held up his hands. "It's not like a serious relationship couldn't happen. It wasn't that long ago that Mark Byler joined our church and married Miriam Troyer."

"I know. But Summer hasn't ever shown she'd want to do that." He couldn't go down that path . . . They were good friends. Two very good friends.

They stopped at Mervin's store first when they got into town and delivered the first of the furniture pieces they'd completed.

"*Gut* work," Mervin said as they carried them inside. "I can always depend on you two to do *gut* work." He rubbed his hands together. "I'll have the *fraa* write you checks."

"If she has the time," Abram told him. "Otherwise she can put them in the mail."

"Just take a few minutes." He strode over to speak to her, then returned. "Say, did you hear Isaac Zook needs help tearing down his barn next week?"

Abram nodded. "*Ya.* I asked him if I could have some of the wood."

"What do you want old wood for?" Wayne asked.

"The *Englisch* like things made out of it," Melvin said. "They call it reclaimed wood. Maybe make a big dining room table out of it. What do you think?"

128

"I could do that," Abram told him.

"What if he makes it and no one wants it?" Wayne wanted to know.

Mervin walked over to his wife's desk and returned with checks and a home decorating magazine. "Elizabeth showed me this the other day," he told them, flipping to a page that had been earmarked. "There's several pages of things made of reclaimed wood. See? Tables, sliding barn doors for inside the house. It's apparently a big decorating trend."

"Interesting." Abram glanced through the section. "I'll start with the table after I finish my orders, see how it goes."

"Remember what a customer paid for that six-foot table you made last winter? I think they'll pay 50 percent more for something like this." He pointed at the table in the magazine.

"I'll have it for you in a few weeks."

Melvin turned to Wayne. "What about you? Do you want to think about making something out of reclaimed wood?"

"I could make a bookcase, I guess. See how I like working with it."

Their checks tucked in their wallets, Abram and Wayne picked up some supplies at the feed store and stopped for lunch on the way home.

Abram ordered the meatloaf sandwich and was delighted to see the cook had given him a large serving of mashed potatoes and gravy. A chicken salad sandwich in the hospital cafeteria hadn't been much of a supper the night before. By the time he'd gotten home he'd been too tired to fix a snack, and this morning he'd barely had time for a fried egg sandwich after doing chores before Wayne arrived to go to town with him.

"Look who just walked in," Wayne said as he buttered a roll.

Abram glanced over at the entrance of the restaurant. The bishop and his *fraa* followed the hostess to a table on the other side of the room. He returned his attention to his food.

"I was thinking you should invite Summer to church."

"Oh?"

Wayne nodded. "She looked like she really enjoyed it last time. And you know what a comfort church is when you've been going through a tough time. You know, like she has with her mother."

Abram waited for it.

"She could invite Kim," Wayne said casually. "She might like to see what one of our church services is like. We could all go out to lunch afterward."

He shook his head and chuckled. "You are so predictable," he told him. "So utterly predictable."

"Well?"

"Well what?" Abram took a sip of his iced tea and enjoyed watching Wayne's frustration at his pretending not to understand the question.

"Will you think about inviting them?"

"I'll think about it."

But as he ate he couldn't help thinking Wayne had a very *gut* idea indeed. About inviting Summer, that is.

Sixteen

Done.

Summer turned in her final exam and placed her final paper on top of the stack on the desk in front of her professor. He glanced up from grading an exam and smiled at her.

"Enjoy your break," he whispered.

"You too."

Kim was sitting on a bench out in front of the building. "I was beginning to wonder if I should have gone over my exam again."

"Not a good idea," Summer told her. "I realized I was second-guessing my answers." She sighed. "I am so glad that's over. How do you think you did?"

"Really good. Our study session helped."

"I think so too." She yawned. "Sorry. I was up late finishing my paper. I wish papers and projects weren't due in the last week when we have final exams."

"Me too. I'd have liked to have the paper due the week before." She stood. "Well, I'm going home and crashing. You?"

"The same." She rose and they began walking toward the parking lot. "Remember to bring your daughter out to the farm on Saturday."

"You sure you want to have us come? We made those plans before your mom had to go to the hospital."

"I'm sure. Mom loves showing kids around the farm."

"Okay. See you!"

Summer got into her car, locked the door, and dialed Carl's cell phone. "I'm on my way home," she said when he answered.

"No hurry," he told her. "Your mom and I are sitting here playing cards."

"Okay, bye." She smiled as she put the phone down on the passenger seat. Carl had come over earlier in the day bearing a bouquet of flowers for her mother and a bag of groceries.

"Can't have that Abram outshining me," he told Marie as he handed her the bouquet.

"They were from his friend Wayne too." She blushed as she sniffed the pink roses. "So pretty. Thank you."

He pulled a package of steaks, baking potatoes, and a bag of pre-cut salad mix from the bag. "Thought I'd cook dinner for us since you've fixed me so many meals over the years."

Summer kissed him on the cheek as she left to take her final and made him blush. Carl had done many kind things for them through the years, but knowing he would be spending the evening with her mother meant she wouldn't worry about her when she needed to concentrate on taking the exam.

Now that classes were over for the semester, she could turn her attention to the upcoming holiday. December wasn't the easiest month, since her father died just a few days after Christmas. She'd brought him her laptop and helped him order a book of poetry, and when it arrived helped him wrap it while her mother was running errands one day.

Last year she'd ordered a book of poetry for her mom and put his name on the tag before placing it under the tree. Maybe tonight she'd look online for her mother's gift. It would be such a relief not to have to sit at the laptop and write a paper or study for a test.

Two whole weeks off from classes. She felt almost giddy at the thought of not having to go to class or study or write a paper.

She passed Abram's house and saw that the windows were dark. She wasn't surprised since it was after ten.

Maybe tomorrow she'd call him and set up a time for them to go out for the dinner they hadn't been able to go for because of her mother's emergency.

They needed to talk.

She pulled into her drive and shut off the engine. Gathering up her book bag and purse, she got out of the car and walked up the porch steps. The porch light was on, and when she opened the back door she found Carl and her mother laughing at the kitchen table.

Although she'd told herself everything would be okay—that Carl would call her if her mother had any problem—she felt a sense of relief that all seemed well. He winked at her as if to say he knew what she was thinking.

"You're early," her mother said, glancing at the kitchen clock.

"Final didn't take as long as I thought it would," she explained as she dumped the book bag and purse on the bench near the door.

"We saved you a plate," Carl said. "It's in the refrigerator. Just take a minute to warm it up."

"Thanks, but I had a sandwich with Kim when we had a quick cram session before the exam."

"How do you think you did?" her mother asked her.

"Good." She yawned. "Sorry. I'm ready for bed." She bent and kissed her mother's cheek. "See you in the morning."

As she left the room she heard Carl challenging her mother to one more game of cards.

Exhausted, she climbed into bed and snuggled in. And slept.

It was her favorite time of the year. Christmas break was coming, and before it the Christmas play. Her teacher had said she was her best scholar and asked her to be in the play everyone attended that was such an important part of the holidays. It meant memorizing lots of lines, but she didn't mind that. She knew hochmut—*pride—wasn't their way, but secretly she was so proud and so happy to not only be in the play, but be asked to be the female lead.*

How she loved schul. *While some of her friends were looking forward to graduating this summer, sometimes she wished she could go on—attend four more years like the* Englisch *did. But that wasn't the Amish way. Some would go on to apprenticeships, learn a craft, or take a bigger role in the family farm or business, and, of course, just because you weren't in* schul *didn't mean that you stopped reading or learning . . .*

Still, sometimes she wished she could spend more time in class, learn more, ask more questions of a teacher, work on essays and projects, and . . .

Summer woke and blinked.

What a bizarre dream. She'd gone to bed so grateful classes were over for the holidays, and here she was dreaming she wanted to be in class more.

And then she remembered it was another of her dreams of being an Amish *maedel*. Funny how she'd never had one where she'd longed to be a student and attend school after the eighth grade. Maybe she should be grateful for the opportunity, she mused. She punched her pillow and got more comfortable and closed her eyes, willing sleep to come.

And slept dreamlessly.

SSS

Abram heard a car pull into the driveway as he was working in the barn. He opened the door and saw Summer getting out of her car. He waved to draw her attention from the house.

She brightened when she saw him and waved back. "Hello!"

"Hello. How did your exam go?"

"I think I did well. And now I'm on break. No classes for two weeks!"

It did his heart *gut* to see her grinning from ear to ear. "That's wonderful."

"I wanted to thank you again for coming to the hospital to be with me the night Mom was there. It meant a lot."

"It was nothing."

"No," she said seriously, walking closer. "Having you there meant a lot to me. You kept me calm, made me eat." A gust of wind caught her hair and she pushed it back. "You've been such a good friend."

"It's cold out here. Come inside."

"Oh, you're working on a dresser," she said as she stepped inside and he closed the barn door. "It's beautiful."

She laughed as Joe and Shadow stuck their heads over their stalls. "Hi, guys! Good to see you." She walked closer to stroke their noses. "I wish I'd brought something for them."

"They're happy just to have some company besides me, I'm sure," he told her.

"So I thought I'd stop by and ask you to dinner. We didn't get to go that night."

"That'd be great."

"I should have called first," she said, chuckling.

"It's no problem. I don't have plans. Give me a few minutes to clean up." He screwed the lid on the jar of stain he'd been using. "Do you want to come in the house, have some coffee?"

"I'd rather you got me something I can give these guys and stay here. I miss having a horse."

"Sure. I'll be right back."

When he came back he had apples for both horses. "I'll just wash up and change."

"No hurry." She turned to Joe and Shadow. "Who wants a treat?"

Abram rushed to wash up and change, but when he returned to the barn, he saw he hadn't been missed. Summer was clearly enjoying herself with his horses. Her cheek rested against Shadow's and she spoke softly to him.

"You keep that up, he'll be following you home."

She smiled. "He's a sweetie. Such a shame when people mistreat animals." She passed by Joe, giving him a final pat. "Bye, Joe."

"So where shall we go?"

"You choose," she said as they walked to the car.

He named the restaurant favored by tourists and locals alike, and they drove into town. "I've been so busy I didn't realize how soon Christmas will be here," she said as she took in the sights of the shops decorated for the holidays.

She pulled into the restaurant parking lot and shut off the engine. They were seated quickly at a table under a handmade quilt mounted on the wall.

"How is your mother doing?"

"There haven't been any more fainting spells, but she still doesn't seem herself. Carl fixed her dinner and stayed with her yesterday so I could take my exam without worrying."

"That's good."

"He also brought flowers. Said he couldn't have you showing him up." She glanced at him. "She sends her thanks and hopes to thank you in person one day."

"No need. Glad she enjoyed them."

Two women were seated at a nearby table. One woman set her shopping bags in one of the empty chairs and gave a self-deprecating shrug when her companion shook her head.

"I need to get some Christmas shopping done," Summer told Abram after they ordered their food. "I haven't gotten my mother's gifts yet. I get one from me and one from my dad. I promised him I'd see she'd get something from him each Christmas."

"That's a nice thing to do."

"He died two days after Christmas," she said softly. "I was so afraid he wouldn't make it. Christmas was their favorite holiday."

She traced a pattern on the condensation on her glass of iced tea. "I remember the last gift I helped him buy and wrap—a book of poetry. The next Christmas, when I brought out the boxes of Christmas ornaments and wrapping paper, I found Mom had saved the paper, ribbon, and tag from the present from the year before. She told me it was the last time he wrapped a present for her and wrote on the tag and she cried. So now I have to wrap her book in the paper and ribbon and make sure his tag is on it." She blinked hard. "I don't know what I'll do when that paper wears out."

Abram reached for her hand. "I know you're worried about her. I want you to call me if I can help in any way. No matter what time it is." He wanted to take care of her, have her turn to him. She had such a generous spirit, cared so much about other people, and worked so hard . . .

"I appreciate that." She looked at him and something passed between them, something strong and true. The noise of the restaurant around them faded. "Abram I—" she stopped, shook her head. Her eyes were wide and wondering. "Abram, we need—"

"Abram!"

He started and jerked his head up. Fannie Mae, one of the women from his church, stood beside the table, staring with shocked eyes at his hand holding Summer's.

Summer tried to pull her hand away, but Abram held it firmly.

"Fannie Mae," he said calmly. "How are you? Have you met Summer Carson?"

"*Ya*. You came to church one Sunday." She turned to Abram. "How are your *eldres*?"

"Doing well, thank you."

"*Gut, gut*. Well, I'm meeting someone. Abram, I'll see you at church this Sunday." She nodded at them and hurried away.

Abram watched her hurry to a table near the back of the restaurant and join another woman from church.

"Abram?"

He tore his gaze away and looked back at Summer. "What?"

"Why didn't you let go of my hand?"

He looked at their joined hands on top of the table, then at her. "Do you want me to?" he asked her.

She shook her head slowly. "No. But I don't want to get you into trouble."

"Let me worry about that," he said.

"But—"

"I mean it. Let me worry about that."

Seventeen

Summer looked down at their clasped hands.

A gesture of comfort had suddenly become one of attraction, of deeper feelings.

She wasn't quite sure how she felt. That phrase so many people used casually when asked about their relationship on social media—"It's complicated"—came to her mind. She knew she felt more than friendship for this special man sitting opposite her, who looked at her the way she'd so often wished a man would.

But it was complicated. Hadn't Fannie Mae just shown that?

He was Amish. She was *Englisch*.

That they had become such good friends wasn't altogether unusual in this area where the two mixed to do business. But she couldn't ignore the fact that they both felt more than friendship now. She pushed aside her plate.

"Don't let her bother you," Abram said.

But she noticed that he'd stopped eating as well.

"Can we go?"

"Sure." He signaled for the check and the server came over and frowned.

"Is anything wrong?"

Summer shook her head. "We just need to go. Could we get some boxes to take this home?"

The woman's face cleared. "Sure. Be right back."

When she returned she put the check beside Abram's plate and scooped their meals into the take-home boxes herself.

They walked outside and got into her car. The temperature felt like it had dropped ten degrees. "It'll take a minute for the heater to get warmed up," she warned him.

He chuckled. "You're forgetting I ride in a buggy in the middle of winter."

"Yes, I guess I did."

Summer fell silent, and he didn't say anything either as they drove through the town of Paradise. Her thoughts drifted to the temptation of holding his hand again. She glanced at him and felt her cheeks warm. She hoped he didn't notice in the dim light inside the car.

"Speaking of buggies," he said. "If we were riding in my buggy, I could hold your hand again."

It was as if he'd read her mind . . .

She gave him a brief glance and then took her right hand off the steering wheel and held it out to him. "Only for a minute," she warned with a smile. "I need both hands to drive."

"I see a lot of people driving with a cell phone in one hand," he told her, giving her hand a squeeze.

"I'm not one of them," she said. "I promised my mom when I got my first cell phone that I wouldn't use it when I drive."

It wasn't easy to concentrate on her driving when he was touching her. She felt a mixture of relief and regret when she had to let go to put her hand on the steering wheel and make a turn.

"We didn't get coffee at the restaurant," she told him. "Want to stop for some?"

"That would be great. Maybe one of the burger places that has pie? We didn't get that either."

She laughed and shook her head. "Didn't get all your dinner but you want dessert. Typical man."

"Tell me you can turn down pie."

"I can turn down pie. Especially the pie at a burger place."

"I'm not choosy. I haven't had it for a while. Besides, I'll eat my dinner when I get home."

So she drove them to a nearby burger restaurant that had pie. She parked and they went inside. They sat in a booth and drank coffee and ate pie, and, while it wasn't bad, she decided she'd bake him a pie while she was on break. There was time to bake some Christmas cookies with her mother too. Her mother always loved baking for the holidays, and recently they often baked together so she wouldn't feel as if she were hovering, worried her mother would burn something and not smell it . . .

"You're looking worried."

"Just thinking about Mom."

"Didn't you say Carl checks on her whenever you're away from home?"

She nodded and sipped her coffee.

"Then she's fine."

"I know." With a sigh, she pushed her unfinished pie toward him. He grinned as he finished it. "What's your favorite pie?"

"Pie."

"Seriously."

"Seriously. I can't remember ever not liking one."

It was her turn to grin. "I bet. I was thinking I have some time to do some holiday baking. Maybe I'll make you one."

"I won't turn it down."

The door opened, and Summer looked up, then down again at her coffee when she saw it was an *Englisch* couple.

"If we're going to see each other—"

Her head shot up.

"—you have to get over worrying that someone will—"

"See us?" she asked. "Is that what we're doing? Seeing each other?"

"I think we want to be more than friends," he told her quietly. "Don't you?" He extended his hand, his gaze intent on her.

Summer stared at his hand for a long moment. And then took it. "Yes," she said slowly. "Yes."

♪♪♪

Abram had been taught all his life to maintain decorum in public, but right now he wanted to jump up and shout with joy. He forced himself to stay seated and look calm when he felt anything but.

"The thing is . . ." Summer began.

His spirits sank. This didn't sound good.

"Where can this take us?" she asked him. "We come from different backgrounds. We—"

"Can't we take it one day at a time?"

"One—"

"When you start seeing someone, do you always try to see all the way down the road?"

She bit her lip. "Well, no, I guess not. But at least when I date someone who's *Englisch* like me, I know it can have a future."

He leaned back in the booth and studied her. "Okay, you have a point. But how do you know we can't have a future?"

"Isn't that obvious? One of us would have to make a big change."

"Lots of couples do. Lots of couples have."

Summer nodded. Mark Byler had joined the Amish church and married Miriam Troyer. She knew of one or two other couples who'd done the same.

But there'd been only a few Amish who'd left the church and married an *Englischer.* The Amish shunned those who left the church . . .

Marriage was hard enough without such a radical change of religion, wasn't it?

"Can't we just be a couple who wants to be together? For as long as we want to be?" he pressed her.

She stared at their clasped hands. Looked into his eyes. And, again, felt that connection she hadn't felt with a man before.

"Please think about it. That's all I'm asking."

"That's a lot."

"True."

A staff worker holding a broom stopped at their table. "Sorry, folks, we're closing."

Summer glanced at her watch. "I had no idea it was this late." She stood and began putting their cups and paper plates on their tray.

"Don't worry about that," the woman said. "I'll get it. You folks have a good evening."

Abram lifted his head and sniffed when they walked outside. "Early snow's coming."

Summer nodded. "I can smell it too."

"Farmer's daughter."

She smiled. "I am. Dad left the farm to Mom and me, but he and Carl ran the farm together so Carl's continued. It's probably time we found him some help. I don't have any time—with college and work."

"At least winter gives him a break."

"True." They got into the car. She started the car, adjusted the heater, and backed out of the parking lot. "We were talking about Christmas. Are your parents planning on coming back?"

"No. My brothers, their families, and I will get together without them Christmas Eve."

"I'm sorry they won't be here, but it's nice you'll be with family." She drummed her fingers on the steering wheel. "You're welcome to come to dinner with us Christmas Day. Carl always comes."

"I'd like that."

"We eat at four. That gives you time to do Second Christmas with your family. You know, when I was a kid, I was always so jealous of the Amish. Two days of Christmas! It wasn't until I got older that I found out that the first day was for a spiritual time with the family, and gift-giving didn't happen until the second day. And school kids didn't get as long a Christmas holiday break as we did. Amish kids went back sooner after holiday break because the school year ends early. Everyone's needed to help with harvest."

"Seems I heard the Jewish people celebrate Hanukkah for eight days."

"Yeah. I was jealous of them too until I realized no Christmas tree. No Santa." She fiddled with the radio—she'd finally had the time to find the security code—and Christmas music filled the car. "I should take Mom for a ride one night. The Christmas lights are always so pretty in town."

"I'm glad we got out tonight," he said when she pulled into his driveway. He held out his hand and she took it. "Thanks for coming to ask me to dinner."

"First time I asked a man out."

"Well," he said. Then he thought, *That's the best you can do?* He released her hand and took his takeout box. "Don't forget your dinner."

"I won't. Have a good night."

"You too."

He watched her back out of the driveway and sighed. What a turn the day had taken. He needed to think about that. He went into the house, set the box down on the table, then went back out and checked on the horses one last time before going to bed. After assuring himself that all was well, he headed into the house, ate the dinner he'd brought home, then made his way upstairs.

It was late, but after he got into bed he found it impossible to sleep. He replayed the time he spent with Summer like it was one of the movies he'd seen with Wayne during Wayne's *rumschpringe*. Only this one was more exciting.

He frowned when he remembered Fannie Mae stopping by their table at the restaurant and being so obviously disapproving when she saw him holding Summer's hand. Turning on his side, he closed his eyes.

Finally he slept.

Frost covered the ground, crunching under his boots as Abram walked to the barn early the next morning. He was dressed warmly, but the wind was sharp, biting, and he was grateful for the warmth of the barn when he entered it. Working methodically, he cleaned stalls, fed the horses, and headed back into the house to make breakfast.

He was working on a four-drawer dresser when he heard a buggy entering the driveway. Before he could find a place to stop and check the drive, the barn door opened.

"*Guder mariye*," Fannie Mae said, stepping inside and closing the door with a snap. "I thought I'd find you out here. We need to talk."

Abram wanted to roll his eyes. He knew what was coming. Fannie Mae had a reputation for being outspoken about the rules of the community. She'd graduated from *schul* just two years before him, yet she always looked stern, acted older, and was faintly critical of anyone she considered wasn't as strict about the rules of the community as she was.

"Do your *eldres* know that you're dating an *Englisch* woman?"

Well, that was blunt. But wasn't Fannie Mae always so?

He straightened. "I'm a grown man, Fannie Mae," he said.

"So they don't know," she pounced.

"We haven't talked about it yet."

"I've known you and your family all my life. I feel you should think about what you're doing. Perhaps you should talk to them. Or the bishop."

He studied her. First the bishop, now Fannie Mae. "I've talked to the bishop," he said slowly. "If I feel I should talk to my *eldres*, I will. Now, if you'll excuse me, Fannie Mae, I have chores to do."

Frustrated, she shook her head, then spun on her heel and strode out of the barn with a decided flounce.

Dating was a private matter in this community. *Eldres* were often the last to be told about a couple's plans. He still didn't know where things were going with Summer. When it was time to talk to his *eldres*, he would. But not on anyone else's timing. Not Fannie Mae's and not the bishop's.

Eighteen

"We have company," Marie announced as she looked out the kitchen window. "Your friend is here."

Summer felt her heart leap. Abram had stopped by? Then she remembered that Kim was coming by with her little girl today. Before she could get up from the table, her mother was flinging open the door and welcoming Kim and her daughter inside.

"This is Gabby, short for Gabrielle," Kim said. "Gabby, this is my friend, Summer, and her mother, Mrs. Carson."

"So nice to meet you, Gabby," Marie said. "How old are you?"

"I'm five," Gabby told her, holding up five fingers. Her eyes were big and bright green like her mother's. Mother and daughter wore their curly red hair in braids.

"Your mom says you want to see our farm."

Gabby nodded vigorously, making the pom-poms on her knitted cap bob.

"Then let's go straight outside and have some fun," Marie said with an enthusiasm Summer hadn't seen in a while. She bundled into her jacket and hat and then handed Gabby the egg basket.

"Let's go see how many eggs the girls have laid."

"Girls lay eggs?" Gabby asked her mother.

"Hens. Chickens, sweetie," Marie explained as she took Gabby's hand. "I call them my girls."

"Silly mama," Summer told Gabby. "I'm her girl."

Gabby giggled. "You're a big girl!"

"I am." Summer pulled on her jacket and knitted cap.

They walked outside and found Carl waiting with a cart for them to ride hitched behind his tractor. He helped them climb into it and take seats on the benches.

"Too bad you couldn't come when the fields were bare," he said as he started the tractor. "That there is where Summer and her ma have their garden with fruits and vegetables, and it's my job to plant on the rest of the acreage."

He stopped in front of the elaborate chicken coop he and Summer's dad had built, shut off the tractor, and came around to help everyone climb out of the cart.

"She's been looking forward to this for days." Kim said, grinning as Marie handed Gabby a basket to gather eggs.

Gabby gasped when she saw the hens inside. "Can I hold one?"

Marie nodded. "Emmy here likes to be held. Just hold her carefully and not too tightly, okay?"

Gabby held out her arms and giggled when the hen was placed in her arms. "She's so soft. Her fur tickles."

"Feathers," Kim corrected her. She pulled one from Gabby's jacket and showed it to her. "Hens have feathers."

"Let's gather some eggs," Summer told Gabby. "You can take the eggs home with you and have your mom cook them for you."

"And I can take Emmy home with me too?"

"'Fraid not, baby," Kim told her. "Emmy has to stay here in her house. We can't have her in our apartment."

Gabby pouted, then looked at Summer. "You got horsies?"

"Not anymore," Summer told her. "But we have one pig in the barn. Let's go see it."

"You keep a pig in a barn?" Kim asked as they walked to the barn.

"Too cold outside right now. And I'm surprised Mom doesn't keep Billy in the house. She treats him like a pet."

"I do not," Marie protested.

But when they went into the barn Marie cooed and baby-talked at Billy, and she and Gabby petted him like a dog. Billy responded by pushing his snout into Gabby's hand, so Marie let her feed the pig.

"No horsies," Gabby said sadly as she looked around at the empty stalls.

"I miss them too," Summer told her. Then inspiration struck. "But I know someone who has horsies. I mean, horses."

"I wanna go see them!" Gabby cried. "Can we go see them?"

Marie gave Summer a knowing look. "I can guess where you want to go."

"Me too," Kim said, grinning.

"We'll just make a quick visit." Summer pulled her cell phone from her pocket and sent Abram a text.

A few minutes later he responded and said to come right over.

"I'll stay here and make some hot chocolate," Marie said. "And some coffee for our tour guide."

Summer climbed into Kim's car, and they drove over to Abram's farm with Gabby strapped in her car seat in the back.

"I'm sorry about the tune," Kim apologized as Gabby sang "Old MacDonald" exuberantly.

"I'm glad she's so excited. I loved growing up on a farm." She glanced over the seat. "Gabby, my friend Abram has four horses."

"Four!" Gabby cried. "Can I ride one?"

Summer looked at Kim and saw her friend had paled. "Probably not today," she told Gabby. "Maybe next time. But you can pet them. And I bet Abram has an apple you can feed them."

Kim shot her a grateful look. "Thanks."

"You're welcome." She told Kim where to turn, and soon they were pulling into Abram's driveway.

"Well, well, look who's here," Kim murmured.

Wayne stood with Abram at the barn door. He wore a big grin as he walked toward Kim's car.

♫♫♫

"He was here working on a furniture piece with me when you texted," Abram told Summer as she watched Kim unbuckle Gabby from her car seat. "I didn't call him. Honest."

"Well, look who's here," Wayne said in a jovial voice as Kim set Gabby down next to her car. "It's Mini-Me!"

"I'm Gabby, not Mini-Me!" she told him indignantly.

"You saw *Austin Powers?*" Kim asked.

"Sure. During my *rumchspringe*. And all of the Star Wars movies."

"Gabby, this is Wayne and this is Abram."

She immediately abandoned her mother and grabbed Abram's hand. "You got horsies?" she asked him, gazing up at him adoringly.

"I sure do. Come meet Joe and Shadow."

Summer grabbed Abram's other hand and stopped him in his tracks. "Kim says no riding!" she whispered in his ear.

He gazed down at her, mesmerized by her closeness. "Okay," he said slowly.

"Horsies!" Gabby prompted him.

"Sorry." He tightened his hold on Summer's hand while the other little charmer skipped along holding his hand.

"I have horsies," he heard Wayne telling Kim behind him.

Kim laughed. "That's good to know."

Abram had to let go of the hand of one of the females to open the barn door. Reluctantly he released Summer's hand, and when he reached for it again she'd moved forward so he couldn't hold it again. With a sigh he watched her caress Shadow's nose, then Joe's.

"They're big!" Gabby told him, awed.

He reached down and picked her up. "You can pet Joe, see? Nice and soft on his nose."

"Mommy, feel!" she told her. "Nice Joe."

"I got Shadow recently and he'd been abused," he told Kim. "So I'm letting him get used to people. But he's met my nieces and nephews and he's gentle as can be."

"He's sweet," Summer agreed.

"Smart too. Likes women," Wayne offered when Shadow nodded as if in agreement and Kim jumped.

"I told Kim you might have something her daughter could give the horses," Summer said meaningfully.

It took Abram a minute to figure out what she was saying. "Oh, sorry." He reached in his jacket pocket and gave Gabby a small apple for Joe.

"I—be careful," Kim told him, moving closer.

Joe took the apple delicately then crunched it with his big teeth.

Abram pulled out another and gave it to Gabby to offer Shadow. He took the fruit with the same delicacy.

Abram wondered if it was his imagination that Shadow seemed to smirk at Kim.

"I'm guessing you haven't been around horses much," Wayne said to Kim.

"No, I haven't. I guess it shows. I don't know where Gabby got this interest in them."

"I got my first horse when I was eight," Summer told her.

"We always lived in an apartment. Hard to have one there."

"I guess," Summer said, chuckling.

"So you gonna let Gabby sit on Joe?" Wayne asked.

All three adults shushed him, but it was too late.

"Sit on horsie?" Gabby cried. "I can sit on Joe?"

"Now you've done it," Abram told him.

Gabby turned to her mother and gave her a pleading look. "Please, Mommy, please!"

"No."

"I want! I want!" Her face screwed up and she began to sob piteously.

"I told you that you couldn't today," Kim began, but Gabby became inconsolable and refused to let her mother take her from Abram's arms. She twined her arms around his neck like a vine.

Abram turned to Summer. "Help?"

"Gabby, stop!" she told her firmly. "Let me talk to your mother." She pulled Kim aside. "Abram can hold her on Joe's back in the stall for a few minutes. He won't let go of her."

"I shouldn't let her get her way by having a tantrum."

"Then tell her that." She patted Kim's shoulder. "I promise Abram will be careful with her if you allow it."

Kim moved closer to her daughter. "Gabby, if you say you're sorry, I'll let Abram sit you on Joe for a few minutes. If you fuss when I say it's time to get off, we won't come here again." She gave Abram a side-long look. "Not that you're likely to ever invite us again."

He grinned. "Of course you're welcome. It's another matter for Wayne here."

"Sorry," Wayne muttered.

"I sorry too," Gabby said as she looked up at him under lashes sparkling with tears.

Abram's heart melted. "Thank you. Wayne, will you open the stall so we can go in?"

"Sure." He opened it so Abram could carry Gabby inside, then closed the stall.

Abram tossed a blanket on Joe's back and set Gabby on him. He held her firmly as he talked quietly to Joe.

Gabby leaned forward and kissed Joe on his mane and then looked at her mother. "I love Joe. And Abram."

"I may not let you take her home," he told Kim.

"She knows how to charm to get her way."

Abram looked at Summer. "When did you sit on a horse for the first time?"

"My mom has a picture of me on one when I was three. My dad was holding me like you are Gabby now."

He stood patiently with the child on the horse until Kim walked forward. "Nice Joe," she said as she stroked his nose with a hesitant hand. "Thank you for being so good with my little girl."

"Standardbreds are known for their calm natures. Shadow seems to love children too."

"My mom said she was going to make us hot chocolate," Summer told Gabby. "Say goodbye to Joe. Tell him thank you."

"'Bye, Joe. Thank you."

Abram lifted Gabby from the horse and handed her to Kim. "Thank you, Joe," he said. "You made one little girl's day." He glanced at Shadow as he let himself out of Joe's stall. "Your turn next time."

"Don't I get thanks for suggesting it?" Wayne asked as they walked to the car.

"No!" the three adults told him simultaneously.

"Gee, can't a guy make a mistake?" He hunched his shoulders, then shot Kim a grin. "How can I make it up to you? Maybe if you come—"

"Don't say it," she warned. "Whatever you were going to suggest, you whisper to me first where she doesn't hear." She jerked her head meaningfully at her daughter in her arms.

"Oh, okay." Wayne leaned close and whispered in her ear.

"I'll think about that."

She opened the back door to her car, set Gabby in her safety seat, and buckled her in. Then she turned to Abram. "Thank you again."

"Anytime." He looked at Summer. "I'm glad you asked to come over."

"Come to supper tonight?"

"I'd love to."

Abram stood with Wayne watching the car roll down the driveway.

"Huh?" Abram realized Wayne was talking to him when he elbowed him.

Wayne slung a companionable arm around Abram's shoulders. "You're one lucky dude."

"Yeah," he said. "Yeah, I am."

Nineteen

"This is going to be fun," Summer told her mother as they drove into Paradise. "We haven't gone shopping together in ages."

"I love this time of year," Marie said as they searched for a parking place. "Everyone looking so happy. The shops decorated for Christmas."

"We'll drive in one night so you can see all the lights." Summer squeezed into a spot that opened up. "It's so pretty."

They wandered the streets, mixing with locals and tourists. Sure, it was crowded, but that was part of the fun. Every shop seemed to invite "come inside" when you looked into its display windows.

"Let's stop here first." Summer pointed to the toy store. "I want to get something for Gabby."

The toy store was crammed with parents loading their baskets as they held long lists in their hands. Summer debated between choosing a stuffed chicken that looked a lot like Emmy and a brown horse. She remembered the look of pure joy Gabby had worn as she sat on Joe and chose the horse.

"Then I'm getting this one," Marie said and reached for the chicken.

Next was the card and gift shop, where they chose a box of Christmas cards to send out together. Summer let her mother have her choice: a snowy farmhouse scene.

A crafts store where crafts made by local Amish were sold drew them in. Ornaments made of quilt scraps were displayed on a Christmas tree. The Amish didn't have Christmas trees, but the shop used the tree as a way to show off the ornaments. They each bought one to add to the tree they hadn't yet put up in their living room.

"I can make some like these next year," Marie said when they were outside the shop. "I have an old quilt that's falling apart I can cut and sew into ornaments."

"Marie, haven't seen you in town for ages!" a woman exclaimed and rushed up to hug her.

"Ellen, good to see you."

Summer said hello and then used the opportunity to slip into the nearby bookstore and pick up the book of poetry she'd decided on for her mother. When she came back out the women were finishing up their conversation.

"What did you get?" Marie reached for Summer's shopping bag.

She batted away her mother's hands. "Christmas secrets."

Marie pretended to pout. "Spoilsport."

The display window of the quilt shop beckoned. In it a family of Amish dolls clustered around a little fireplace. Evergreens were draped on the mantel, and a battery-operated light imitated the glow of a fire in the hearth. The father read his newspaper while the mother sewed her quilt and the children sprawled on a rag rug to play the card game Dutch Blitz.

Marie filled a basket with thread and some fabric she needed to complete a project. Summer hesitated over some gorgeous dark chocolate-brown yarn that reminded her of Abram's eyes. It would make a handsome muffler to wrap around his neck on chilly days. She fingered it. The yarn was so soft and yet sturdy.

Marie whispered over Summer's shoulder. "You should get that. Someone we know has brown eyes that'd match."

She turned. "I don't have time to make it."

"Sure you do. A muffler takes no time at all. And you're not studying every evening now."

That decided it. Summer put the yarn in her shopping basket. Then she added a pretty bottle green to make a muffler for Kim. Gabby had been bundled up warmly in a pretty jacket and cute knitted muffler and cap with a pom-pom, but Kim had worn a plain beige muffler. She'd worn no hat. Summer added another ball of yarn and hoped she'd have time to knit a simple cap—and that Kim liked them. Maybe Kim didn't wear a cap because she didn't care for them. But as Summer stepped outside and the cold hit her, she saw nearly everyone wore a cap or a hat or a hood. She decided she'd take a chance.

"Lunch," Marie announced. "Let's put the bags in the trunk and go eat. I need a sit down and some coffee. Maybe some nice soup."

"Sounds good to me."

They had to wait for a booth in the restaurant Summer and Abram had visited. Like many in the area it served Amish favorites so it was popular. While they waited Summer glanced around and wondered if she'd see anyone she knew.

She just hoped she wouldn't run into Fannie Mae again . . .

A server stopped to show the waiting guests a tray of desserts. All had to sigh over the warm bread pudding that smelled of vanilla and cinnamon, apple dumplings, gingerbread, and of course shoofly pie.

"I'm on a diet," a customer said with a sigh.

"There are no calories in these," the server assured her.

Everyone laughed.

Summer and Marie looked over the menu when they were finally seated. "Their vegetable soup is homemade here," Marie said. "I'm having that and a half sandwich. Then I'll still have room for dessert."

"Or we can always take it home."

She laughed. "We should do that anyway."

Summer was glad to see her mother looking happier than she had recently. It was good they'd been able to get out and do something happy today.

Their soup came, warm and rich with chunks of vegetables and beef. Both of them had half a grilled cheese sandwich that was crusty and delicious.

"I invited Abram to dinner tonight. I'll cook."

"Be my guest."

An Amish woman passed their table and Summer scowled.

"Why the frown?"

"Hmm?"

"You're frowning."

Summer hesitated. "When Abram and I ate here. I was telling him how I was worried about you, and he touched my hand in sympathy. And just as he did this woman he knows stopped at our table, saw what he was doing, and looked like she was going to say something."

"I see."

"Mom, we're going to see each other," she said, choosing her words carefully. "We're feeling like we're more than friends, but we don't know where it's going."

Marie looked thoughtful. "I've been sensing something between the two of you. I haven't seen that with you and anyone else you've dated and brought to meet me."

Her mother went back to eating her soup. Summer waited as she finished it, then smiled and thanked the server when she cleared the bowl and topped off her coffee.

"That's it?"

"No, I have to have dessert. Who can turn down one of their desserts?"

"I meant . . . that's all you have to say about me seeing Abram?"

"You're smart, Summer," Marie said calmly. "You know the risks of being involved with a man who's not only not of our faith but from one that is very . . . restrictive." She poured a dollop of cream into her coffee and stirred it. "You've been fascinated by the Amish since you were a little girl—even before you found out about your grandmother. You would come to the breakfast table and tell me about your dream the night before. I always wondered about cell memory."

She looked up. "It would mean a big change for one of you if you married. A huge one." She reached across the table and took her hand. "But life's short. I was married for more than thirty years to your father, but it still wasn't enough."

Summer stared down at her mother's hand. It was so thin and blue veins showed under the fragile skin. But her grip was firm and steady.

"I just want you to be happy."

"I know, Mom. Thanks."

"So," the server said brightly as she appeared at the side of the table. "What are you ladies having for dessert?"

∽∽∽

Abram pulled into Summer's driveway and wondered if he'd been invited to dinner because she didn't want to risk being seen with him again in public. He sat there for long moments thinking about it. Well, so what if that was the reason for the invitation? What difference did it make? He didn't care if anyone said anything to him, but wanted whatever made her comfortable. He wished he'd been able to stop Fannie Mae from stopping by their table . . .

"You getting out anytime tonight?"

Abram jerked. Carl was staring at him quizzically as he stood beside the buggy.

"Yes. Just thinking."

Carl rocked back on his heels. "Well, don't want to interrupt a man's thinking."

"No, I'm coming." He got out.

"Let's put Shadow here in the barn. Cold tonight."

"That would be wonderful. Thanks." He unhitched the horse and the two of them walked him into the barn and put him in a stall. Abram saw it was lined with fresh straw.

When he glanced at Carl, he shrugged. "Marie told me you were coming for dinner."

Abram gave Shadow a final pat, and he and Carl headed to the house. As they approached the back door he saw one of Rose Miller's Christmas wreaths hanging on it. Carl opened the door and gestured him inside.

Summer looked up from the stove and smiled at Abram. "Hi."

"Hi."

"Yeah, hi, Carl, how are you?" Carl asked with some irony.

She made a face at him. "I just saw you five minutes ago when you were sniffing out what we were having for dinner."

"Figured I'd better check on whether I needed some Pepto Bismol."

Summer put her hands on her hips. "And what is that supposed to mean? Are you giving me grief about my cooking again?"

"Well, you remember that episode with the chili." He looked at Abram. "I think she dumped the whole jar of chili powder in it."

"That was years ago. Are you ever going to forget it?"

Carl rubbed his stomach. "My stomach never did."

Marie burst out laughing. "Carl, now you stop."

"Yeah. Stop." Summer turned to Abram. "Take off your jacket and have some coffee. Dinner's almost ready."

Carl poured a mug and handed it to Abram after he shed his jacket. "Yeah, Abram, have a seat and forget what I said."

"You could always leave and eat your own cooking. I believe that's usually a Hungry Man frozen dinner when you're not eating with us, right, Mom?"

"I'm staying out of this," she said, grinning.

Abram pulled out a chair and sat. "I've eaten Summer's cooking and it's very good," he said diplomatically. "Smells fantastic." It really did. The kitchen was warm, the aromas enticing.

But more, he felt welcome here, so very welcome.

"Thank you." Summer pulled a ceramic baking dish from the oven and carried it over to set it on a hot pad on the table. "Just a baked chicken."

"Mmm, looks good," Carl said.

Summer gave him a sour look. "Don't try to charm me now." She returned to the stove and brought a basket of golden-brown biscuits to the table.

Abram loved biscuits. He hoped they tasted as *gut* as they looked. He hadn't had a biscuit since his *mudder* had left for Pinecraft.

Marie got up from the table and opened a cupboard and poked around in it. "Summer, where did you put the aspirin?"

She walked over and located the bottle of Tylenol and handed it to her mother. "You take this, remember? What's the matter? Do you have a headache?"

"Knees are achy. Back too. Guess I'm just not up to daylong shopping jaunts," she said, smiling as she sat again.

Summer took her seat next to her mother and all bent their heads to say grace.

"So you two bought out the town today?" Carl asked.

"I wouldn't go that far," Summer told him. "Just a few Christmas gifts. I don't have much time to make things this year with school. I can't wait to see what Gabby thinks of the stuffed horse we found her at the toy store."

"Good chicken," Carl spoke up as he took a second helping.

Summer grinned. "Glad you like it. I'm making the turkey for Christmas this year."

"Oh my." Carl clapped a hand to his chest. "Marie, remember the first year she baked the turkey?"

Summer rolled her eyes. "I forgot to take the neck out of the inside of the turkey. Big deal. Nobody died."

"'Cept the turkey," Carl chortled.

"I had no part in his demise. I simply baked him. And I never made that mistake again." She narrowed her eyes at him. "You don't have to come." She turned and smiled at Abram. "I hope you won't let Carl's teasing keep you away."

"I won't." Abram grinned as he looked at Carl eating with obvious relish. "And I don't think he will either."

He considered himself a lucky man he'd been invited to supper tonight. And to Christmas Day dinner. Summer was a very *gut* cook. And so pretty to look at. Forget the food. He could just sit here and stare at her all night.

"Oh dear," Marie said and slumped against Summer.

"Mom?" She grabbed her mother's shoulders before she could slip to the floor. "Mom?"

Her mother's eyes were closed and her face was bone white.

Carl pushed back his chair so quickly it fell. He rushed over. "Marie? Marie? Honey, are you all right?"

She blinked and sat up. "My goodness, Carl, I'm fine. Just got a little light-headed there for a minute." She looked at Summer. "Sorry if I scared you."

Abram filled a glass with water and handed it to Summer. "Have her take some sips of this."

Her eyes were terrified. "Maybe we should call 911."

"Let's give it a minute," he said, laying a hand on her shoulder. "See how she does."

"Just got light-headed," Marie repeated.

"I think we need to get you checked out," Summer told her.

Marie accepted the glass of water and gave Abram a tremulous smile. "Thanks. No, Summer, we did that last time and the doctors at the ER couldn't find anything wrong, remember? I'm not going through that again. I just probably overdid today."

"Sip it nice and slow," Abram cautioned when Marie took a long drink.

"You sound like you have some experience with this sort of thing," she told him.

"My oldest sister fainted a lot when she was expecting her first baby."

Marie coughed on a mouthful of water and he patted her gently on the back. She chuckled. "I think we can rule that out."

Summer shook her head. "You two stop it. She scared me to death."

Carl walked over to the stove, picked up the teakettle, and filled it at the sink. Then he set it on a burner and turned on the gas. "A nice cup of tea should help. You didn't eat much yet, Marie. Can you eat a little more?"

"We had a big lunch."

"That was hours ago." Summer stood. "I can make the tea, Carl."

"Sit and calm yourself down," he told her quietly as he rested a hand on her shoulder. "You're looking almost as pale as your mother."

She looked into his eyes and nodded. "I'm okay. Thanks."

Carl fixed the tea and Marie sipped it, then picked up her fork and ate a little more. Summer served dessert—apple dumplings she and her mother had brought back from the restaurant. Then Summer got her mother to go upstairs and go to bed.

"Looks like you and I are on cleanup," Abram said to Carl as he rose and began clearing the table.

"Seems fair." Carl went to the sink, turned on the faucet, and squirted dishwashing liquid into the water. "Gonna take Marie in Monday to be checked again by the doctor if I have to pick her up and put her in the truck myself."

Abram nodded and remembered how the man had called her "honey" and wondered if Summer knew how much this man cared about her mother.

Time would tell.

Twenty

Summer sat in the waiting room of the doctor's office with her mother.

When she'd called, the doctor's nurse had told her to bring her mother right in, and they would work her in. So far they'd been sitting here for nearly two hours. The waiting room was full.

"Not a good place to be when you're not sick," her mother murmured as the woman sitting several seats away sneezed.

Summer couldn't have agreed more but what could they do. There wasn't a separate waiting room for the contagious. Restless, she considered picking up a magazine, but when another patient coughed and sneezed she reconsidered touching something that might have germs on it.

"Should have brought your knitting," her mother told her.

"I had other things on my mind."

The door to the exam rooms opened, and a nurse stepped out and called Marie's name.

"Come on," Marie said as she stood. "You were the one who insisted I see the doctor."

Summer didn't remind her that Carl, too, had insisted but had stayed behind at the farm.

The nurse took her mother's blood pressure and temperature, then weighed her. "BP's up a little, weight's down another five pounds. Doc's not going to be happy about that. Too bad I can't give you five of mine."

"I'm sure I'll make it up over the holidays. Everyone gains then."

"Eats like a bird," Summer muttered.

"I don't work on the farm with your father anymore," Marie told her. "I shouldn't eat as much as I used to."

"But you're losing," the nurse said as she led them to an exam room. "Sit down." She took a seat on the little rolling stool and entered the pre-exam data into her computer.

"You told me on the phone you felt faint last night. Did you do anything out of the ordinary yesterday?"

"We did some Christmas shopping, had lunch in town."

"Sounds nice. I haven't done any yet. Where were you when you felt faint? What were you doing?"

"I was sitting at the table eating dinner. I didn't even have to cook. Summer cooked."

"Mom complained about her knees hurting," Summer remembered. "She took something for pain."

"Joints have been feeling achy," Marie admitted.

"She's been having trouble sleeping, and then after she takes the antidepressant she's drowsy."

"Any other symptoms?"

"Hot flashes. And I thought those were over two years ago."

"You didn't tell me that, Mom."

Marie shrugged. "It's not a big deal. They're mostly at night."

Summer had to say it. "Mom's having trouble with her memory."

The nurse turned to them. "I know that always worries people. But like the doctor will tell you, most of the time if you're worried about your memory it's fine." She stood. "The doctor will be in shortly. We're a little backed up. Cold and flu season."

It was more than a half hour before the doctor came in looking harried. She greeted both of them, sat on the stool, and scrolled through Marie's records. Then she had Marie sit on the exam table and did a brief exam, listening to her heart, peering into her throat and ears. "I think you may have a touch of the bug that's going around," she said. "Get some rest, plenty of fluids, and give us a call if you don't feel better in a few days."

"But what about her memory problems?"

The doctor gave Summer a kindly look. "Everyone complains about them. Even people your age."

"Summer, I'm fine," Marie insisted.

There was a knock on the door.

"Come," the doctor said.

The nurse poked her head in. "I need you. It's urgent."

"Sorry," the doctor said, jumping up and rushing out of the room.

A few minutes later the nurse returned. "Sorry. The doctor is with a patient we've had to call an ambulance for."

"Well, we don't need to be bothering you when you have really sick people," Marie said, standing up.

"No, wait, Marie, the doctor wants me to do the Mini-Cog on you. It'll just take three minutes." She pulled a piece of paper from a drawer, sat on the stool, and began reading from it. She read a list of three words and asked Marie to repeat them.

Marie repeated the three words.

"Good." She handed her a pad of paper and pencil on which she'd drawn a circle. "Now put the numbers where they belong as if on a clock."

"I'm not an artist," Marie warned her, but she did as she was told.

"And finally, put the hands at ten past eleven," the nurse requested. She took the paper back when Marie finished doing what she'd asked and glanced at the clock on the wall. "Now, tell me the three words I mentioned a few minutes ago."

Summer found herself holding her breath, but her mother repeated the words without mistake.

"Good."

"I passed?"

The nurse nodded. "This isn't a complete test, but it's a simple one we start with. I'll tell the doctor. Do you want to wait and see her again?"

"No," Marie said firmly as she stood and gathered up her jacket and purse. "Thank you."

"Okay, the doctor wants you to get some rest, plenty of fluids, and give us a call if you don't feel better in a few days."

Summer had no choice but to get up and follow her mother out of the office. After the tension of the visit, she felt like she needed some rest as well. She drove home, fixed a quick and simple lunch, and gave her mother a look when she said she wasn't hungry.

"Fine," Marie said and sat at the kitchen table. She ate a bowl of soup and a half sandwich and then announced she was going upstairs for a nap. "I'm sorry I was so much trouble this morning," she said, bending to kiss Summer on the cheek.

"You weren't any trouble. I'm just worried about you."

"Well, don't be."

Summer cleared the table, did the dishes, then debated going upstairs for a nap herself. But she felt too restless to sleep. She got her yarn, settled in the recliner in the living room with the television tuned to a home decorating show, and began working on the muffler for Abram. Knitting always relaxed her, but she hadn't had time in months to do it.

❧❧❧

Abram saw Summer's car parked in her driveway when he drove by in his buggy, but he forced himself to keep going. He didn't want to make a pest of himself. There were errands to run. He'd finished two more furniture pieces for Mervin, he needed to mail his gifts to his *eldres* in Pinecraft, and he'd promised to stop by Mark Byler's house. So Abram went on into town, wishing when he saw the line at the post office that he'd thought to go a week ago. After an interminable wait, he saw his package off to Florida. His *mudder* had been much better about mailing his gift. It had already arrived in a box full of presents he was supposed to pass along to his *bruders, schweschders,* and their *kinner* on Second Christmas.

He dropped off the two furniture pieces and chatted briefly with Mervin about the last orders he had to complete. Mervin's question about whether his parents were returning for the holiday suddenly reminded Abram that he didn't have anything for Summer. He was going to her house for Christmas Day dinner. Wait, that meant he should probably have something for her mother as well.

Panic set in. What could he make them? He wanted Summer to have something nice, but it couldn't be too big or too elaborate. The gift for her mother to thank her for the hospitality of her home should be something thoughtful. So he decided to look through the store catalog again while Mervin's *fraa* wrote out his check. But all the custom wooden furniture pieces in the catalog were too much for a gift to a woman you were dating. And Summer's house had a spice rack for the kitchen.

So with the check tucked in his jacket pocket he decided to take a stroll to some of the nearby shops to see if he could come up with any ideas. He looked in the window of the quilt shop and hesitated. He'd never set foot in the shop in his entire life.

"Won't kill you," his *mudder* had told him once when he was in town with her and his *dat*. He'd joined his *dat* sitting on the bench outside while she got what she needed.

But today he was a desperate man. Every time he came to town it was busier, traffic crowding the streets even more. If he could find something while he was here it would be best.

So he pushed open the door and went inside. He walked the aisles and looked at the goods. Fabric. No. Yarn. No. Sewing basket. No, he'd seen one sitting on the kitchen counter of her home. He didn't know if it was Summer's or Marie's. He kind of doubted Summer had much time for sewing with her college classes and part-time job.

Abram spied a display of thimbles painted with flowers and decided to take a chance on Marie being a sewer. One had little violets painted on it. Hmm. Pretty and it didn't cost too much so he'd look like he was trying to impress her.

He paid for it, tucked the bag in a jacket pocket—there, no letting other men know he'd been inside the quilt shop, he thought with a grin—and walked out.

Two doors down a shop that sold Amish crafts had a display of candles and wooden candlesticks in the window.

Perfect. He went inside, studied the wooden candlesticks with an eye to making some himself, and chose two vanilla-scented candles to go on top of them. There were some small candles in glass holders that smelled of bayberry and cinnamon and pine. He scooped up several to wrap for gifts for his *schwaegem*. They'd probably appreciate them more than the little gifts he hadn't yet made for them.

He breathed a sigh of relief as Anna, a friend of his *mudder's*, wrapped the candles in old issues of the *Budget* before putting them in a bag.

"So, is that it for your Christmas shopping?" she asked him with a twinkle in her eyes.

"I think so."

"Be *schur* to tell your *eldres* we're hoping they have a nice Christmas down in Florida."

"I will."

He left the shop, walked to Mervin's store, and got into his buggy in the parking lot behind it. After a quick stop at the bank to deposit his check, he went through the McDonald's drive-through for a quick lunch. On his way home, he passed Rose's stand outside her farmhouse and waved to her. She was doing a brisk business as usual with her handmade crafts, like the wreath on the kitchen door of Summer's house.

And that made him think of Summer again. He was pleased with the idea he'd come up with. It wouldn't take long to make the candlesticks, and he hoped it would mean more to her that he'd carved them just for her.

His last stop was at Mark's farm. Mark came out of the barn as he pulled into the drive.

"I got the copies of the deed for you inside," he told him. "Let's go in, have coffee and look them over."

"Great."

Mark opened the kitchen door.

"Da-da!" a toddler cried from where she sat in a high chair.

He grinned and leaned down to rub his nose on her cheek. "Emma!"

She squealed and reached to tug at his beard, but he was too fast for her and pulled away.

"Hello, Abram," Miriam said with a smile as she pulled a tray of gingerbread men from the oven. "Would you like a gingerbread man and some coffee?"

"I would love both."

"Have a seat," she invited as she used a spatula to transfer the cookies to a cooling rack. She brought a plate of cookies over to the table, set them before him, then gave one to Emma.

"She's growing so fast."

"*Ya*," Miriam said with a smile before she turned to slide another tray of cookies into the oven to bake.

Then she chuckled when she saw her *dochder's* face covered with gingerbread crumbs. She lifted her from the high chair and sent Emma into a fit of giggles when she kissed her chubby cheeks. "Bath for you." She turned to Mark. "Get the cookies out if the timer goes off before I come back."

"*Schur.* And Abram and I will eat all of them too," he told her as he poured coffee into mugs.

"Better save one for me." She carried Emma from the room.

Mark went to a cupboard to retrieve a manila envelope, handed it to Abram, then sat. "So, the farm is officially in your name," Mark told him.

Abram opened the envelope and scanned the paperwork. So many emotions swept over him: gratitude, joy, and a little fear about having such a responsibility for carrying on the legacy.

"It's a lot to take in, isn't it?"

He looked up and saw understanding in Mark's eyes. He took a deep breath. "Did you feel a little bit scared when you took over the farm from your *grossdaadi*?"

"You bet. I had worked alongside him for many summers when my parents let me visit, but I'd been an *Englisch* attorney living in Philadelphia for years," Mark said, looking off into the distance as he remembered. "The farm had been in the Byler family for generations. What if I messed up?" He chuckled and shook his head. "Not the best way to say it but that's how I felt. But Granddad was here to give me advice when I asked for it—still does—and I found that all I had to do was ask others in the community when I needed help."

Abram stuffed the paperwork back in the envelope and set it on the seat of the chair beside him so he wouldn't spill his coffee or cookie crumbs onto it. He stirred cream and sugar into his coffee. He chose a cookie and wondered if he should ask a question that weighed on his mind.

"Something you want to ask?"

His head jerked up. He stared at Mark. "How did you know?"

"When I was an attorney, I had to be good at reading facial expressions and body language," Mark reminded him. "I'm sensing this isn't a question about the farm deed."

"You seem happy. Contented," Abram said finally.

Mark grinned. "I am."

"Few *Englisch* join the Amish church."

"True. The Amish way of life isn't easy. But if it's the right one for you . . . it's the right one," he said simply. "The transition was easier for me since my grandfather was Amish, and I spent summers here with him from a young age. My dad decided he didn't want to join the church when he came of age, but my parents encouraged me to spend time with Granddad."

The oven timer dinged. Mark got up, turned it off, and used a potholder to pull the tray of cookies from the oven. He set it on top of the stove and transferred cookies from the tray to the cooling rack like Miriam had done.

"You're good at that."

Mark grinned. "I'm good at observing, remember?" He turned off the oven and took his seat again. "Since I'm Amish now, and we're not supposed to pry into whether two people are seeing each other, I won't ask you if there's a personal reason for your curiosity about whether I'm happy with my choice. But let's just say I observed the way you were looking at Summer Carson when she attended one of our church services."

Abram frowned. "Fannie Mae saw the two of us holding hands at a restaurant in town and came over to see me the next day," he found himself blurting out. "Seemed to think she should lecture me about being with an *Englisch* woman."

"Oh. Well. I'm surprised that the news hasn't reached Miriam and me yet. The Amish grapevine is faster than the internet."

"That's odd."

"Maybe she decided to keep it to herself."

They looked at each other. "Nah," said Mark. "I can't see that. Fannie Mae can't keep something like that to herself."

"Fannie Mae can't keep what to herself?" Miriam asked as she walked back into the room.

"She has an opinion about me seeing Summer Carson," Abram told her.

"Oh, well, Fannie Mae has an opinion about everything," Miriam said and she chuckled. "Many in the church don't think we Amish should date, let alone marry, an *Englisch* person." She reached for Mark's hand and gazed at him with love, then she turned to Abram. "Are you going to listen to them or to your heart?"

Twenty-One

Knitting calmed Summer the way nothing else did, but she was a bit surprised to find out how much she enjoyed knitting the muffler for Abram. The muffler used a simple stitch, and it didn't take long to produce a pretty decent length. She held it up and loved the way the brown wool looked.

A massive yawn overcame her. She let the knitting fall into her lap and closed her eyes. The morning had been so stressful. She just needed a moment to rest her eyes. Then she'd do some more knitting, think about what to fix for dinner.

She woke to find her mother shaking her arm. "Why don't you go upstairs and take a nap, be more comfortable?"

"The chair is pretty comfortable," Summer told her. "Now I know why Dad used to fall asleep in it so often." She glanced at her watch. "I only slept a half hour but I had the nicest dream. I was about eight and we were in the fields, with me trying to walk in his footsteps. I pulled a carrot out of the ground, wiped the dirt on my jeans, and began eating it. He turned and saw what I was doing and told me not to do something like that in front of you. That a little dirt didn't hurt anyone, but moms didn't feel that way."

"You two were good at keeping secrets like that." Her mother grinned. "I found out he was the reason you had too many cavities after I took you to the dentist. So I started asking your dad questions. He confessed he bought you candy whenever the two of you went into town. He knew better."

"He liked to spoil me," Summer told her, grinning. She looked down at the muffler in her lap. "I got a lot done before I fell asleep."

"You did."

She began knitting again. "I forgot how relaxing it is."

Marie stood. "What would you like for dinner?"

"I don't know."

"I don't think I have a recipe for that."

"I don't care."

"Nope, no recipe for that one either."

Summer laughed. It was an old family game. "Dad and I only did that with you because we honestly didn't have any ideas. Besides, we liked everything you cooked."

"Maybe because the two of you didn't like cooking?"

"Maybe. I can cook tonight. What do you want?"

"I don't know," Marie said dryly. "I don't care."

She chuckled. "Got me." Summer set the knitting aside, got up, and slid her arm around her mother's waist. "Let's go see what we can rustle up."

Carl walked in and found them sitting at the table eating ice cream. He tried to hide his expression of disappointment.

"Timing's off," Summer said with a chuckle as she dipped her spoon into the ice cream in her bowl.

"I didn't come hoping for dinner," he told her quickly.

"Didn't say that you did." But she struggled to hide her grin. "Mom and I decided we'd have dessert first. Want some?"

"Sure. But I came over to see what the doc said."

Summer let her mother tell him while she fixed him a bowl of ice cream. But Carl frowned as she set the bowl before him. "Don't look like you got a bug to me." He shrugged. "What do I know?" He dipped his spoon in his ice cream but just sat staring at it. "Something don't sound right."

"Well, I agree. But that's what the doctor thinks, and she said if Mom doesn't feel better in a few days we should come back."

"Guess that's all you can do." He ate a spoonful of ice cream. "If she's got a bug, then why haven't we gotten it?"

"Maybe your immune systems are better," Marie said as she finished her ice cream and set her spoon down. "Who knows? All I can say is that I hope you don't have to go into a doctor's office anytime soon. The place was a hotbed of germs today."

Summer stood, took her and Marie's bowls to the sink, then went to the refrigerator to stare into it. She pulled out a plate with the remains of the leftover chicken and shook her head. "I have no idea why I put this back in. I made sandwiches out of the leftover chicken at lunch and there's nothing left but bones."

"Don't throw it out," Marie said. "We can make bone broth out of it."

She put it back in the refrigerator and looked into the freezer. Hmm. A frozen package of stew meat, hamburger, and chicken breasts. They'd need to be defrosted and then cooked. She closed the freezer. "Why didn't I set something out to defrost earlier? Well, I guess I could defrost the hamburger and make spaghetti."

"Don't you worry about it," Carl said. "I'll order us some pizza. My treat. You both up for our usual?"

"Sounds good to me. Mom?"

"Sure."

Maybe ice cream and pizza weren't the kind of menu a sick person should eat, but Summer figured if her mother ate beyond a few nibbles, it was a good thing.

Carl went to the kitchen phone and dialed the number.

"Knew it by heart, did you?" Summer teased when he hung up.

He had the grace to look embarrassed as he sat down at the table.

Summer's phone vibrated on the table. She picked it up, glanced at the display, and saw that Abram was calling. "Excuse me, I'm going to take this in the other room."

"I hope I'm not calling at a bad time," Abram said. "I just wanted to know how your mother is doing."

Summer gave him a quick summary of her mother's diagnosis.

"Hmm. She doesn't seem like she has what's going around. The flu or whatever."

"That's what Carl said. If Mom's not feeling better in a few days we're going back."

"Good. She just doesn't look well." Silence hummed. "Summer, I want to see you, but I know you're worried about leaving your mother by herself right now."

She heard laughter from the kitchen. "I don't think Carl would mind spending an evening with her again. He's over here now talking to her."

"Tomorrow night?"

"Sounds good." She bit her lip. It was getting so cold out. "How about I pick you up?"

"Okay."

"Six?"

"Good. Have a good night."

"You too." She disconnected the call and walked back into the kitchen. No, from the way Carl and her mother were chatting, Summer had no doubt he wouldn't mind being with her tomorrow.

SSS

Abram walked out the minute she pulled into the drive.

"You look pretty," he told her and she blushed.

"Thanks. I started to put on a dress but then I decided to go for warmth tonight. So the dress went back into the closet and out came a sweater and slacks. Big snowstorm coming tomorrow," she said.

Maybe she was as nervous as he was. After all, this was their first date since they'd agreed to see each other.

"I thought we could have supper first." He named a local restaurant. "Then you can tell me what you want to do."

"Do?"

He shrugged. "We could go to a movie if you want."

"I haven't been to one in ages. Haven't had time."

"Me either. But not for the same reason as you."

"Do you *want* to go to a movie?"

He looked at her. "I want to do whatever you want to do. I don't know what the *Englisch* do on a date."

"Sometimes they go to a movie," she said slowly. "But I never much cared for that. At least not at the beginning, like a first date. I mean you go out with someone to get to know them better and then you sit in the dark with them and you don't get to talk to each other. Doesn't make sense."

"Well, there's one plus," he blurted out before he could stop himself.

"What's that?"

"Guys put their arm around their dates' shoulders."

She laughed. "Yeah. It's always fun to see a teen boy work up his nerve to do that. He'd act like he was stretching and then lay his arm carefully around his date's shoulder. Sometimes she'd allow it. Sometimes she wouldn't." She slanted a glance at him. "I thought you were going to say the advantage was popcorn. The Amish aren't into PDAs—public displays of affection—in the community or on *rumschpringe*."

"Movie popcorn *is* the best."

"Agreed. I can eat a big bucket of it even after having dinner before going to the movies." She pulled into the restaurant parking lot. "This place is expensive."

"Oh. You've been here before? I was hoping you hadn't."

"Family celebration. Let's go Dutch."

"I asked you out. I pay," he said firmly.

"Then I'm asking you out next time and I'm paying," she said just as firmly.

Their gazes met. Warmed. "You realize what you're saying?"

Summer smiled at him. "I do."

They went inside and were led to a booth in a secluded corner. Abram liked that. They'd be able to talk quietly without interruption. Not that it was likely Fannie Mae or someone from his church would be out in the evening—especially to an expensive restaurant.

"You could call this a celebration," he told her after they looked over the menu and placed their order. "Mark Byler had me pick up the deed to the farm today. It's officially in my name now."

"That's wonderful. Congratulations."

"Thanks, but I didn't do anything."

"You did. The Amish don't give the farm to the eldest automatically. If you didn't show that you deserved your legacy, that you would take it over and care for it and make it prosperous, they wouldn't have transferred ownership. And your parents will continue to live there, in the *dawdi haus*, and be cared for if needed."

He watched her hesitate, and he wondered for a moment if she was trying to show him how much she understood about his life.

"I know sometimes the eldest makes some form of compensation as well. Whether or not that's true in your case is beside the point. Your parents made the decision, and I'm sure you'll look out for them in the coming years."

"I'd do that whether I inherited the farm or not," he told her. "Just as I know you will if your mother needs you to care for her. I've seen that you love her and take the responsibility."

Her lips trembled and he could have kicked himself for saying it.

"She's my mother. I love her. And I made a promise to my dad. He always saw himself as a protector, and when he realized he wasn't going—" she stopped, composed herself. "When he saw he wasn't going to make it, he made me promise I'd look out for Mom."

"Family's everything. And she looks out for you. I remember you telling me she packs your lunch for you on days you have to work or go to school."

She looked surprised. "You listen."

"Everybody listens."

"Not like you."

"Then maybe you've been talking to the wrong people."

"Maybe." She smiled as she ate the last bite of her chicken cordon bleu and set her fork down with a sigh. "This is nice, but we didn't have to go someplace this fancy. I'm just as happy with a hamburger and a drive."

"I know. But I wanted our first date to be special."

His heart skipped a beat when she reached across the table for his hand.

"Did you folks save room for dessert?" their server asked.

"Of course," he said at the same time that Summer shook her head. "Your dessert sampler. Two forks."

"I couldn't possibly eat another bite," Summer told him as the server chuckled and took their plates. But when the sampler came and she saw the double chocolate cake, she sighed and picked up her fork.

Wayne had told him women always refused dessert—and always ended up reaching over with a fork and eating more than a bite of yours. While Wayne had dated more women, both *Englisch* and Amish, than he had, Abram knew he didn't know everything about women.

But Wayne had been right about women and dessert. The plate was empty when the server returned to top off their coffee and discreetly leave the check.

Abram tucked bills in the leather check holder and looked at Summer. "There's still time for a movie if you want."

She shook her head. "Let's just take a drive and look at the Christmas lights. I'm a sucker for them."

He decided the date was going very nicely indeed when she took his hand and didn't let it go as they left the restaurant and walked to the car.

"It's snowing!" she cried, delighted as the flakes fell gently from the sky. "Nothing better than a first snowfall and a full moon." She sighed. "What a wonderful night."

He looked at her staring up at the sky, the moonlight bathing her face and thought, *Ya, wunderbaar* indeed.

No matter what happened, he would never forget this night with a woman named Summer.

Twenty-Two

Too restless to sleep, Summer pulled on her robe, shoved her feet into slippers, and padded downstairs. She put the kettle on to boil for a cup of tea and sat down with her laptop at the kitchen table. An email from the college marked "urgent" caught her attention. It announced a hike in tuition. She sighed. Just what she needed. She wondered what Kim thought and wrote a quick email to ask her. After she fixed a cup of tea, Summer decided to check her bank balance online. She typed in her password, and when the screen popped up, she stared at the amount of money in her checking account.

Ouch.

Maybe she shouldn't have spent quite so much Christmas shopping the other day, but it had been so nice shedding worries and spending time with her mother, buying presents, and eating out the way they used to. Well, she wasn't going to be sorry. They'd deserved that day out and she wasn't going to regret it.

But now it was time to get back to reality. She sat there, sipping her tea and thinking. The past semester had been stressful and they still didn't know what was wrong with her mother. She just didn't think it was a bug.

She heard footsteps and saw her mother descending the stairs.

"I'm sorry, did I wake you up?"

"No. Just not sleeping well," her mother said as she sat down.

"You're not running a fever?"

Marie shook her head.

"Want some tea?"

"That would be nice."

Summer jumped up before her mother could get it herself. "Maybe some chamomile?"

"Yes, thanks." Marie glanced at the laptop. "You're not doing homework? I thought you were done for a couple weeks."

"I am. Just checking email." She poured hot water into a cup, found the box of chamomile teabags, and set both in front of her mother. "Are there any of those cookies you baked left?"

"You'll have to look in the cookie jar. Carl likes to sneak one now and then. Your dad used to do that. I guess it's a guy thing."

"Uh, well, sometimes Dad took the blame for me when I was a kid," Summer told her with a chuckle. She found there were still cookies in the jar, so she placed some on a plate and brought them to the table.

"I suspected that." Marie shook her head when Summer offered her a cookie, then relented and took one when Summer insisted.

Summer took her seat and bit into her cookie. "Mmm, I love sugar cookies. I remember how much I loved helping cut out all the different shapes when I was a kid. You must have a hundred different cookie cutters."

"Well, not quite that many. They'll be yours one day. I hope you'll have children to make cookies with." She finished the cookie and sipped her tea. "How was your evening?"

She noticed her mother didn't use the word *date*. "Very nice." She frowned. "But Abram took me to that new restaurant outside town. It was very expensive. I told him that wasn't necessary. He said we could call it a celebration. The deed came transferring the farm to him."

"That *is* worth celebrating."

"True. But I don't want him thinking we have to go someplace like that often. We all know when we live on a farm we have to be careful with money." She took a deep breath. "One of my emails was from the college. They're raising tuition. Again."

Marie sighed. "College is just getting more and more expensive. I wish you'd stayed full-time. You might be finished now and not be having to deal with it."

"We've had that discussion," Summer reminded her. "I wanted to help with Dad. And I'm glad I came home. I got to spend time with him. Who knew he wouldn't make it. I never knew anyone who was so alive, so vital."

Nodding, her mother reached over and squeezed her hand. "It surprised all of us." She sighed. "I guess you were right to come home."

Summer listened to the kitchen clock tick away minutes. "Mom, I'm not going to take two classes in spring semester."

"Oh, no, if you need money—"

"It's not just that," she hurried to say. "It's just too much with my part-time job and my business. And I want to spend more time at home."

"I'm not having you putting off school to hover over me," Marie said firmly. "I'm going to be fine."

"It isn't that either." Part of it *was* that she wanted to be around more until she felt better about her mother's health, but she wasn't going to tell her that. "Remember I told you I want to plant a bigger fruit and vegetable garden and can more. I want to use more of Grandmother's recipes." *Please remember.*

"That's right. I remember." Marie smiled. "I didn't know her for many years. She died just a few years after your father and I were married. You were barely a year old. At least she got to meet you. She was thrilled to have a grandchild." She pushed aside her empty cup. "But we're getting off the subject. I don't want you going down to one class. Let me give you some money. I have the insurance money from your father, remember?"

"And you need to hold onto it. Be careful with it. Taxes went up this year, and we never know what will happen with crops. I want to do this, Mom."

"You're just like your father," Marie said. "Stubborn as an old mule."

Summer nearly spit her sip of tea. "I am not!"

"You are."

She stood and leaned over to kiss her mother's cheek. "But you love me."

"I do. Just like your stubborn old mule father."

Laughing, Summer carried their dishes to the sink. "I'm going to bed."

"We're not finished discussing."

"You mean arguing."

"Discussing." But Marie smiled.

Summer decided she wouldn't mind "discussing," if it meant her mother would be around longer.

$$\mathcal{SSS}$$

Abram listened as Summer told him about her decision to take only one class in the spring semester. "I thought you wanted to get finished," he said as he stained the chest of drawers he was finishing. "If it's a matter of money I can help."

"Absolutely not!" She stared at him, looking appalled. Then she took a deep breath. "Thank you for the offer but no, I can't take money from you. Besides, it's not just money. I'm worried about Mom. I'd like to stick around home more. Work in my garden. Keep an eye on her."

He stopped and stared at her. "Did you tell her that?"

"Of course not. Do I look crazy? She'd have had a fit. But I'm not sure she didn't figure it out." She eyed him. "Does this mean you're siding with her?"

"Yes. She's right."

She got up from the bale of hay she'd been sitting on and looked over the chest of drawers. "Nice work."

"Thanks." He set down the brush. "You're changing the subject."

"I made up my mind."

"I can change it." He walked toward her with a gleam in his eyes.

She backed up. "What are you doing?"

His gaze shifted to her mouth. She had such pretty, rose-colored lips. She seldom wore makeup. He knew *Englisch* women were good at making it look natural, but he could tell the color of Summer's lips and the glowing skin on her face were all her own, not the artifice of makeup.

"You forgot to put the top on the can of stain."

Abram turned, saw that he hadn't closed the can. "You distracted me." He walked back and put the lid on, tapped it to make sure it was securely closed.

And told himself to behave.

"Aren't you going to finish?"

"I have to let that dry then do another coat. Ready for some lunch?"

"Sure am. Let's go get a burger and French fries. Lots of French fries. I always take a bag lunch to work and eat at my desk so I can leave at four. It'll be fun to eat lunch with you."

He grinned. "I agree." His grin faded. "But we're not done talking about the college thing."

"My mother called it discussing. And it won't do any more good for you to discuss it with me than it did for her," she told him as they walked out of the barn and shut the door. "She says I take after my dad and I'm as stubborn as a mule."

"That so? Well, my mother said I was her most stubborn child. So I think I can take you on."

"Ha!" she said. "Race you to the car. Loser buys." She took off and made it there before him.

"I would have won if you hadn't surprised me with that."

She got in the car and then looked at him. "Did you let me win?"

"Why would I do that?" He gave her an innocent look as he buckled his seat belt. "I know you can eat your weight in French fries."

She laughed. "I'd be insulted if that weren't true. But you can eat your weight in pie."

"I'd be insulted if that weren't true."

They went to their favorite burger restaurant and she doused an enormous pile of French fries with ketchup.

"Is that your friend Kim?" he asked and his eyes widened as she curved her hands protectively around the fries before looking.

"Yes, it is." She waved and Kim waved back from where she stood in the order line with Gabby.

"What's that about?" he asked her, gesturing toward her hands.

She laughed. "Oh, I thought you were playing the game my mom and I always have. She'll say she doesn't want fries or potato chips, then she always tries to distract me so she can steal one of mine."

"But I have my own fries."

"Old habits die hard."

"I'll remember that. You have such a nice relationship with your mother."

She smiled. "Different from the one you have with your mom, I'm sure."

"Yeah. But I did play jokes on her," he said as he picked up a fry and ate it. "Typical boy stuff."

"Abram horsie!" a high-pitched child's voice cried.

"Gabby! How are you?"

"I got a hamgerber and fresh fries."

"Hamburger and French fries," Kim translated with a chuckle. "And sorry, you've been 'Abram horsie' since we came to your farm."

"It's fine. I like it," he told her with a grin.

"Sit with Abram horsie?"

"No, sweetie, remember we're taking lunch home to Grandma and eating with her."

Gabby thrust her lower lip out. Abram knew what was coming. He had nieces and nephews.

"Kim, will you have time this week?" Abram asked quickly, locking gazes with her and hoping she'd get his message without him inviting them to the farm in front of Gabby. He'd learned to get parental approval from his brothers and sisters before offering a treat to his nieces and nephews.

"Time?" Kim stared at him, looking confused. Then her expression cleared. "Oh, yes, I hope so. Can I call you?"

"Sure. Summer can give you my number."

"Gabby, tell Abram we'll see him later."

"Horsie?"

"Yes, you can come see the horses again with your mother," he told her. "You be good for her and she'll bring you when she can."

She grinned. "Bye!"

"Gabby, say goodbye to Summer too."

Summer laughed.

"Bye, Summer."

"Bye, Gabby and Kim." She watched them leave, then looked at Abram. "I sure know where I stand."

"You're number one with me."

"I bet you tell Joe and Shadow that too."

Now it was his turn to laugh. "No."

"Well, it's been very nice eating lunch with you today."

"I wish we could do it every day."

She smiled. "Me too."

"You'd have to buy your own French fries sometimes, though. Otherwise I couldn't afford it."

She tossed a fry at him. "Thanks a lot!"

He remembered how the night before she'd told him he didn't have to take her someplace expensive—that she'd love just going out for a hamburger. Today he saw she was enjoying the meal with him just as much as she had the expensive food. Well, maybe she didn't want to go to the place with the fancy food. But that didn't mean he'd only take her out for a burger.

He wasn't far off teasing her that she ate her weight in French fries.

Twenty-Three

It was back to work the next day.

As Summer sat in the employee break room—she was determined not to eat at her desk just one day—she ate the sandwich her mother had packed and thought about how much fun she'd had eating lunch with Abram the day before. She sighed.

"One of those days, huh?" Doris, one of her coworkers, asked as she joined her at the table.

"I had lunch with a friend yesterday. It was a nice break from a sandwich at work."

"Tell me about it." Doris, a cheerful woman in her late fifties, unpacked her lunch. It was the same thing every day: a ham sandwich with mustard on rye. A couple of slices of dill pickle packed separately in a piece of paper towel inside a plastic sandwich bag so they wouldn't make the bread soggy. Carrot and celery sticks. An apple and a thermos of coffee. Doris always brought her own coffee. She said that the office coffee was dreadful. Summer remembered Doris had started saying that the day the staff was told the price was going up.

Summer ate two of the cookies her mother had packed and drank the bottle of juice that was tucked in the lunch bag and kept everything cold. Then after using a wet wipe, she picked up her knitting tote. She'd brought it to work so she could work on Abram's gift during her lunch break.

Hank, one of her male coworkers, glanced at it as he pushed coins into the soft drink machine near them. "My grandmother knitted," he teased.

Summer just ignored him.

"I used to knit," Doris said. "Don't know why I stopped. It relaxed me. I think it's doing the same for you. You're looking calmer today."

"I'm on break from school," Summer pointed out as she knitted.

"That could explain it," Doris said as she crunched on a carrot stick. She glanced around the break room the staff had decorated the previous week. "I miss the Christmas tree."

Most cities had stopped decorating their offices for Christmas and now used the term "holiday." Summer missed the office Christmas tree but remembered the look on a coworker's face when he'd been given a Christmas tree decoration at the office party. He was Jewish and no one had remembered.

"The Amish don't put up Christmas trees," Summer told her.

"Don't believe in Santa Claus either. I figure they got that right."

"I don't know. I loved believing in Santa when I was a kid."

"Teaches kids the wrong thing."

She had a point. Summer glanced up at Doris. "We're decorating the house tonight. Mom promised she wouldn't drag the boxes down from the attic while I'm at work. I hope she listened to me."

"Is she feeling any better?"

Summer shook her head. "We went to the doctor again. She thinks she has the bug going around. But I don't think so."

"Sometimes it feels like forever before you get a diagnosis," Doris said darkly. "Took five years for them to diagnose my sister's fibromyalgia."

Hank wandered over and eyed the baggie of cookies. Summer picked it up and held it out for him to take one.

"So when are you going to plan the office holiday party?" he asked Doris.

"Why's that always the job of the women in the office?" she responded tartly.

He held up his hands. "Hey, you know what it'd be like if us guys do it?"

"Excuses."

"You *are* going to bring your coconut cake, aren't you? Never tasted better."

"Sure. What are you bringing? Something you made your wife cook?"

He chuckled. "Nobody should want me to decorate or bake." He wandered over to a table where some male coworkers sat.

"We women end up doing everything around here," Doris groused. "I guess I should start the donation list going around. So what are you bringing?"

"Christmas cookies, I think. Everybody liked them last year."

"Especially Hank."

She laughed. The two of them often traded barbs this way, but last year when Hank was hospitalized Doris was the one went around the office and got everyone to volunteer to take meals to his house. She glanced at the clock on the wall. Time to get back to work. She tucked the muffler back into the tote.

"Making that for someone special?"

"Sort of." Summer felt her cheeks warm.

Doris grinned as she put the wrappings from her lunch into her tote. "Didn't know anyone blushed anymore. You're just an old-fashioned girl, aren't you? Chip off the old block. Your mom's like that." Doris knew. She'd been a family friend for years and hadn't just attended her father's funeral but had visited her mother frequently since then.

They went back to their desks and things were so busy Summer didn't talk to Doris again until it was time to go.

"You tell your ma I'll stop in to see her tomorrow evening if she's home."

"She'll be home. She doesn't go out much lately."

Summer stopped at the grocery store on the way home. The day was bitter cold and the snow was still coming down, but they needed some things. She had taken on the job of shopping the past couple of months. Pulling out her list, she went down the aisles and filled her cart with flour and sugar and everything needed to make all the cookies they liked to make for gifts. She looked over the lettuce and tomatoes and sighed as she put them in the cart. There was nothing like going out to your own garden and picking a head of lettuce and tomatoes right off the vine. At least they had a basement filled with jars of fruits and vegetables that they had canned at the end of summer.

Standing in line waiting to check out, she gazed at the bright covers of December issues of magazines. She splurged on a couple of her mother's favorites, including the big weekly magazine that always had a feature article about the latest diet promising you'd lose ten pounds a week—and photos at the bottom of cookies and cakes you could bake for the holiday. It would be nice to flip through the magazines on a cold winter night and see the recipes and decorating ideas.

She flinched when she checked out and saw the total bill. How did people with bigger families manage when she and her mother saved so much baking their own bread and raising so much of their own fruits and vegetables?

Carl came out of his cottage when she pulled into the driveway. He walked over to help her carry the bags inside. "Caught your mother hauling boxes of Christmas stuff down from the attic," he told her as they walked into the kitchen.

"You tattling on me, Carl Smith?" Marie demanded as she turned from the stove.

"You bet." He set the bags down on the counter. "I made her sit and got the rest of them down."

"Thank you, Carl. Mom, you promised."

"Oh, don't fuss. The ones I carried down weren't heavy. And it gave me a chance to see something I've been meaning to give you."

"Oh?"

"Not now," her mother said mysteriously. "Let's get those groceries put away and have dinner. I can't wait to decorate. Carl got us a tree today, and he's already set it up in the living room. Got the lights on too."

"Well, thanks again, Carl."

He shrugged. "Got some Christmas cookies out of it."

Summer wondered if he thought he was hiding his pleasure at being asked to stay and help decorate after he shared dinner with them. As he hung ornaments with her mother and bickered over the best placement, she saw the glances they shared and felt the bitter-sweet pang of a daughter seeing her mother beginning to care for another man.

She took a deep breath and tried to be happy for her. She'd heard her father making her mother promise that she'd marry again.

Promises, she thought. And blinked hard against the tears that burned against her eyelids.

Abram stood in the doorway of his barn at dawn and watched the snow come down. It was a *gut* day to be at home, to have work to do and not have to be on the road.

Then he thought of Summer. She had work today. *Nee*, this would have been declared a snow day, wouldn't it? Now he was going to worry until he heard from her. She often called at the end of the day. He debated calling her and then decided to text her so he wouldn't disturb her at work. While he did, he thought about how he shouldn't be seeing a woman outside his community, let alone looking forward to her phone calls and texts. The bishop would no doubt have even more of something to say about it. And while Abram believed that the heart guided in ways of this sort, he had moments when he felt torn.

An hour later, when she texted back that she'd made it in safely and signed it with a smiley face, he felt relief. He should have known. Phoebe, one of the members of the church, always said it was arrogant to worry, that God knew what He was doing.

He decided to go inside and fix himself some lunch. And that reminded him again of Summer and the lunch they'd shared. He had the purely selfish wish they could have lunch together every day.

Miriam had given him a loaf of bread when he visited. He sliced it. She didn't have the light touch his *mudder* did—the bread was a little heavy—but it tasted fine. It was nice when a friend shared baked goods, especially when you were a man and didn't know how to make them. The plastic container of gingerbread cookies would last a while too if he rationed them carefully.

He ate his solitary lunch, enjoyed a couple of the cookies, and drank a cup of coffee. Determined to have something more than a sandwich for supper, he assembled the ingredients for a big pot of soup, then set the flame low under it to simmer while he worked in the barn. Then he took a couple of apples out to the barn and delighted Joe and Shadow with the treats.

Back to work. He checked the second coat of stain on the chest of drawers, but it was drying slowly with the dampness in the air. So he turned to the wooden candleholders he was making for Summer's Christmas gift. He was carving the foot high holders by hand and liking the way they were turning out. He'd stain them the same color as the chest since she'd admired the color. He kept an ear out for the sound of a vehicle entering his driveway, not that he expected her on a workday. But it wouldn't do for her to show up and find him making her gift.

It had always been a bit tricky to make Christmas gifts since family was always around. Many times he'd come upon someone in his family who suddenly covered up something when he walked in. His *mudder* always had a twinkle in her eye and told him to mind his business when he'd asked her what she was doing. "Christmas secrets," she'd tell him. Yet she seemed to wander into the barn more during the weeks leading up to Christmas than other months. And the barn was the only place his *dat* had to make gifts.

Now he missed being on the alert while he made gifts. He sighed. While he was glad they were enjoying some warm weather in Pinecraft after so many long, bitter Pennsylvania winters, this would be the first Christmas they wouldn't have the whole family here. He sighed again. Then he reminded himself that it would be the first Christmas he'd share with Summer and her mother. That cheered him.

The afternoon passed in the usual routine of winter with equipment repair, planning, and carpentry, instead of the work in the fields he liked much better. Still, it was all much easier work than the back-breaking routine of spring planting and harvesting in blinding summer heat. *To everything there is a season . . .*

And he reminded himself he was grateful God gave him a strong body to do whatever work came his way in whatever season.

He sanded the candleholders and applied the stain, then did his evening chores of feeding and watering the horses. Rolling his shoulders, he said *gut nacht* to them and opened the barn. He stopped. Snow had piled up another two feet. Resigned, he turned back and grabbed a shovel and cleared a path to the kitchen door.

The aroma of beef vegetable soup greeted him when he walked inside. He washed his hands and then stirred it. Looked okay. He turned off the flame, ladled up a bowl, and set it on the table. With Miriam's bread and some butter, he had a nice hot meal. Not bad for a bachelor, he told himself.

He washed up, took a cup of coffee into the living room, and started a fire. Snow continued to come down, but it was warm inside and he had a *gut* book to read. If this was spring or summer, he might have been doing the same thing after supper, but half an hour after he settled down to read he'd be nodding off from exhaustion. It wasn't an evening with Summer, but being awake and having time to think was giving him an idea.

His brother Eli had a sleigh he rented out to Amish and *Englisch* alike this time of year to make a little extra money. His *fraa* Mary would even make up a basket with a thermos of hot chocolate and gingerbread for a few extra dollars. He'd stop by their farm tomorrow and see about renting it one night. *Ya. Gut* idea, he told himself. It was a chance to go out and be together for a few hours without spending a lot of money. He just had to hope the sleigh wasn't booked up after this snow.

His cell phone on the table beside his recliner rang. He grinned when he saw the caller was Summer.

"Just thinking about you," he told her.

"I'm not calling you too late?"

"I don't go to bed at seven."

She laughed. "Sorry. I know you get up earlier than I do."

"Are you busy tomorrow evening?"

"No."

"Good. Let's go for a drive."

"You mean if we're not up to our ears in snow? It was quite an adventure getting to work today. I followed a snow plow in."

"So the county didn't declare a snow day for employees?"

"No. I wish they had."

"Snow won't be a problem. But dress warm." He heard the ding of the oven timer in her kitchen.

"Sorry, let me turn that off. Then I just need to get this last pan of cookies out of the oven."

He heard the clang of metal on metal and could visualize her opening the oven door, getting the cookie sheet out, setting it on the stove. Could almost smell the cookies, taste them.

Then she was back on the phone. "Mom and I baked Christmas cookies tonight. This is the last pan."

"Maybe you'll save me a couple?"

"Maybe. But what if they're not the kind you like?"

Now it was his turn to laugh. "I never met a cookie I didn't like."

"I'll remember that. We decorated the house for Christmas last night, so now begins the cookie baking."

They talked for a while longer. It was an evening ritual he'd come to look forward to—one or the other of them calling to see how the day had gone for the other. Big things, little things. Just a way to connect when they couldn't see each other. After they hung up, Abram lingered by the fire, but the book didn't interest him any longer. Instead he thought about what route they could take the next day in the sleigh, imagining being out in the open under the stars with her.

He banked the fire and went up to bed. As soon as he'd done his morning chores, he was going to find out what the weather was expected to be tomorrow evening and see if the sleigh was available for rent.

Summer had delighted in the snow falling the night he took her to the restaurant for their first date. He hoped she'd enjoy a sleigh ride under the stars.

Twenty-Four

Summer smiled when she saw that Abram was waiting for her on his porch. How nice to have someone waiting to see her. He hurried out to the car and got inside.

"Hello." His gaze was warm when it met hers, his smile wide and welcoming.

"Hi." She checked traffic then pulled out onto the road. "Where are we going?"

"Eli's farm. Half a mile down, on the right."

"Eli's farm," she repeated.

"You'll see," he said mysteriously.

He told her where to turn and she pulled into a drive. Eli stood there beside a horse-drawn sleigh.

A sleigh.

"What's this?" she asked Abram.

He grinned. "You haven't ever seen a sleigh before, *Englisch* girl?"

"Never up close. Are we going to ride in it?"

"That's the plan. If you ever get out of the car."

She turned off the engine, slid out of the car, and tucked her keys in her pocket.

"Are you going to be warm enough? It's pretty cold." He took her hand to lead her to the sleigh.

"I'm plenty warm."

"*Gut-n-owed*, Eli," he said.

"*Gut-n-owed*, Abram, Summer." Eli touched the rim of his black felt hat at Summer.

She murmured a greeting to him, too awed to take her eyes off the sleigh.

"A sleigh. You have a sleigh." Summer stared at it.

"Eli rents it this time of year," Abram told her.

She'd only seen sleighs from a distance before. This one was big, with a long carved wooden carriage, wide seats, and metal runners. A Standardbred, bigger than Shadow or Joe, waited patiently at the head of it. A collar of bells hung around his neck and when she walked toward him, he shook his head and they rang musically.

"I've never ridden in a sleigh."

He held out his hand and helped her up into it. "Then let's get in and get started."

There was a big woolen blanket to spread over their laps and a basket on the floorboard. When she looked curiously at Abram he told her Eli's *fraa* had packed hot chocolate and gingerbread.

"When did you arrange all this?"

"I came over to ask him this morning," he said. "I'm sure I wouldn't have gotten it on such short notice in another week."

"The snow's so pretty," she said, gazing at the tall white drifts. "Oh, it's just feeling like it's Christmas."

Dusk was falling, casting blue and purple shadows over the snow. Abram clicked on the battery-operated sleigh lights, called "giddyap" to the horse, and they were off.

"Have a good time," Eli called after them as they started down the snow-covered path at the back of his farm.

The sleigh slid over the snow, the only sound the sleigh bells on the horse ringing merrily as Abram guided the horse along the path. Tall, bare trees stood like sentinels on each side of the path. As night fell stars came out. Summer leaned back and gazed up at them. "Starry, starry night."

He glanced over at her. "Enjoying it?"

"Who wouldn't? She wrapped her arms around herself. "It's just so beautiful tonight."

"You're beautiful."

She felt her cheeks warm. "You're too kind."

"I'm honest. Still warm enough?"

She nodded.

"I thought we'd stop down by the pond and have the hot chocolate," he said after they'd ridden for a time.

"I've skated on that pond. It's pretty this time of year."

He stopped and she pulled the thermos and cups from the basket and poured the rich, dark chocolate into them. "Mary even put a package of marshmallows in the basket."

"I'll take a couple."

She pulled out the plastic baggie, poured several of the mini marshmallows into both their cups, and they sat sipping the drink.

"I've got to have some of that gingerbread," he told her and reached for it. "I could smell it the minute we got in the sleigh." He spread open the gingham napkin that covered it and broke off a piece for each of them. "Mmm, one of my favorites."

"Mom and I made gingerbread cookies last night. I'll make sure to save some for you."

"I'll have to find a reason to stop by tomorrow."

"I notice Carl has a sixth sense about knowing when we've been baking." She ate her gingerbread and sipped the last of her hot chocolate.

She realized he was watching her. "What?"

"You've got something on your face." He reached over to stroke his forefinger along her bottom lip, showed her the white dab of melted marshmallow, then surprised her by licking it. "Mmm. Sweet."

She wondered if he'd try for a kiss, but he continued drinking his hot chocolate and watching the snow fall lightly. "It's so pretty . . . until it piles up and you have to drive to work in the morning."

He nodded. "I worried about you driving in it."

Her heart warmed remembering how he'd texted her.

"I remind myself God knows what He's doing."

"Look at all the stars."

"All I want to do is look at you."

"You say things like that, take me for a sleigh ride. I don't know what to think."

He held out his hand, and she put hers in it. "My grandfather called it courting."

Stunned, she didn't know what to say.

◇◇◇

If only moments like this could be frozen in time.

Abram figured this was one of the better ideas he'd ever had. And it hadn't cost half the price of the fancy restaurant dinner. If only they could stay out longer.

But it was getting late, the temperature was falling fast—each time they talked they saw little clouds of white emerge—and it was time to call it a day. Reluctantly he released Summer's hand and picked up the reins. "I guess we have to go."

"I'm glad you thought of it. I loved every minute," she told him. "I hope it wasn't too expensive."

"You don't need to worry about my wallet. Eli is very reasonable."

An owl hooted from a nearby tree, then flew over them in a sweep of broad wings. It was the only sign of wildlife as God's creatures burrowed into the woods and huddled together to stay warm.

Eli came out of his house when Abram pulled the sleigh up before the barn.

"We had a wonderful time," Summer told him as she got out of the sleigh. "Tell Mary that the hot chocolate and gingerbread were very good."

"I'll tell her. I'm glad you liked them."

"I'll tell everyone at work about it. You'll probably be booked solid."

"Thank you."

Abram walked to the car with Summer. He hoped the heater would work better than usual and get the car warm quickly. He was afraid she was cold and not willing to tell him.

"So would you like to come to dinner tomorrow night?"

Abram grinned. "Then I wouldn't have to think of an excuse to drop by for those cookies."

"There's that," she said dryly.

The car heater barely had a chance to warm up by the time she pulled into his drive. He wondered if her car really was any warmer than his buggy in the winter. But she didn't appear to mind.

"See you tomorrow. Around six."

"I'll be there." For the second time that night he thought about kissing her and then decided to wait. He didn't want to move too soon.

"'Night."

"Goodnight, Summer. Sleep well."

He stood and watched her drive away as he always did and wished she didn't have to leave. Turning, he did a last check of the horses, made sure the barn door was securely closed, and went into the house.

Earlier he'd wished a moment with Summer could be frozen in time and he'd wanted to stay out on the sleigh ride forever. Now he couldn't wait for tomorrow to come.

The next day started out like so many with morning chores but went rapidly downhill. Shadow huddled in a corner of his stall and glanced at him with misery in his eyes when he walked into the barn. Abram stroked his nose and found it warmer than usual. After he put him in an empty stall so he could clean the other one, Abram found evidence the horse had been sick during the night. After he led Shadow back to a clean stall, he offered food and water and Shadow turned his nose up at both.

Joe also seemed listless. He didn't seem warmer than usual but he, too, didn't want to eat. Feeling uneasy, Abram cleaned Joe's stall as well, then went into the house to wash his hands and fix his own breakfast. The kitchen faucet decided to spring a leak, so he spent the next hour under the sink fixing the problem before he could cook breakfast.

Abram wasn't the best of cooks on a good day, but, distracted by worrying over the horses and plumbing, he managed to not only burn his bacon but his hand as well. After tossing the burned bacon in the trash, he settled for scrambled eggs and decided not to risk trying to toast bread in the oven.

When he returned to the barn neither horse had eaten. He checked the chest of drawers he'd put a coat of stain on before the sleigh ride, but it hadn't dried. He'd hoped to deliver it to the furniture store today. Well, with two horses acting under the weather it was probably best to stay close to home instead.

Hours passed as he worked on another project and went back and forth looking after the horses, who continued to reject their food.

Wayne stopped by at noon and looked over Joe and Shadow. "I haven't heard of anything going around," he said. "I think they're both just feeling a little off. I don't think it's anything serious. Give it another day and if they don't perk up call the vet."

"I was invited to supper at Summer's tonight, but I'm wondering if I should cancel."

"Don't do that. I'll come over and check on these guys for you."

Abram stared at him, surprised. "That would be great." Then he narrowed his eyes at him. "What do you want?"

"You wound me," Wayne said, looking hurt. Then he chuckled. "Maybe you could let me know the next time Kim and Gabby come over."

"I knew you had an ulterior motive."

Wayne slung his arm around Abram's shoulders as they walked into the house to have lunch.

So Abram's day got better. That evening, he was more than ready to head to Summer's house—not a short walk, but it hadn't snowed all day, and the temperature had gone up a good ten degrees. If conditions changed, well, he was a healthy Amish man. He could walk home or ask Summer to give him a ride in her car.

He wasn't canceling an evening with Summer if he could help it.

Even before he got to her house, he saw that her saying she and Marie had decorated for Christmas was an understatement. A huge Christmas tree strung with colored lights shone in the front window when he walked up the drive. He kept going around to the back door. One of Rose's wreaths still hung there, but miniature white lights that must have been battery-operated had been woven into it. When Summer opened the door, she beamed at him and invited him into the kitchen that had baskets filled with evergreens and Christmas decorations on every available surface.

"Wow," he said as he took off his jacket and hat and hung them on pegs by the door.

"You ain't seen nothing yet," she told him with a chuckle. "Wait until you see the living room."

"I saw the tree in the front window when I walked up."

"Walked?"

"Joe and Shadow are a little under the weather. Wayne said he'd check on them later for me."

"You should have called me. You're *not* walking home." She took his hand. "Come with me."

She showed him the living room where two stockings hung from the mantel strewn with more evergreens. One of the stockings bore her name, the other her mother's. Ornaments that ranged from expensive-looking glass balls to those obviously made by a child with Popsicle sticks decorated with colored stones and glitter hung on a tree with a star that nearly touched the ceiling. Figurines of angels and Santas and elves were everywhere.

"Kind of overkill," she told him. "I know it's not at all what your family probably does."

"Families are different." He shrugged. "It's pretty."

They returned to the kitchen and he sat at the table drinking coffee while she finished cooking supper.

"Where's Marie?"

"Having dinner with Carl. I think they're trying to give us some time together." She turned and smiled. "And having some of their own. Carl's always been a friend of the family, but I think he wants to be more than that with my mom now."

"I think so too. How do you feel about that?"

"Carl's one of the best men I know," she said simply as she brought a platter of pot roast to the table. "I'd be happy for them if they decided to get married."

His bad day became a distant memory as he sat in the kitchen that smelled of evergreens and pine and bayberry candles and ate pot roast that melted in his mouth.

"I thought *Englisch* women didn't like to cook much," he teased.

"Some do. Some don't have time. But when you grow up on a farm you don't go running out for takeout. And I love growing things and then cooking them. Nothing beats fresh."

They chatted about their day as they ate, but he noticed that she wasn't eating much.

"You okay? You seem a little quiet tonight."

"I'm fine. Ready for dessert?"

"Always."

Later, long after he'd had two helpings of Summer's apple crisp, Marie came in looking wan. She greeted him with a smile, and after kissing Summer on the cheek, said she was going up to bed.

"Still no improvement?" he asked Summer quietly, as Marie left.

She shook her head. "I'm taking her back to the doctor next week whether she likes it or not."

Summer bolted out of her chair when they heard a thump on the floor overhead. She raced upstairs.

"Summer? You need some help?" he called up the stairs.

"No, thanks."

A few minutes later she came downstairs looking worried. "Mom said she didn't fall, but she looked shaken when I got upstairs. She's in bed now." She sighed. "Abram, you didn't have to do the dishes."

"Seemed fair to me. You cooked." He dried the last plate and put it into the cupboard. "I should go." He grabbed her arm when she started for her jacket hanging on a peg. "No, I can walk. You need to stay with your mother."

"She's in bed and was almost asleep when I left her room." She pulled on her jacket, searched in her purse for her wallet and keys and started for the door. Then she stopped. "I almost forgot." She picked up a plastic container decorated with a sprig of holly and handed it to him. "The gingerbread cookies I promised."

He took the cookies and wished the holly was mistletoe.

When she pulled up in his drive and stopped the car she turned to him. "I hope your horses are better."

"I'm sure they'll be fine."

Then she grabbed his arm and pulled him toward her. Before he knew what she was up to she kissed him on the mouth and then sat back. "Good night. And thank you for coming to dinner."

"My pleasure," he managed and walked to his door on legs that felt a little unsteady.

Twenty-Five

Two days later, Gabby fairly danced into the kitchen when Summer opened the door.

"Remember what we talked about," her mother warned Gabby.

She nodded vigorously as her mother unzipped her jacket and removed her hat. "No touching."

"That's right."

"Children are welcome here," Marie told her firmly. "My theory is that if you don't want a child to break something, you put it up where it can't get broken. I remember my mother bursting into tears when my sister accidentally broke a sugar bowl her mother had left her. I was only ten, but I remembering thinking, 'Why didn't you put it up in a cabinet if it meant that much to you?' She really hurt my sister's feelings over a sugar bowl."

Marie held out her hand to Gabby. "Come with me, sweetie, and see our tree."

They walked away as Kim took off her jacket and muffler. "Your mom is so sweet. Is she feeling any better?"

"No. We have an appointment in a few days."

Kim hugged her. "I'm sorry. Mom and I have been praying for her."

"Thanks. I appreciate that." She smiled as she stood back. "I'm glad you came today. Mom's been looking forward to it."

They joined her mother and Gabby in the living room. Summer smiled when she saw her mother sitting in the rocking chair with Gabby on her lap, reading her a Christmas story she remembered from childhood. Kim pulled out her cell phone and snapped a photo and Gabby never stirred, too absorbed in the story.

"She loves to be read to," Kim whispered as she showed Summer the photo and then tapped the screen. "I sent it to you."

"Mom'll love it."

They took seats on the sofa and listened to Marie read. When she said "the end," Gabby clapped.

"Now presents?"

Kim groaned. "Kids."

"Presents!" Marie said firmly, making a face at Kim. "I want them too."

So Summer knelt beside the tree and pulled out the presents so Gabby could carry them to the recipient. To Gabby's delight her pile was the largest.

The adults watched Gabby open her presents first. "Horsie!" she cried when she tore the wrapping from the stuffed toy horse from Summer. She hugged it to her chest. "Thank you, Summer."

"You're welcome."

"We go to see Abram horsie?"

"We'll see. He's going to call me." He'd told her that Joe and Shadow were back to normal, but she wanted to be sure before she brought over an energetic child.

The toy chicken Marie had bought for Gabby was almost as popular as the stuffed horse.

"Oh, Summer, I love it!" Kim said when she unwrapped her green muffler.

"I made it, so don't look too closely or you may find a dropped stitch or two."

"You made this? Wow, I'm impressed. When did you find the time?"

"Doesn't take long. A muffler's pretty easy. And being out of class helped. I had time to make two."

"Yeah? Wonder who the other one was for?" Kim teased.

"His is plain brown."

"Well, green would be too *Englisch*, right? And if I remember correctly, his eyes are brown."

A warm chocolate brown, thought Summer. But she wasn't going to say so.

"Maybe you can show me how to knit sometime."

"Sure. Some people think it's something only grannies do," she told her, remembering what her male coworker had said.

Kim rubbed the muffler against her cheek. "I'd love to learn how to make something so pretty and warm."

Gabby came over to look at the muffler, her stuffed horse clutched to her chest. "Mommy, see Abram horsie now?"

"Gabby, you didn't give Summer and Marie our presents," Kim reminded her. She handed her daughter two small boxes. "They're not much," she said. "Dollar store."

"I love it!" Marie told them when she unwrapped the bud vase. "I can put flowers from my garden in it. Thank you."

"And I love my hair scrunchies," Summer said.

As soon as the presents were opened Gabby went to her mother. "Horsies now?"

"And not have some Christmas cookies first?" Marie asked.

Summer didn't like how her mother frowned and rubbed at her knee before she stood.

"Christmas cookies!" Gabby tugged at her mother's hand.

So everyone had to troop into the kitchen and eat some cookies and drink hot chocolate. Summer watched how her mother doted on Gabby and wondered for the first time if her mother ever hoped for a grandchild. She'd never hinted she wished Summer would get married and give her one.

Summer texted Abram and he told her to come whenever they were ready. Joe and Shadow were fine. She caught Kim's eye, pointed to her cell phone, and gave her a thumbs-up signal, and Kim nodded. They waited for Gabby to finish her cookies and hot chocolate and then told her Abram was looking forward to them visiting.

She was out of her chair in a split second.

Marie laughed and helped Gabby get her jacket and hat on.

"Are you coming with us this time?" Kim asked Marie.

"I don't think so. Maybe next time."

"I guess we'll see how often Abram lets us come."

Summer pulled on her own jacket and cap. "He enjoyed having

you both. The Amish love children, consider them a gift from God. And they're so good, so patient with them."

They walked out to Kim's car, and Summer told her about attending the Amish church one Sunday with Abram where a little Amish boy had sat quietly next to her during the long, long service. And then he'd leaned against Summer's shoulder and fallen asleep.

"Sounds like he felt comfortable with you," Kim said as she strapped Gabby into her car seat. "You're good with Gabby. Do you want kids?"

"One day."

"How are things going with Abram?" She gave Summer a mischievous smile as she started her car.

"Good. He took me for a sleigh ride the other night."

"Ooh, how romantic."

"Yeah." Summer smiled as she remembered. "I thought he'd kiss me then but he didn't."

Kim put the car back in park. "Are you saying he hasn't kissed you yet?"

"No. He's very much a gentleman." Now it was her turn to give Kim a mischievous smile. "So last night when he came to dinner and I drove him home, I grabbed him and kissed him."

Kim laughed and did a fist bump with her.

"Mommy! Abram horsie! Now!"

"Nag, nag," Kim said with a chuckle as she resumed backing up. "We're going to see Abram horsie."

Summer wanted to see Abram even more than the little girl in the back seat did. Her spirits rising, she began singing "Jingle Bells" and Gabby joined in.

SSS

The sound of a vehicle entering the driveway had Wayne bolting toward the barn door.

"Hey, try to restrain yourself," Abram called to him. "They're not coming here to see you."

"Sure they are," Wayne said, shooting him a cocky grin over his shoulder. "They just don't know it yet."

Abram just shook his head and stroked Shadow's nose. "Good thing you guys are feeling better. One little girl wants to see you almost as much as she wants to see Santa."

Wayne went out and returned carrying Gabby with a stuffed toy horse under her arm.

"Abram horsie!" she cried.

He didn't have hurt feelings when her gaze went straight to Joe and Shadow.

"Up, up on horsie!" she demanded. "Please?"

"Hi, Abram," Kim said. "It's up to you. She's pretty wired from looking forward to this and sugar cookies and hot chocolate at Summer's house."

"She'll be fine, right, Abram?"

"Sure. We'll do the same thing as last time," he said easily. "Gabby, Joe and Shadow want you to pet their noses first to say hello."

"Okay," she said. "Hey, Mommy, hold my horsie."

Kim moved forward to take the toy. Gabby stroked Joe's nose and then Shadow's, crooning to them. When the horses reacted as calmly as they always did to people—even excited little girls—he opened Joe's stall. Wayne walked in, put a blanket on the horse, then lifted Gabby up and set her on the horse's back.

Kim moved closer and watched as Wayne held her daughter firmly while she sat on the horse.

"Love Joe," Gabby said and wrapped her arms around the horse's neck.

"I hope now that she has her own horsie, she won't be asking to come so often," Kim told Abram as she held the toy to her chest.

"I'm glad to have you." He smiled at her, then turned his gaze to Summer. She stood there watching, looking thoughtful. She hadn't said anything beyond saying hello.

He walked over to her. "How are you today?"

"I'm good. You?"

"Always better when you're near." He watched her blush and dart a glance at the others, then she looked back at him.

"I don't know what to say when you talk like that."

He touched her cheek. "You don't have to say anything," he told her. "Just know it's true."

Abram wished his visitors could stay all afternoon, but when Gabby's eyelids drooped and she yawned, Kim moved in. She lured her daughter off the real horse with the new toy one and a promise they'd return another time.

Wayne walked them to their car and then, saying he had to get home, left.

Too soon the barn was quiet except for the shuffling of the horses in their stalls. Abram realized he was restless and decided to load the now dry chest of drawers into his buggy and deliver it to Mervin. He stopped in a nearby coffee shop for a cup he didn't make himself—he really wasn't very *gut* at it—and treated himself to some of the shop's brightly decorated Christmas cookies. At least he knew the sugar wouldn't make him hyperactive like Gabby.

As he sat at a table next to a window that overlooked the sidewalk, he watched people passing by. So many *Englischers* spending so much money, he thought. Summer had even admitted she and her mother had enjoyed a day Christmas shopping. He sipped his coffee and wondered if she could ever lead a simpler life.

An Amish life.

They'd agreed to date and not think about the future. But the more he was with her, the more he wanted to be with her. Permanently.

"All done?" the server asked with a smile as she gestured at his empty plate.

"Yes, thanks. They were good."

"I'll take the plate then. Don't go rushing off. Enjoy your coffee."

But several customers walked in and looked around for a table and he realized he should give his up. He swallowed the last of his coffee, stood, and carried his empty cup over to the table set up for used cups and plates.

He left the shop and decided to stretch his legs and walk a bit in the brisk air. It was nice not to feel as driven as he had last time he was in town when he needed to get gifts. He noticed that a couple of shoppers passing him had the same look he'd probably worn that day. Especially the occasional male shopper he passed.

A window display caught his eye. A jewelry store window. He stopped out of curiosity and stared at the rings sparkling in the late afternoon sun. A sign over the display of the rings nestled in bright red or green velvet boxes declared them "Perfect for your Christmas engagement." If he was *Englisch* and asking Summer to marry him, he'd be going inside and buying her one.

He shook his head as if to clear it of the thought. Where had that come from? He wasn't *Englisch*, and it was too soon to think of marriage. He was Amish and the Amish didn't wear engagement or wedding rings. And if he wanted to marry Summer, one of them would have to change his or her whole way of life.

But he wanted . . . what?

Abram turned suddenly, bumping into a shopper, and quickly apologized. Home. He needed to get home, away from displays of rings and thoughts of a future he couldn't have with a woman he'd grown to care for too much. He walked quickly back toward the furniture store parking lot. Then he realized someone was calling his name. Turning, his spirits sank as he watched Fannie Mae hurrying to him.

"I called and called your name," she told him breathlessly when she reached him.

"Sorry, couldn't hear you over the Christmas music," he said, gesturing at the speaker on a nearby storefront.

This was the second time she'd run into him in town. Just how often did she come to town? Then he chided himself. She couldn't run into him here if he wasn't in town as well, could she?

"Out Christmas shopping?"

He shook his head. "Just delivered a piece of furniture to Mervin and took a little stroll, had some coffee."

"So you were just window shopping?"

Abram had always wondered why they called it window shopping. When you window shopped you didn't buy anything.

"Well?"

He realized he hadn't been paying attention. "I'm sorry, what?"

"Not thinking of buying anything from the jewelry store you were looking at?"

He'd grown up minding his tongue but now he felt like saying something rude at least in his mind. But Fannie Mae was so nosy she'd probably be able to read his mind. Honestly, why did the biggest gossip in the Amish community have to see him looking in a jewelry store window in town?

"I was just looking in shop windows before I head home. Didn't buy anything." He held up his empty hands. "And why would I need anything from a jewelry store?"

"That's what I wondered."

She eyed him for a long moment, her small, dark eyes narrowed, her bonnet ribbons flapping around her black bonnet. Tall, skinny, dressed in severe black, she reminded him of a crow. He chided himself for such a thought.

"Maybe you were buying a gift for the *Englisch* woman," she said finally.

"She has a name."

"I'm aware of that."

Annoyed, he blurted out, "Why haven't you told the bishop that you saw me holding hands with Summer at the restaurant that night?"

She tilted her head and studied him. "I thought about it. But I decided you're not a flirt like your friend Wayne. You're steady, you've been a *gut* Amish man. I'm going to trust that you'll remember our way and not be tempted. I'm *schur* you don't have to be reminded what the Bible says about—"

"*Nee*, I don't," he cut her off. "I have to get home, Fannie Mae. You have a *gut* afternoon."

He left her standing there on the sidewalk, and if she called after him again, he didn't hear her.

Twenty-Six

Summer didn't usually find herself nervous about new people and new situations, but she didn't know all of Abram's family members and Christmas Eve was such a private, sacred occasion.

"You're sure I'm invited?" she asked him when they spoke on the phone just before she left.

"It's my home," he pointed out.

So she showed up and found several buggies already parked in the driveway.

He opened the kitchen door and his smile warmed her. "Hello." He reached for her hand, drew her into the room, and took her coat when she shed it. "You look pretty."

"Thank you."

The kitchen was crowded with three women who were his *schweschders*. Summer would have known they were related even if she'd never met them. All had the same chestnut brown hair and brown eyes Abram had. She'd met two of them at the church service she'd attended some time back. Another was introduced as the youngest sister, who told Summer she'd moved to Ohio to avoid always being treated as the youngest and therefore fair game for teasing.

"Abram was the one who teased you," Ruth said. "We were only trying to help you learn things."

Naomi Rose just rolled her eyes.

"I'm an only child," Summer told her. "I always wished I had brothers and sisters."

A little girl ran into the kitchen and tugged on Naomi Rose's apron. "*Daed* says come on so we can start."

"Tell your *Daed* we'll be there in a minute." She opened the oven door and the delicious scent of honey-baked ham drifted out.

"I brought scalloped potatoes," Summer told them as she lifted the dish out of the basket. "It should stay warm in its dish until we eat."

The sister called Ruth cleared a place for it in the center of the big kitchen table crowded with dishes and bowls and plates of cold cuts.

Abram left the room to hang up her coat, leaving her with the women.

"Everything looks so good," she said, suddenly nervous as she felt all eyes on her.

"We're glad you could come," Ruth—Abram's oldest sister—said politely. But she stood stiffly and her expression was far from warm.

Summer eyed her uncertainly. Everyone she had met in the Amish community had always been polite if reserved. But she still had the feeling of being observed, measured. Why was she here as Abram's guest? She could almost *feel* the sisters thinking it.

Then Anna, the second oldest sister, turned from the oven and said hello and smiled warmly and Summer felt a little better.

Eli, the next oldest brother after Abram, came in with his wife, Mary. He deposited the heavy basket of food he carried and then went into the living room. Eli went to join the men and Mary excused herself to nurse her youngest child she carried in her arms.

Another little girl ran into the kitchen, an older version of the one who'd come in earlier. When she spotted Summer, she walked over to her and eyed her curiously. "Is your name really Summer?"

"I—er, yes."

"Why?"

She told her the story she told everyone about why she had the name and the little girl smiled.

"I like it." She gazed at Summer's dress. "Pretty."

"Thank you."

Abram came back in and looked from one sister to the next, then at Summer. "Well, have my sisters been grilling you?" he asked her.

"Most certainly not!" Ruth glared at him.

"They haven't," Summer said quickly.

Was it her imagination that he appeared relieved? "Let's go in the living room and get started."

Summer said hello to Abram's three brothers and met Naomi Rose's husband. The men were polite but reserved and resumed their seats. She tried not to notice that they studied her when they thought she wasn't looking.

Summer had never been in the house and now, as she sat in a chair, she glanced around at the spacious room. The furnishings were simple but well made; some of it she was sure Abram or his father had crafted. Abram's farmhouse was bigger than the one she lived in with her mother. Abram had once told her that there were eight bedrooms. The size wasn't uncommon since the Amish had large families. The *dawdi haus*—just off the kitchen—would be occupied by his parents when they returned from Florida.

Evergreens were draped on the mantel and paper snowflakes obviously crafted by his nieces and nephews were hung from them. She saw a child-sized wooden table and chair set in the corner of the room and paper, coloring books, and crayons were scattered on it. Children were obviously welcome here, whether they were visiting Abram or his parents.

Summer counted more than a dozen children sitting quietly on the rag rugs in front of the adults. Unlike the adults, each one of them had a shy smile for her when they looked at her.

She watched Abram take the leather chair beside the fire. As the eldest, it was his role to open the family Bible and read the story of the birth of baby Jesus on a night so long ago and so far away. His voice was deep and reverent, and from the way he looked up from the print he obviously knew the story by heart.

The children listened with rapt attention, their faces lit by the firelight. Summer listened just as intently. She didn't think she'd ever been so touched by the story of that night when Joseph and Mary hadn't found room at the inn and baby Jesus had been born in a stable. Her throat tightened with unshed tears as she felt her heart stumble and fall for this strong, handsome man who read with slow, steady, devout care.

When he finished, he closed the Bible and their gazes locked.

"Let's eat," someone said, and Summer was barely aware that the others rose from their seats and hurried from the room.

"Are you all right?" he asked as he got up and walked over to her.

"Yes, why?" she managed to say.

"I don't know. You got a strange look on your face."

Summer stood and brushed at her skirt, afraid to meet his eyes. "No woman wants to hear that."

"Did I tell you how pretty you look tonight?"

"I think you mentioned it. But thanks."

He started to say something and then Eli walked into the room with a loaded plate.

"We'd better go get something to eat before it's all gone."

"Try the ham," Lester, Ruth's husband, advised her. "Ruth does quite a job with it."

Abram filled his plate and went to sit in the living room with the men and some of the older children. Summer thought how, whether families were Amish or *Englisch*, mothers always seemed to be the ones who helped the children with meals. She hung back to help fix plates for the youngest ones, and after they were seated at the big table, it seemed expected that she should sit with them and their mothers.

"Abram tells us you're going to college," Naomi Rose said. "I always loved school."

"Some think we're not educated because we don't go to school after the eighth grade," Ruth said, frowning. Her mouth thinned as she cut into her ham.

"Ruth," Anna said quietly.

"I don't think that way," Summer told them politely. "I've lived here all my life, and I know the Amish have apprenticeships for jobs, and what some of us *Englisch* would call homeschooling in the responsibilities of running a home and a farm. Most of what I know for my part-time job came from what my father taught me on our farm, not from college classes. But the job requires a college degree these days."

She sipped her tea. "My mother was a teacher, and she says a smart person never stops reading and learning."

"How is your mother doing?" Naomi Rose asked her. "Abram told us she's been unwell."

"Not any better. I think we'll be seeing the doctor again soon. I've been glad to be on break so I can stick around the house more."

"That's as it should be," Ruth said abruptly. "Family takes care of family. At least here." She glanced pointedly at the *dawdi haus* door. Then picked up her empty plate and stood. "I'll take coffee in to the men."

"Abram's never invited a woman to a family occasion," Anna told her quietly as they cleaned up the kitchen after the meal and packed up leftovers. "It's obviously a little hard for Ruth to accept."

"You mean an *Englisch* woman."

"No, any woman."

"I . . . see." Ruth reminded Summer of the way Fannie Mae had looked that evening she'd seen them holding hands at the restaurant.

Ruth returned with some used dishes, set them in the sink, and filled it with warm water and dishwashing liquid.

Summer picked up a clean dishcloth. "I'll dry."

"No need," Ruth said. "You might collect dishes from the other room if you want."

"Okay." Summer went out into the living room and picked them up and felt the men staring at her while Abram sat on the floor helping one of the children put together a puzzle. She felt like the elephant in the room no one was talking about. Anna and Naomi Rose came out to pass out Christmas cookies, so Summer took a deep breath and headed into the kitchen, knowing Ruth was in there alone.

"It was nice to be invited tonight," she began as she handed Ruth the plates she'd collected.

Ruth glared at her. "Abram invited you. Not me. He's evidently forgotten about what the Bible says."

Summer waited, knowing what she'd hear.

"Be ye not unequally yoked together with unbelievers: for what fellowship hath righteousness with unrighteousness? and what communion hath light with darkness?" Ruth quoted sternly. She turned back to the dishes when Anna and Naomi Rose came in.

Her spirits sinking, Summer chose not to make things worse by saying anything. She finished helping and decided to tell Abram she was leaving.

A little girl tugged on her skirt. "Are you going to marry *Onkel* Abram?"

"No, sweetheart," she said, and fought back tears. "We're friends."

Time to go. The family would be leaving soon, and in Abram's world, a single woman and a single man weren't supposed to be together in a home.

Abram looked concerned when she went to say goodbye to him and his family.

"You're sure nothing's wrong?" he asked as he walked her to her car. "No one said anything? I know Ruth can be a little . . . tart sometimes. Did she say anything to you?"

"No," she lied. "I need to get home and see that Mom is okay. I'll see you tomorrow."

She got into the car before he could try to kiss her.

✀✀✀

Christmas Day dinner at Summer's house started very differently from the meal at his house the night before. For one thing, the kitchen was quiet—it was just Summer. She greeted him at the door with a sober expression and then invited him to sit while she finished up cooking.

Today she wore a bright red turtleneck sweater, jeans, and earrings that were little red, green, and white rhinestone bows that had little jingle bells hanging from them. It was a very different look from the quiet long gray dress she'd worn the night before.

"You're staring at me."

"You look different."

Summer glanced down and then back at him. "We're casual for Christmas dinner."

"Pretty."

"Thanks."

The table was set for four, but it wasn't covered with so many serving bowls and platters that the wooden surface wasn't visible. Here it was fine china, not sturdy everyday stoneware. Fancy silverware. And wine glasses. A big platter sat in the center of the table ready for the turkey he could smell baking in the oven.

With luck he'd go home with some turkey along with the ham left from the night before. He was set for meals for the next few days.

"Help yourself to some snacks. Dinner will be ready in about half an hour." She set a cup of coffee before him and pushed little bowls of nuts and cheese and crackers closer to him.

"You okay?"

"Yes." But she went back to stirring something and didn't say more.

He chose a cracker and a piece of cheese. "Where's Marie?"

"She went to get Carl."

How different that was from the night before, he thought. Summer couldn't be alone with him at his house in his community, but Marie could be with Carl at his place. And he could sit here in the house with Summer.

The kitchen door opened and cold air rushed in as Marie came in with Carl. They brushed snow off the shoulders of their coats before shedding them and hanging them on pegs.

"Merry Christmas!" Marie exclaimed when she saw Abram.

"Merry Christmas."

She wore a bright green sweater with a grinning reindeer on it, jeans, and walnut-sized Christmas ornament earrings that hung almost to her shoulders. Her cheeks were rosy, but he could tell it was from the cold and not from feeling better.

Carl nodded at Abram and then looked at Summer. "Sure smells good in here."

"I made sure to take the neck out of the turkey first," she said, sending him a mock glare and waving the turkey baster at him. "So don't you start on my cooking."

He just chuckled and held up his hands. "Won't bring it up again."

Marie sat at the table with a cup of coffee. "Abram, did you have a good Christmas with your family?"

"I did. And everyone stopped by for Second Christmas with gifts today."

"We had a nice Christmas Day service at church this morning," she told him as she stirred cream into her coffee.

Abram had been in the act of picking up a cracker and stopped. It occurred to him that Summer hadn't asked him if he'd like to go with her.

He picked up the cracker and put it in his mouth and wondered why she hadn't asked him. Maybe she just hadn't wanted to invite him.

"Carl, would you hand me the platter?"

Abram watched Summer transfer the turkey to the platter and carry it to the table. She brought the rest of the dishes to the table and then sat. They gave thanks for the meal and Carl carved the turkey. Abram filled his plate with turkey, dressing, mashed potatoes and gravy, sweet potatoes, and green beans that had been canned at summer's end. Summer's yeast rolls were light as a feather, and the scent from the pumpkin pie sitting on the counter sent a promise it would be just as *gut*.

He found himself hoping he'd be offered some of the sides as well as turkey to take home . . . he was enjoying the food so much it took a while to realize Summer was being unusually quiet.

Her mother noticed too.

"Honey, are you okay?"

Summer nodded and pushed food around on her plate.

When they finished the meal everyone agreed that they were too full for dessert and went into the living room with their coffee to open presents. Summer chose a rocking chair instead of the sofa he sat on. He wished she'd sat beside him, but it felt awkward to say anything.

It was a different experience to sit in an *Englisch* living room before a Christmas tree lit up so brightly and open presents in fancy wrapping paper. The gifts he'd received from his family earlier in the day had been wrapped in brown paper and tied with string, and they'd been made by hand. But when he opened the gift from Summer, it was a woolen muffler of a deep brown that she told him she had made.

"You knit?"

"I'm more domestic than I look." She sounded defensive.

"It's just you're so busy with college. Thank you." He wrapped it around his neck. "Feels soft. It'll be welcome on these cold mornings for sure."

When she opened her gift from him, her eyes widened when she saw the candleholders he'd made.

"Thank you." Her eyes met his briefly.

"Summer, put them on the mantel. Let's see how they look," her mother said when she sat with them in her lap, unmoving.

She put them on the mantel and set the vanilla scented candles on top of them and lit them. The delicate scent wafted from them and cast a glow in the room. But she stood there looking so quiet.

Carl reached for presents under the tree and gave Abram's gift to Marie. She liked the thimble painted with violets he'd found in the quilt shop.

"So pretty," she said, putting it on her finger and admiring it.

Abram was surprised when Carl gave him Marie's gift and he found it was a tin of his favorite candy she'd made.

"Summer told me you like peanut butter fudge."

"I do." He immediately had to have a piece and invited the others to have some.

Carl got a tin of peanut brittle from Marie. She didn't seem surprised when he gave her a box of chocolate covered cherries.

"He gets me the same thing every year," she said happily as she opened the box and after taking one passed it around for everyone else to enjoy.

"What works, works," he told them with a grin.

They returned to the kitchen and ate the pie—as *gut* as any he'd ever eaten—and then Carl told Marie he wanted to go for a drive and see the Christmas lights. Soon Abram and Summer were alone in the kitchen.

He helped her put leftovers away and dried the dishes she handed him after she washed them.

"Why didn't you ask me to go to your church this morning?" he found himself blurting out.

Surprised, she stared at him. "I'd have asked you to go, but I knew your family would be stopping by your house for Second Christmas," she told him.

"I could have told them to come to the house later."

She nodded and said nothing.

"You're sure that's the reason you didn't ask me?"

"Sure."

But she stared down into the dishwater.

He took her by the shoulders and turned her to face him. "Is something bothering you? You've been quiet all evening."

"I'm fine." She walked to the refrigerator, got out a plastic container, and set it on the table. "Mom made you a container of leftovers."

"Thank you." He stood there, uncertain what to do. "Summer, do you want me to go?"

She put the teakettle on a burner and turned up the flame under it. "It's getting late. It's not safe for you to be out on the road in your buggy late."

"Tell me what's wrong."

"I told you, I'm fine. Just tired." She got a mug from a cupboard, put a tea bag in it, and still wasn't looking at him.

"Summer, I can't fix what's wrong if you don't talk to me."

She looked at him then. "I don't think we should see each other anymore."

"What?"

The teakettle began shrieking.

"Summer."

"Please, just go."

"Fine. I'll go." He stalked over to his coat and snatched it off the peg. As he yanked open the door he turned back and saw her standing by the stove, her face in her hands.

He got all the way home and realized he still had the little plastic bag of mistletoe he'd bought at Rose's stand in his pocket. He'd planned to kiss Summer beneath it tonight.

Twenty-Seven

Abram cleaned the stalls and fed and watered his horses the morning after Christmas, trying not to think about what had gone wrong the night before. Miserable, he moved around doing the chores, shoulders slumped, his head downcast, until Shadow butted his shoulder with his nose.

"Sorry, guy. I'm just feeling moody." He caressed the horse's nose, then sat on a bale of hay. Shadow stared at him patiently with liquid brown eyes, listening as Abram poured out his feelings.

Roy had always done that—seemed to read his moods, listen to him, and provide a sympathetic shoulder. Abram never talked about that with his friends, but they'd all been quick to come over when Roy died and express their sympathies and help him bury the horse. So maybe they had had the same kind of relationship with a horse once.

Finally, his tale of woe finished, he got up and did the last of his chores.

The wind was bitter, slapping him in the face when he left the warm barn and started for the house. This would have been a good morning to wear the muffler Summer had made him. He'd forgotten to take it with him when he stormed out of her house the night before. He wondered if she'd bring it to him. No way was he going to go get it after she hurt his feelings the way she had.

What a mess things were. He went into the house, washed up, and took off his coat. He'd had a cup of coffee before starting out to the barn, so he heated it up while he looked in the refrigerator and tried to drum up enthusiasm for breakfast. He wasn't hungry, but a man couldn't get through a morning of work without eating. So he took out a couple of eggs and set them on the counter near the stove. Then he remembered his *schweschders* had left him some baked goods Christmas Eve . . . he looked in his breadbox and *schur* enough, there was half a loaf of pumpkin bread. He figured he could force down a slice or two with a couple of scrambled eggs.

He had the bread in his hand when it struck him. His *schweschders*. Had they said something to Summer? She'd told him they weren't grilling her when he walked into the kitchen after putting her coat in the front bedroom with others. But later, when the women cleaned up the kitchen, she'd been in there with them and he'd been with the men in the living room. She'd been one of the first to leave . . .

Perhaps it was time to talk with his *schweschders* and see what they knew. He ate quickly, donned his jacket, and went out to hitch up his buggy. As he started out of his drive, he debated which *schweschder* to visit first and decided it should be Ruth. She was the oldest and the one who always seemed to feel she knew what was best. If she didn't know anything, he'd work his way down the list of his *schweschders*.

Ruth looked surprised to see him. "We're just having breakfast," she told him as she flipped pancakes onto a plate and set it before her *mann*. Her *kinner* were quiet as they wolfed down pancakes. "Have you eaten?"

"*Ya, danki.*"

"Then sit. Want some coffee?"

"*Nee, danki.*" He took off his jacket and sat and watched as Ruth's family ate.

After assuring herself that everyone had all they needed, she sat with a cup of coffee. "So what brings you here?"

He glanced at the *kinner* and hesitated. When he'd made the sudden decision to come here and talk to her, he hadn't considered she'd be busy with her family. Then he realized after the *kinner* looked up and smiled at him and then went back to eating that they were completely absorbed in their breakfast. He'd had Ruth's pancakes so he totally understood.

"I just wondered if you knew any reason why Summer would be upset."

She stiffened. "I'm *schur* I wouldn't know. Who knows how an *Englischer* thinks."

"They're human just like we are," he said mildly.

Her lips thinned and she lifted her chin. At that moment she looked older, stern . . . judgmental.

"She left early that night. Before anyone else."

"That's as it should be. You weren't planning on having her be there after the family left, were you? That wouldn't be proper."

"Ruth." Her *mann*'s voice was low but held a warning note.

"Someone has to say it."

Now it was Abram's turn to look at her sternly. "I don't need anyone to tell me what's proper."

She sniffed. "Well, I didn't tell her to leave, if that's what you came over to ask me."

Lester pushed aside his plate and stood. "Time to finish chores."

The boys rose and put their empty plates in the sink, put on their jackets, and followed him out the door. The girls cleared the table and began washing dishes.

"Maybe you didn't tell her to leave," Abram said quietly. "But did you make her feel unwelcome?"

"Did she say I did?"

"*Nee*, or we'd be having a different conversation."

"Well, I can't help it if she realized she didn't belong there."

"She was my guest. And she's important to me."

"How important?"

Her question struck him like a blow to the chest. Just how important *was* Summer to him? He got to his feet and started for the door.

"Abram? How important?"

He turned. "I love her," he said simply.

"Abram! Come back here! Abram, you can't mean that!"

He kept walking out the door.

His next stop was Summer's house. Her car wasn't in the driveway, but he stopped anyway and knocked on the door.

"They're gone," Carl called out from his front porch where he was shoveling snow. "Went to see some friends, I think."

"You okay?"

"Yeah." What else could he say? He didn't want to tell the man he'd upset Summer. "Guess I'll leave a note on her door."

Carl nodded and went back to shoveling snow.

Abram found a piece of paper and a pen, wrote a note to Summer and left it on the back door. Then he climbed back into his buggy and returned to his farm.

Now all he could do was wait for her too call.

Summer swallowed a couple of aspirin with a glass of water for her headache. She fixed a cup of tea and when she went to the refrigerator for some milk to put in it she saw the plastic container of Christmas dinner leftovers her mother had made for Abram sitting on the top shelf. He'd left without it.

She sighed and made a mug of tea. She carried it into the living room and sat in the recliner. The lights on the Christmas tree blurred as she gave up on blinking back tears and they ran down her cheeks.

What an ending to the day. She should have called Abram and made up some excuse, told him not to come today. Instead she'd bottled up her feelings, thought she could get through the evening, and botched everything by fighting with him before he left.

What had she expected following a night tossing and turning and barely sleeping after the evening with Abram and his family? Sure, she and Abram had agreed they were just seeing each other. They had been careful to say they weren't looking to a future together. But the evening had shown her that his family wouldn't be happy if he continued to see her.

Miserable, she reached into the deep pocket of the recliner for the packet of tissues her mother kept in it, found them and the Christmas magazines she'd bought at the grocery store. She dropped them into her lap, pulled a tissue from the pack to wipe her tears away, and blew her nose.

Well, what had she expected anyway? Who got into a relationship saying "we won't think about the future"? They came from two different worlds, and if they didn't consider what could happen if they developed feelings for each other . . . it wasn't like two Protestants marrying. Even when a Protestant or Catholic married someone of the Jewish faith, it wasn't necessary to convert. Sure, they had to find someone to marry them, but they didn't have to change the way an *Englischer* and an Amish person had to . . . either she had to become Amish or Abram had to leave his church and be shunned. Shunned.

So she sat there staring at the Christmas tree and thought about how this holiday—a time that should have been one of joy and celebrating the birth of Christ with family—had instead driven a wedge between them.

Her gaze fell on the chair Abram had been sitting on. He'd left more than the turkey dinner leftovers. He'd left his Christmas gifts.

Seeing them brought more tears. She remembered how he'd looked when he unwrapped the muffler and found out she'd knitted it for him. She squeezed her eyes shut hard and the tears finally stopped.

Reaching into the recliner pocket for the remote, she turned the television on and dispiritedly channel surfed. All that she found on were bright and cheerful Christmas programs. She caught the last few minutes of a romantic movie where the couple was getting engaged before the Christmas tree.

She hit off and reached for her tea and found it had grown cold.

Sighing, she looked down at the magazines in her lap. She and her mother always enjoyed buying several of the Christmas issues so she'd picked them up at the store. Her mother had obviously read the *Martha Stewart* issue since there were pages turned down and one page with recipes had been torn out.

She set it aside, too depressed to look at how to decorate a house for the holidays and turned to a different magazine. But she couldn't get interested when she read the headlines on the cover and saw how many articles dealt with romantic relationships. No, not what she needed right now. She tossed it aside.

Then she saw that mixed in with the Christmas issues she'd

picked up a November issue of a women's magazine her mother favored. "Reclaim Your Energy," it proclaimed. Who wouldn't like to do that? she wondered as she read the text under the headline. *Tick-borne infections are up . . . chronic fatigue, joint aches, memory loss . . . what you need to know because your doctor doesn't.*

Tick-borne infections. Lyme disease.

She flipped quickly to the table of contents, found the page the article was on, and read it avidly. The author said the infections were up hundreds of percentage points and were reported in every state. Older women were especially vulnerable because their immune systems were weaker as they aged. Sometimes the women thought their symptoms were caused by menopause. Hmm. Her mother had complained about hot flashes and night sweats and had many of the symptoms listed in the article.

Even though she'd been somewhat reassured her mother didn't have dementia or early Alzheimer's after the recent doctor visit, Summer had worried about what *was* the problem.

She heard the kitchen door open and her mother and Carl arguing. After she swiped at her wet cheeks she set the magazines aside, got up, and walked into the kitchen.

"Don't you go telling Summer," her mother was saying.

"Don't tell me what?"

Marie started guiltily and when she swayed on her feet, Carl grabbed her by the waist and steadied her. "Oh, I fell asleep in his truck. Big deal. It's been a busy week, that's all. And the medicine makes me sleepy. You know that."

"She fainted," Carl said bluntly. "I had to stop and pat her cheeks to get her to snap out of it."

"I fell asleep," Marie insisted. She frowned at Summer. "Have you been crying?"

"I was watching television. You know *It's a Wonderful Life* always gets to me." Well, she wasn't entirely truthful. She'd been watching television and the movie was a sentimental favorite of hers and the ending always made her cry. She just hadn't been watching it when they came in. One look at her mother's pale cheeks told her that she needed to get to bed regardless of whether her mother or Carl was right.

Besides, she couldn't handle talking about how she'd told Abram she didn't think they should see each other anymore.

"Thanks, Carl. I'll help Mom up to bed."

"Need help?"

Marie stepped away from him. "Don't go acting like I can't get myself to bed," she said tartly.

"Fine, fine." He sent Summer a worried look. "You call me if you need me."

"I will, Carl. Thanks."

Carl leaned forward and kissed Marie on the cheek. "Merry Christmas, honey."

Her shoulders sagged. "Oh, Merry Christmas, Carl. Sorry I'm such a grump lately."

"You're the grump I love."

Touched, Summer smiled at him and after he left, locked the door. "Come on, let's get you to bed and I'll bring you up a cup of tea. I could use one too."

Her mother let her lead her upstairs and then insisted she could get herself to bed. Summer turned down the covers and lingered while her mother went into the bathroom and when she came out handed her a nightgown.

"I'll be right back."

Hurrying downstairs, she put the teakettle on and then unplugged the tree and turned off the television. The magazine she'd been reading lay on the chair. She scooped it up and went into the kitchen to make tea and set mugs on a tray. When she got upstairs she found her mother already asleep. She set a mug on the bedside table, turned the lamp on low, and left the room. She'd share the magazine article with her mother in the morning and call the doctor. They were going to get an appointment and get her mother tested for Lyme disease as soon as they could get in to see the doctor.

Lyme disease. Not early Alzheimer's disease or some other terrible condition. Lyme was serious but there were treatments, the article said.

During this holy season maybe she had her miracle. "Thank You, God," she whispered.

$$\mathscr{SSS}$$

Summer was sitting at the kitchen table sipping hot tea when her mother came downstairs.

She hoped her mother would be as hopeful as she was after she read the article.

"Sit down. I want you to read something." She got up and poured a mug of hot water, dunked a tea bag in it, and set it before her mother.

Then she sat beside her and showed her the article she'd torn from the magazine. "I found this last night. I want you to read it."

Tears began slipping down her mother's cheek as she read.

"Mom, please don't get upset," Summer murmured and leaned over to hug her mother.

Marie shook her head. "No, no, I'm not. This would be so much better than what I was afraid it might be." She pulled a tissue out of her pajamas pocket and wiped her tears. "The memory problems have scared me to death."

Summer hugged her. "I know. Me too." She glanced at the clock on the wall. "I'm calling the doctor's office as soon as it opens."

"I kind of doubt they'll be there, do you?"

"I have my fingers crossed."

There was a knock on the door and Carl strode in. He stopped and stared. "What's wrong?"

"Look what Summer found." She handed him the article.

He scanned it then stared at them, his eyes wide. "You think this is what's been making her sick?"

"We don't know," Summer told him. "I'm calling the doctor's office to see if we can get her in today."

Marie went upstairs to get dressed, and Summer made the call. They were in luck. The doctor's receptionist said they were open and could squeeze them in later that morning if they didn't mind waiting.

"Good, good," Carl said when Summer hung up the phone and gave him the news.

Summer had been concerned that Lisa, the nurse practitioner at the doctor's office, might not like being asked to look at the magazine article, but she seemed receptive and began scanning it. "I'll order the tests right now."

"I don't remember ever being bitten by a tick," Marie told her. "And I never developed any rash. But the article says people don't always notice a tick bite and some never develop a rash."

"It's right. But you show a lot of the symptoms. The lab will have my order this morning, but call them at the number listed on the form before going there. I'm not sure of their hours this week."

"We will."

"If the test comes back positive, then I'll have you come back in and discuss a treatment plan. If it's not Lyme we're going to find out what's wrong." She squeezed Marie's hand. "Don't lose hope."

"I won't."

"In the meantime, move carefully and try not to put yourself near something like a glass door or whatever if you feel faint again."

"Thanks, Lisa. I'm glad you could see us today."

Lisa smiled. "You're welcome. And never be afraid to ask questions or bring in an article. Dr. Wilson and I don't pretend to know everything."

They walked out of the office building and into the cold wind that whipped their coats around them.

"Go back inside and I'll get the car, Mom."

Marie took a deep breath and gazed up at the cloudless sky. "No, it feels good to be cold. Makes me feel alive." She grinned as she looped her arm through Summer's and they walked to the car. "Let's call the lab, find out if they're open today, and if I can have the blood drawn. Oh, I wonder if I should have fasted."

"We'll look at the information in the car. If not, I'll call on the cell. Then let's have lunch out. My treat."

"Sounds good to me."

Summer felt some of her stress over her mother melt away as they ate lunch out. But it was hard to hide how miserable she was feeling about Abram—especially when she saw an Amish buggy pass by the window that overlooked the road.

She drove them home and was about to turn into their driveway when she saw Abram's buggy parked there. She drove on.

"You back again?"

Abram was climbing into his buggy when he heard Carl call out.

"Yes sir."

He squinted at Abram. "You two have a fight?"

"Did she say we did?"

"Nope. But she looked like she'd been crying when I brought Marie home. Tried to say she'd been watching a Christmas movie. But she looked like she'd been bawling her head off. I know the difference between the way a woman looks after she's been crying over a movie and when her heart is broken."

He gave Abram a steely look. "I think you broke my girl's heart."

"I didn't mean to. I love her."

"Then how you gonna fix this, son?"

Ya. How are you going to fix it? he asked himself. "I don't know."

Carl clapped him on the shoulder. "Come on, let's have a cup of coffee and talk in my place. I got a soft spot for a man in love right now."

"It shows?"

"Takes one to know one. I've been carrying around an engagement ring for Marie for a week now. Wanted to give it to her last night but . . . well, I'll give it to her soon." He held the door open and Abram stepped inside.

"Honey, you went past our house."

"I know, Mom. I thought we'd enjoy driving a little bit. See the Christmas decorations."

"Did you forget I did that with Carl? Besides, it's better at night when the lights are on."

"We can still take a drive. Unless you want to go home right away." She hoped she didn't.

"This have anything to do with the fact that Abram's buggy was parked at our house?"

"You saw." Summer sighed.

"Did you have a fight? I felt like something was wrong during Christmas dinner. That's why Carl and I took a drive. So the two of you could talk."

Summer stared ahead. "Mom, what was I thinking? That relationship couldn't go anywhere. We come from two different worlds. I told him I didn't want to see him again."

"So you came to care for him more than as a friend."

Surprised, she looked over at her and then back at the road. "Yeah."

"I figured. Otherwise you could still see him." Marie leaned back in her seat. "So how long are you going to drive us around?"

"I don't know." Miserable, she blinked at tears that threatened to fall.

Marie reached over and patted her hand on the steering wheel. "We'll drive around a little bit and then I'll call Carl and see if Abram is still there."

"Good idea." She tried not to notice that they were approaching Abram's farm.

"Looks like someone's waiting for Abram," her mother remarked.

Summer glanced over and saw Naomi Rose, Abram's youngest sister, walking back to the buggy after evidently finding he wasn't home. She looked away quickly and hoped the woman didn't see her passing by.

"Okay if I use your phone? I'm going to call Carl and see if Abram's left," her mother told her. "Don't worry, I'll be careful what I say."

She made the call, saying quickly, "Carl, don't say my name. We saw Abram's buggy in the drive and Summer doesn't want to come home until he's gone. Uh-huh, okay. Love you too. Bye."

"Carl said he left a few minutes ago."

She sighed. "Thanks, Mom."

"Carl said Abram's upset."

Summer bit her lip. "Well, he'll get over it, marry some nice Amish girl, and be happy."

"Oh, sweetheart, you don't mean that. Think about it and cool off some, then go talk to him."

"I don't want to talk to him and I don't want to see him. Promise you'll tell him I'm not home if he comes back."

"I can't do that."

"Then just tell him I don't want to see him. Please."

Now it was Marie's turn to sigh. "It's against my better judgment. People need to talk things out."

"Talking's not going to change the facts. I shouldn't have ever started seeing him. We're total opposites."

"You're two people who love each other," Marie said firmly. "Now let's go home."

Summer checked traffic and made a U-turn.

Home sounded good right now.

SSS

Abram returned to his farm disappointed he hadn't been able to see Summer.

It was kind of Carl to invite him in and offer him coffee and talk to him. Clearly the man considered Summer to be like a daughter to him, but he'd treated him with caring and respect and talked to him when he saw he was upset.

Now he had to think about how he was going to fix things between them. Summer wasn't answering his phone calls or his texts. And he didn't think it was because she was still at the doctor's office with her mother.

So he went back home where he found a note from his *schweschder* Naomi Rose on his kitchen door. She wanted him to call her. He put the note in his pocket. Maybe he'd do it later. Not now. He felt too miserable to talk to anyone.

Right now he needed to do the only thing he knew. He worked on his furniture order and talked to his horses and did his chores and ate a solitary supper and when it was time, he went to bed.

A day without talking to or seeing Summer was a very long day.

The next day Naomi Rose stopped by again. She found him in the barn working on a bookcase for the furniture store.

"I talked to Ruth," she said simply as she sat on a bale of hay and watched him work. "Abram, Ruth wasn't as friendly as she could have been, but I don't think she said anything deliberately hurtful. I was there."

"Doesn't take words to hurt."

"True. And Ruth has always been so stern. I'd be the first to say so. She's always thought she should be the one to tell us what to do even though you're the oldest. Maybe she thinks of herself as a second *mudder* since she helped *Mamm* with all of us." She smiled. "You know if she hadn't run herd on you boys, you'd have driven *Mamm* mad."

Abram shrugged but he couldn't help grinning. She was right. "Still, from what Summer said when we had a fight, it sounded as if she didn't feel like my family liked her or wanted her to see me."

Naomi Rose was the youngest and had always had a tender heart. Her face immediately registered distress. "Oh, Abram, I'm so sorry! She seems like a lovely person. Maybe I might have spent more time talking to her if I hadn't been, well, thinking about myself." She hesitated and then she smiled. "Abram, I'm having a *boppli!*"

Abram dropped the sandpaper he'd been using. "A *boppli?*" he repeated.

She nodded and her eyes shone with excitement. "We're not telling anyone else right now. But maybe I didn't pay as much attention to Summer that night as I should have."

"You're just a *boppli*," he said and he folded her in a hug.

She laughed. "I'm twenty!"

"When did that happen?" He shook his head.

She laughed. "I'm sure that's what *Mamm* will say when we tell her. *Schur* wish she and *Daed* would come home."

"Me too." He released her and went back to his sanding. "I wish they'd have had a chance to know Summer."

"*Ya*, me too," she said thoughtfully. "Well, I have to go. I'm *hungerich*. Seems to be all the time these days. Bye!"

"Bye."

She'd no sooner left than Wayne stopped by. He started off asking if Abram had had a good Christmas with the family and Summer.

Abram frowned and sanded harder. "She broke up with me."

"What?"

He nodded. "Seems to think we can't be together because of our religions."

"Well, it's not easy, but it can work. I mean look at Miriam and Mark Byler."

"Wayne, she attended their wedding, remember? I don't need to remind her."

"Oh, yeah, right." He sat down on the bale of hay Naomi Rose had used. "So what are you gonna do?"

Abram tossed down the sandpaper and picked up a cloth to wipe off the wood. "She won't answer my phone calls or texts."

Wayne grinned. "Say, maybe Kim could talk to her."

He gave his friend a skeptical look. "Oh, and would you call her and ask her to talk to Summer?"

Wayne brightened and pulled out his cell phone. "*Schur*, happy to. You have Kim's number?"

"Put the phone away." Abram put his hands on his hips and regarded Wayne. "You just want an excuse to talk to Kim."

"Well, *schur*, who wouldn't?" He had the grace to look a little shamefaced. "Listen, you need to talk to Summer. Work things out. It's obvious to anyone the two of you really like each other."

"I love her," Abram blurted out.

"Man, then you *have* to talk to her."

"Can't talk to a woman who doesn't want to talk to you."

Wayne appeared to think about it. "I've had them shut me out. Sometimes you just gotta keep banging on her door."

"Didn't an officer of the law once tell you that was stalking?"

Now Wayne looked embarrassed. "Yeah, whatever. I gotta go."

"You just got here," Abram called after him. He shrugged. Who could figure Wayne out sometimes?

He went back to work.

A few minutes later the barn door slid open and Anna walked in.

"Maybe I should put a revolving door on the barn," he muttered under his breath and pasted on a smile.

"Ruth and I talked," she said.

"I'm ready for a break," he told her. "You want some coffee?"

"*Schur.*" She followed him into the house. "She told me you're upset with her."

"To say the least." He took off his jacket, hung it, and washed up. "There's some coffee left from this morning. I can heat it up."

She made a face. "Maybe I could have a cup of tea?"

So he warmed his coffee and heated water for a cup of tea for her. He sliced the leftover pumpkin bread and set it on the table.

"Ruth's not going to apologize."

"Don't expect her to. I know her, remember?" He brought their mugs to the table and sat.

"Sometimes families have a member who isn't the easiest," she began.

"And sometimes they have more than one."

She frowned. "What's that supposed to mean?"

"Nothing. Bad joke." He bit into a slice of the bread.

"I think once they get to know each other—"

"Summer broke up with me."

Her hand flew to her throat, and she looked genuinely distressed. "Oh my."

"*Ya.*" Depressed, he stared into his coffee.

"Talk to her. You can work things out."

"Everyone's saying talk to her!" He jumped up and paced the room. "How do I talk to her if she won't talk to me?"

"You were always a charming *kind*. You could look at us with those big brown eyes and get anything you wanted out of your *mudder* and your *schweschders*."

"Well, it won't work with Summer. I can't use my charm if she won't see me." He returned to his chair and slumped into it.

She put her hand on his and squeezed it. "Keep trying. She's worth it. I saw the way you looked at her that night. I want you to be happy." She hesitated. "Is she willing to join the church?"

"We haven't discussed it."

Worry flashed into her eyes. "Abram, you're not thinking about leaving the church?"

"I haven't thought that far. I only know I love her." He took a sip of his coffee. "And Anna, not everyone's a Ruth."

"Thank goodness. I'm not *schur* the world could handle another Ruth," she joked.

"*Nee*, I meant the biblical Ruth. Why should the woman always be the one to convert?"

"But—"

"Anna, it does no *gut* to talk about this. Summer doesn't want anything to do with me."

"I'll pray for you."

"*Danki.* I could *schur* use your prayers."

Twenty-Eight

Summer had the boxes that her mother stored Christmas ornaments in sitting beside the tree and had resigned herself to taking it down. Family tradition said it came down on New Year's Day, but this year she'd kept putting it off, too dispirited and, yes, maybe too depressed to do it. Her mother was finally on the medications for Lyme and was still easily tired—they'd been warned that it could take five weeks or more to see an improvement—so Summer hadn't let her do it.

"Be careful with that one," her mother said as she supervised from her position lying on the sofa. "It's very fragile."

"Since it's glass I figured that," Summer told her wryly.

She wrapped it in soft batting and set it into its spot in the ornament box. So many of the ornaments were reminders of family interests, travels, mementoes. The ornaments Summer had made as a child were never discarded, even though they were falling apart. She smiled and shook her head. Parents.

"Are you warm enough, Mom?"

"Toasty. It's nice having the fire on."

It was gas, but easier to use than the old wood-burning one had been. Her mother had insisted that she light the vanilla-scented candles atop the wooden candlesticks Abram had given her for Christmas. Both the fire and the candle glow made the room seem warm on the cold January afternoon. Another snowstorm was expected that week.

Summer was already tired of winter.

A car pulled up in front of the house. She got to her feet to see who it was.

"Are you expecting anyone?" her mother asked.

Her eyes widened when she looked out the front window. A taxi was parked out front and an older Amish couple was emerging from the back seat. The man held the woman's elbow protectively as they came up the front walk. Their heads were bent against the wind so she couldn't see who they were, but something about them seemed very familiar.

"Mom, I think it's Abram's parents."

"His parents? I thought they were in Florida." She sat up, brushed at her hair.

Summer watched the taxi leave as she pulled open the front door and the couple climbed the porch steps.

"Mr. and Mrs. Yoder, what a surprise."

He took off his black felt hat. "Isaiah, and this is Lizzie."

"Yes, I remember. Please come in. Mom, these are Abram's parents, Isaiah and Lizzie. They came to Daddy's funeral."

Marie stood and smiled. "I remember. It was very nice of you."

"We thought a lot of Howard," Isaiah told her and his wife nodded. "We remember how he often brought Summer with him when he visited our farm on agriculture business."

Summer hadn't seen the couple in some time and now as they stood there, she thought this was what Abram would look like when he was older—tall, broad shouldered, with chestnut hair and beard that had streaks of silver like Isaiah. Steady, with kind eyes. Lizzie was shorter, rounder, and livelier, but her eyes were a warm brown and her smile reminded Summer of Abram.

"Let me take your coats," Summer said. She collected them and laid them over a nearby chair. "Have a seat. Can I get you some coffee?"

"That would be very nice. We just came in on the bus from Florida." Lizzie looked around. "What a lovely room. Did you have a nice Christmas?"

"We did," Marie told her. "Abram came over for Christmas Day dinner."

"We heard," said Lizzie.

They took seats on the sofa and as she left the room, Summer heard her mother asking them about Florida. Summer hurried through making coffee and setting a carafe, cups, and cream and sugar on a tray. She added some cookies she had baked the day before.

When she returned to the living room, Lizzie was admiring the candleholders on the mantel.

"Abram gave me those for Christmas." She set the tray down on the coffee table in front of the sofa.

"I thought they looked like Abram's work." Lizzie smiled and returned to sit on the sofa beside her husband.

Summer fixed a cup of coffee for her mother and handed it to her and then took a chair. She was too nervous to want anything.

Isaiah chose a cookie and nodded approval after he took a bite.

Marie cleared her throat. "Summer, Lizzie tells me she and Isaiah came back from Florida a little early to talk to you."

"Really?" She rubbed suddenly damp hands on the thighs of her jeans. "Why?"

"I wish we'd been there Christmas Eve," Lizzie told her. "Naomi Rose called me a few days ago. She's concerned that you didn't feel welcome in our family."

"It's all right—" she began.

"No, it's not," Lizzie interrupted her. "It's never all right to make someone feel unwelcome in your home. You were Abram's guest, and I gather my eldest daughter was her usual . . . shall we say . . . judgmental self. Ruth has a good heart, but she sometimes lets her tongue run away with itself."

"The minute Lizzie heard what happened she wanted to come home," Isaiah spoke up.

"Oh no! You shouldn't have."

"Of course we should," Lizzie said quickly. "You're important to Abram and so you are important to us."

"But you barely know me."

"We'd like to know you better." She smiled at Summer.

Her words, her expression, floored Summer. She twisted her hands in her lap and tried to think what to say. "I appreciate you both coming to see me, but Ruth isn't responsible for me breaking things off with your son." She sighed and shook her head. "We started off as friends and it should have stayed that way. But we grew to care about each other, and I didn't see how it could go anywhere. I didn't want to make his family unhappy and worried he'd leave his church over me. So I told him I wouldn't be seeing him anymore. I'm sorry I hurt him."

"It would be hard if Abram left the church," Isaiah said, speaking up for the first time. "The church still expects family to shun the one who's left and keep trying to get them to return."

He stopped and looked down at his hands, then back up at Summer. "We'd hate to see that. But I'm not going to influence my son about this relationship. I don't know what God has in mind for him, who God has set aside for him."

"Did you know that we knew your grandmother?" Lizzie asked her. "Your father's mother, who left her Amish church in Ohio?"

Summer glanced at her mother. "No, I didn't know that."

"Waneta kept her past to herself and didn't tell many people," Marie explained. "But it's interesting that she moved here, where there was an Amish community, when you'd think she'd want to live somewhere else. And she married an *Englisch* man."

"We came to talk to you and apologize for any discomfort you felt," Lizzie said. "It is up to you if you see Abram again. I just want to say that you seem like a lovely young woman, and I can see why Abram cares for you."

Touched, she blinked away tears. "Thank you."

They left a short time later, refusing Summer's offer of a ride, with Isaiah calling the taxi company.

Summer went back to taking the ornaments off the tree and putting them in boxes. "Well, I sure wasn't expecting that."

"They're nice people."

Summer took a papier-mâché butterfly she'd made when she was five from the tree and held it in her hands. Love—hope—seemed as fragile as a butterfly.

When she had wrapped the string of lights around a piece of

cardboard and the tree was bare, she stared down at the base of it. "Mom, there's a present under here." She pulled it out and found her name on it.

"I forgot to give it to you," her mother told her. "So open it."

Summer found a small wooden keepsake box inside the wrapping paper. She opened it and found a *kapp* like those worn by the Ohio Amish women, a packet of letters tied with a ribbon, and trinkets a young girl might collect.

"Your Amish grandmother's," her mother told her. "I found them up in the attic when I went there for the Christmas ornaments. From the time you were a little girl you've told me about your dreams of being Amish. I think Waneta would want you to have it."

Summer stroked the box. "Thank you, Mom. I haven't had those dreams for a week or two. I'm not sure why." She missed the dreams of a simple life as much as she missed Abram. No, she missed Abram more.

That night she dreamed again of being Amish.

❧❧❧

Abram couldn't have been more shocked when a taxi pulled up in the drive and his *eldres* stepped out.

They looked tanned and healthy and greeted him with hugs.

"Why didn't you tell me you were coming?"

His *mudder* glanced at his *dat*. "We made a sudden decision to come back. Let's get inside out of the cold and talk about it."

He made coffee and they shed their coats and settled at the kitchen table.

"Florida was nice but it's *gut* to be home." Lizzie patted his hand.

Isaiah reached for a piece of applesauce cake Abram set on the table while the percolator burbled on the stove. "I see your *schweschders* are keeping you in baked goods."

"Anna brought it. It's not as good as yours, *Mamm*, but don't tell them that."

She chuckled.

"Ruth called us a few days ago," his *mudder* told him.

"She did?"

Lizzie nodded. "She was concerned about you."

Abram rolled his eyes. "I'd say she's still trying to be my *mudder*, but you never acted like her."

She struggled to hold back a smile. "Ruth has always been very *schur* of her opinions." Her smile faded. "I didn't like what I heard. Then Anna and Naomi Rose called."

"All three of them?"

She nodded. "Naomi Rose told me she thought you really care about Summer." She held up a hand when Abram started to speak. "Normally couples don't talk about who they're courting—" She stopped, grinned. "Dating," she corrected herself. "And we've never gotten involved in the relationships our *kinner* are having."

"Up until now," his *dat* spoke up.

Lizzie nodded. "So we went to see Summer."

"You what?"

"We stopped to see Summer before we came here. To apologize if she thought the family wouldn't welcome her."

"Well." He stared at them, not knowing what to say. Then he shrugged. "That's nice, but it won't make any difference. She broke up with me and she won't see me."

"Give her some time. I think we made up for the way Ruth behaved," his mudder said confidently.

Isaiah grunted agreement as he took another sip of coffee. Then he yawned hugely. "Well, Lizzie, you're welcome to talk to our *sohn* some more, but I'm worn out from the trip. I'm heading to bed." He stood, leaned down to kiss her cheek, then clapped Abram on the shoulder. "I like your Summer."

Abram wished she *was* his Summer.

His *mudder* had said to give her time. His *mudder* was right. Two hours later Summer texted him.

Do you want to talk?

His heart leaped. *Yes.*

I'll pick you up in fifteen minutes.

He was outside waiting when she pulled up. When he got in the passenger seat, she gave him a tentative smile. She looked pale, with lavender shadows beneath her eyes, as if she hadn't slept much.

"I'm sorry."

He shook his head. "I am too. I should have known Ruth would make you uncomfortable."

Summer shook her head and pulled out of the drive. "No, she really wasn't as bad as she could have been. She just sort of expressed some of the way I'd been thinking." She glanced at him. "I'm sure Fannie Mae could be worse."

"True."

"Family's important. I don't want to come between you."

"Family should accept the person important to us. Like my parents do."

"They shouldn't have interrupted their time in Pinecraft. But it was very sweet of them." She pulled into the drive-through of the burger place they'd visited before. "I thought we could get some coffee, take a drive, and talk."

They got their coffee and she drove for a few miles without speaking and then pulled off the road. "Where's this going?"

"This road goes to—" He grinned when she shot him an exasperated look. "I know where I want it to go, Summer. I love you."

Her eyes filled. "I love you too."

Abram felt a weight lift off his shoulders. "Marry me, Summer." Before she could speak, he reached for her hand. "Anna and I talked. She asked me if you would be willing to join the church."

"I hope you told her yes."

He stared at her. "No, I didn't. I'm willing to leave, Summer."

"How could you think I'd ask you to do that?"

"Ours isn't an easy life, Summer. You know that."

She nodded. "I do." She reached over the seat and handed him a wooden box. "My mother gave this to me today. It was supposed to be a Christmas gift, but she forgot to give it to me that day. Open it."

He lifted the lid and stared at a *kapp*—the kind worn by Ohio Amish women.

"It belonged to my father's mother. She left the Amish church and moved here, married an *Englischer*, and went to his church. Methodist. I figure I'm doing the opposite."

"Wow."

She laughed. "Yeah. She was a private person and didn't say much about her life before she moved here. But somehow I knew, Abram. My mother says I've been telling her about my dreams of being an Amish girl all my life."

He lifted her hand to his lips and kissed it. "It's not an easy life," he repeated.

"It's not as hard as living without you," she said simply. "Marry me, Abram. Be my *mann*."

He pulled the little plastic bag of mistletoe from his coat pocket and showed it to her. "I brought this over to your house on Christmas Day. I was going to kiss you then."

"It's about time." She laughed. "Kiss me, Abram. Kiss me now."

They kissed, and when they drew apart they were smiling at each other.

A knock on her car window startled them. Her eyes widened when she saw the police officer standing beside the car. She rolled down the window. "Yes, officer?"

"You folks having car trouble?"

"No. We're having a marriage proposal."

He peered into the car. "That so?"

"Yes, sir," Abram said.

"Well, congratulations. Now get off the side of the road before someone hits you," he said gruffly.

"I will. And thank you."

Summer started the car and they drove along the country road.

"Now what?" he asked her.

She shot him a mischievous look. "We find another road to pull off of and hope the officer doesn't patrol it. I want another kiss."

"I'm being serious."

"I know what's involved, Abram. I'll talk to the bishop about the classes I have to take. And I know we have to wait for a lot longer than I'd like to get married. That'll just give us time to get to know each other better, right?"

"If you say so. Right now I'm thinking being able to get married sooner is a very good idea."

She glanced in the rearview mirror, saw they hadn't been followed, pulled over, and smiled at him. "Now where's that mistletoe?"

Epilogue

Summer sat back, wiped the perspiration from her forehead, and thought about taking a break. She'd started working in her kitchen garden right after breakfast, but the heat was already intense. Shading her eyes with her hand, she looked out and watched her husband working in the distant fields.

Husband, she thought, smiling. *Mann.*

A car pulled into the drive and she glanced over. Her mother got out, opened the back door, and reached in. She turned and set a little girl down on the drive. A little girl who rushed across the distance between them.

"*Mamm!* I'm home!" Katie ran toward her, her braids flying, and flew into her arms.

"I see. I missed you so. Did you have a *gut* time with your *grossmudder* and *grossdaadi?*"

"*Ya!*"

"I see you had ice cream." Summer used the corner of her apron to wipe the chocolate from her *dochder's* face. She frowned at her mother as she approached. "I never got ice cream before lunch."

"You weren't my granddaughter," Marie told her, looking unrepentant. "There are different rules for grandchildren."

"You mean no rules."

Behind Marie, Carl chuckled. "We won't talk about how I sneaked you candy when you were a little girl."

"No," Summer said, "we won't."

"Maybe I should have made you pay for some of her cavities," Marie told him as she looped her arm through his.

"Howard was just as bad. Somebody had to balance out all those vegetables you insisted on her eating."

"So tell me how the sleepover went. Be honest, Mom."

"She was an angel."

"Angel," three-year-old Katie agreed, nodding and grinning. The ribbons on her *kapp* bobbed. Her big blue eyes sparkled with mischief.

She bit back a smile. "Really? She didn't tire you out?"

Carl laughed. "We went to bed five minutes after she did." Summer glanced over just in time to see Katie pluck a carrot from the basket beside her and raise it to her lips. "*Nee*, Katie. We have to wash it first."

"Let's just go do that," Carl said, lifting Katie and carrying her toward the house.

"He loves having a grandchild as much as I do," Marie said as she watched him walk away. "Need some help?"

"I was thinking of taking a break."

A shadow fell over Summer. "And I was just coming to make sure that you did." Abram held out his hand.

Summer looked up at her tall, handsome *mann* and took it gratefully. "I was wondering if I was going to have to call you to help me up." She frowned as she pressed a hand to the apron covering her abdomen. This was no longer a baby bump. It was now a small mountain. "But I'm afraid you'll need a team of six horses to pull me up." She sighed and shook her head. "I'm so big and I have two months to go."

Abram laughed and held out both hands. "I think I can manage to help you up."

"I feel huge."

He kissed her hand. "You're beautiful. But you shouldn't be out here working so hard when it's this hot."

"I'll come help you until everything is harvested," Marie said as she fell into step beside them on the way to the house. "And don't you start fussing that I'm not up to it. I've never felt better."

Summer reached out a hand to squeeze her mother's. She did indeed look healthy and happy. Her skin glowed and she'd put on the weight she'd lost. "I'm so glad." It had been a long, hard battle against Lyme disease, but Marie had won.

"But you." Marie shook her head. "I remember being pregnant in late summer. It was so hard. But then I had this beautiful baby girl. And named her Summer."

Tears rushed into Summer's eyes as their gazes met. "That's so sweet."

Marie opened the kitchen door and waited for Summer to walk inside. "You two wash up, sit down, and I'll fix us all something cold to drink."

"We already made them," Carl announced with a big grin. "Isn't that right, Katie?"

"*Ya, Grossdaadi!*" She held out a glass of lemonade to her mother.

"And this is for my beautiful wife," Carl said, handing Marie a glass.

She laughed and gave him a quick peck on the cheek. "What a big flirt."

Summer eased herself into a chair and sighed. She sipped the lemonade and found herself smiling.

"*Gut, Mamm?*"

"Very *gut*," she assured her daughter.

"She got a little carried away with the sugar," Carl murmured. "Your little one moves fast."

"Don't I know it."

"Cookie, *Daedi?*"

Abram glanced over at her then shook his head. "Too close to lunch. After."

Katie frowned. "Before."

"After."

She sighed. "After." She finished her sippy cup and set it down. "*Grossdaadi* read me a story?"

"Sure, we can do that."

She slid from her chair and ran into the other room for a book.

"One book," Marie cautioned. "We have a doctor's appointment in town, remember?"

"Plenty of time."

Katie staggered back into the room with an armful of books. She frowned and looked baffled when Marie laughed.

"What's funny, *Grossmudder?*"

"Nothing, sweet girl. Nothing."

Summer rested her hands in her lap, closed her eyes, and smiled as the *boppli* inside her moved.

Abram dropped down into the chair beside her. "You *allrecht?*"

She took his hand and placed it on her abdomen. "*Boppli's* moving. It won't be much longer before we see him or her." She'd told the sonogram technician she and Abram didn't want to know the baby's sex. They wanted to be surprised. Maybe it was old-fashioned of them but that was the way it was. They'd done the same thing when she was carrying Katie.

Her hand closed over his and their gazes met. In his eyes she saw all the love she'd ever hoped to see. Joy filled her, warm as summer sunshine.

Summer became aware that her mother was moving about the kitchen, getting bread from the breadbox and a plastic container of sliced meats and cheeses from the refrigerator.

"I can fix lunch," she began.

"You just sit, it'll take no time at all. I'll be finished before Carl finishes with Katie's book."

So she sat with Abram and watched her mother fix lunch while the man who'd been like a second father to her after hers died read a story to Katie, and she thought how much her life had changed in just a short time. How she wished her father could be here. She remembered sitting with him in his last days . . .

He'd looked down at her. "I love you, Summer. Promise me you'll always be my little girl."

He loved to say that.

"I promise."

"Promise me you'll always do what makes you happy."

"I promise."

"Promise me you'll always do the right thing."

"I promise."

"Promise me you'll keep God first in your life."

"I promise."

"And promise me you'll always look after your mother if I'm not there to do it."

She'd told him he'd always be there. Now she knew that wasn't true—she'd watched her mother struggle with a serious illness and despaired that she wouldn't overcome it. But she had and now she had a husband to look after her. One Summer loved like a father.

"Where did you go?" Abram whispered in her ear.

Summer turned to him, smiled, and told him about the conversation she'd had with her late father. "I'm so lucky to have all of you."

"It wasn't luck. It was God's plan," Abram said simply. "It was God's plan."

She couldn't have agreed more.

Glossary

aenti—aunt

allrecht—all right

boppli—baby

bruder—brother

daed—dad

danki—thank you

dat—father

dawdi haus—a small home added to or near the main house into which the farmer moves after passing the farm and main house to one of his children

Deitsch—Pennsylvania German

dochder—daughter

eldres—parents

Englisch, Englischer—what the Amish call a non-Amish person

fraa—wife

freind—friend

grossdaadi—grandfather

grossdochder—granddaughter

grossmudder—grandmother

guder mariye—good morning

gut—good

gut-n-owed—good evening

haus—house

hochmut—pride

hungerich—hungry

kapp—prayer covering or cap worn by girls and women

kind, kinner—child, children

kumm—come

lieb—love, a term of endearment

maedel—young single woman

mamm—mom
mann—husband
mudder—mother
nacht—night
nee—no
onkel—uncle
rumschpringe—time period when teenagers are allowed to experience
    the *Englisch* world while deciding if they should join the church
schul—school
schur—sure
schwaegem—sister-in-law
schweschder—sister
sohn—son
wilkumm—welcome
wunderbaar—wonderful
ya—yes
zwillingbopplin—twins

Discussion Questions

Spoiler alert! Please don't read before completing the book as the questions contain spoilers!

1. Why are you interested in reading about the Amish?

2. Summer has dreamed about the Amish. Why do you think that is?

3. Summer has a part-time job doing the same thing that her father did. Have you followed in the same career path or interests as a parent?

4. Abram and his friend Wayne are different in some ways. Why do you think they are still friends?

5. Many Amish own a farm and some *Englisch* think it would be interesting to have one. Do you? Why or why not?

6. The Amish are not all the same just as Christians are not. The Amish in Lancaster County, Pennsylvania, are allowed to own cell phones while other Amish communities forbid them. Do you think cell phones are a positive change for the Amish?

7. Summer has promised her late father that she will always look out for her mother and worries when she becomes ill. Have you had to care for a parent?

8. Do you believe people of differing religions should marry? What challenges do you see them facing? What positives?

9. The Amish believe God sets aside a partner for them. Do you?

10. What is your favorite Christmas memory?

11. Amish young people get to experience *Englisch* life during a period called *rumschpringe*. While some youth use it as a chance to break out of the strict rules of the Amish community, most do not. Do you think teens of either culture need a period of unrestricted time to mature?

12. Have you made a decision others disagreed with but you felt was right for you? What was it and how did it turn out for you?

Amish Chow Chow

4 cups lima beans
4 cups green string beans
2 cups yellow wax beans
4 cups cabbage, chopped
4 cups cauliflower florets
4 cups carrots, sliced
4 cups celery, cut in chunks
4 cups red and green peppers, chopped
4 cups small white onions
4 cups cucumbers, cut in chunks
4 cups corn kernels
4 cups granulated sugar
3 cups apple cider vinegar
1 cup water
1 tablespoon pickling spices
1 tablespoon mustard seed
1 tablespoon celery seed

Cook each vegetable separately until tender but not mushy. When each is finished, lift out of hot water with a slotted spoon and rinse with cold water to stop its cooking and preserve its color. Drain, then layer into a large dishpan. Combine the sugar, vinegar, water, and spices in a 15-quart stockpot (or do half a batch at a time in an 8-quart kettle) and bring to a boil. Make sure the sugar is fully dissolved, then spoon all the vegetables (or half of them, depending upon the size of the kettle) into the syrup and boil for 5 minutes. Stir gently, only to mix the vegetables well. Spoon carefully into hot sterilized jars and seal.

Chocolate Zucchini Cake

2 cups flour
1 teaspoon salt
1/4 teaspoon baking powder
2 teaspoons baking soda
1 tablespoon cinnamon
4 tablespoons unsweetened cocoa
3 eggs
2 cups sugar
1 cup oil
1 tablespoon vanilla
2 cups zucchini, grated, peeled or unpeeled; squeeze dry
1 cup walnuts or pecans

Preheat oven to 350 degrees and lightly spray 13×9 pan with cooking spray. Mix all ingredients in a large bowl until well combined. Pour into pan and bake 50–60 minutes or when a toothpick inserted in the middle comes out clean. Cool completely.

Blueberry Zucchini Cake

2 cups finely shredded and drained zucchini
3 eggs, lightly beaten
1 cup vegetable oil
1 tablespoon vanilla extract
2 1/4 cups white sugar
3 cups all-purpose flour
1 teaspoon salt
1 teaspoon baking powder
1/4 teaspoon baking soda
1 pint fresh blueberries (you can reserve a few for garnish if so desired)

Preheat oven to 350 degrees. Butter and flour two 8-inch round cake pans. Place grated zucchini in a clean dish towel. Squeeze until most of the liquid comes out. You want 2 total cups of shredded zucchini after draining. Set aside. In a large bowl, beat together the eggs, oil, vanilla, and sugar. Fold in the zucchini. Slowly add in the flour, salt, baking powder, and baking soda. Gently fold in the blueberries. Divide batter evenly between prepared cake pans. Bake 35–40 minutes, or until a knife inserted in the center of a cake comes out clean. Cool 20 minutes in pans, then turn out onto wire racks to cool completely. Frost with lemon buttercream. Serves 10–12.

Lemon Buttercream Frosting

1 cup butter, room temperature
3 1/2 cups confectioners' sugar
1/8 teaspoon salt
2 tablespoons lemon juice, about 1 lemon
1 teaspoon vanilla extract
zest of 1 lemon

Beat butter, sugar, and salt until well mixed. Add lemon juice and vanilla and continue to beat for another 3–5 minutes or until creamy. Fold in zest. Makes approximately 4 cups frosting.

Seeds of Hope

HARVEST OF HOPE SERIES

Seeds of Hope is the first book in the
Harvest of Hope series. Here's the
first chapter of the book. Enjoy!

One

Miriam Troyer guided the horse-drawn buggy into the lane that led to John Byler's home. She was lost in the beauty of the scene that unfolded before her. Wind ruffled the tall grasses about to be cut into hay. Livestock grazed in a pasture. The farmhouse itself was a rambling white wooden home that had been added on to by generations of Bylers as the family grew. The old house was the embodiment of Amish peace and tranquility.

John Byler sat on his front porch, his gray head bent as he wrote in a notebook.

How John loved writing letters, Miriam thought fondly. She hated to interrupt him, but when he glanced up and smiled at her, she could tell he didn't regard her dropping by as an unwelcome interruption.

And it wasn't just because he knew she brought baked goods. He had become a good friend, someone who listened and encouraged and offered wise counsel. They were a generation apart, but age had never made a difference in their friendship.

She waved and called for him to stay where he was, but he was already up and making his way to her. He was limping more than usual today. It had rained earlier and she knew his arthritis always acted up worse then. It had become more and more of a problem the last year or so. Still, he was determined to keep going each day and take care of his farm. "If you stop doing, you'll stop being," he'd say when she worried about him.

"It's *gut* to see you, Miriam."

"You too, John."

He reached for the handle of the basket in her hands.

"I'm not some frail *maedel*," she told him. "I can carry this. I put it in the buggy."

They had their usual tug-of-war, which he won like always.

He grinned and laugh lines crinkled around his eyes, the color of faded denim. "We should help each other, shouldn't we?"

"*Ya*," she said with a sigh and a smile. His gentle charm and courtesy reminded her of her *grossdaadi* who had passed years ago.

Both qualities had seemed to be lacking in the men she'd dated.

He set the basket on a small wooden table on the porch and waved a hand at one of the rocking chairs flanking it. "Do you have time to visit a bit?"

Now it was her turn to grin. "And when, I ask you, don't I have time to visit with you? So, how was your day?"

"*Gut*." He gestured at the pad of paper and pen on the table. "Just sitting here writing my *grosssohn*."

She didn't need to ask which one. John had only one. Only one *sohn* as well. Most Amish families had many *kinner* and thanked God for them. John had never complained that he hadn't had a larger family with his *fraa*, long dead now. But he reveled in the times his *grosssohn* visited.

Mark had visited many summers after he turned fourteen. Apparently he'd wanted to know his *grossdaadi*, and his *dat* had decided to let him. He and John had become close.

Miriam had been twelve and just noticing boys. And over the years, she'd developed a fanciful crush on Mark—one that no one but God knew about.

Mark was so different from anyone she knew. She'd been intrigued the first time he'd visited. Years before he became a high-powered attorney, he seemed to carry himself with a confidence the boys she knew lacked. He was outspoken too and had often had spirited discussions with John about the Amish faith and God.

He stood out with his dark good looks too. His black hair shone like the wing of a raven when he stood hatless out in the fields with his *grossdaadi*. His eyes were a vivid blue, stronger in color and more direct than the older man's. She hadn't seen him for a year, but the memory of his face was as vivid as if he were standing right here in front of her.

"Miriam?"

She realized she'd been daydreaming and felt warmth flood her face. "Hmm? Oh, sorry, I was just thinking of an errand *mudder* wanted me to run on the way home."

"You don't have to leave already, do you?"

"*Nee.* So, you were saying you're writing to Mark."

He sighed and leaned back in his chair. "*Ya.* I've asked him if he's coming home to help with harvest."

"He usually does."

John rested his hands on his knees. "The last time he wrote me, he sounded busy with his work at the law firm. But I'm needing his help more than usual." He rubbed at his knee with his big, gnarled hand. "I don't know how much longer I can take care of things. The doctors tried some of the new medicines on my arthritis, but I'm not getting much relief."

John seldom talked about his age and his increasing problems with his arthritis, but Miriam and her *mudder* and other women in the community had noticed and tried to help out by bringing him food. The men in the community helped with chores too.

"I just wish . . ." he trailed off.

"You just wish?" she prompted as he gazed off into the distance.

"I wish there was someone to hand it over to."

"Hand it over?" She wasn't following him.

"My *sohn* didn't want the farm. And I doubt Mark wants it."

She felt her heart leap at the thought and cautioned herself not to show her reaction. "Mark has his work in Philadelphia."

John nodded and looked sad. "I know."

He sat staring out at the fields he'd worked for more years than she'd lived. "There have been Bylers working on this farm for generations. All the way back to the time the Amish first came to Pennsylvania."

"So you've said."

"I don't want it to stop with me." He spoke with such passion she could only stare at him.

"I don't want it to stop with me," he said again, softer now, and he lapsed into silence.

"So you're writing to Mark about harvest?" she prompted again.

John seemed to gather himself and stared at her. "*Ya*," he said. "*Ya*. I was just finishing it." He reached for the pad of paper on the table, ripped the top page off, folded it, and tucked it into an envelope. After dashing the address across it—from memory—he looked at her. "All I need is a stamp."

Miriam held out her hand. "I have one in my purse. I can mail that for you. I'm driving into town."

He handed it to her. "*Danki*, Miriam." He smiled at her. "Mark is a smart young man. A caring one. He'll come and we'll talk."

She bit her lip, worried that John would be disappointed. Mark had a busy, successful career in the *Englisch* world. The last few years he'd visited, he'd driven a fancy, expensive *Englisch* car and worn fancy, expensive clothes. And although he appeared to love his *grossdaadi*, he was the last man she'd expect to be interested in a farm.

John, always the gentleman, walked Miriam back to her buggy, even though she could tell the effort of walking was hard on him.

"Don't forget the basket," she reminded him as she climbed into the buggy. "There's baked chicken and potato salad and a big baked potato and a jar of the chow chow we made today. And a sweet treat that'll be a surprise."

"You make me a happy man," he said. "I know you worry I don't eat right."

She knew his arthritis made it harder for him to take care of the farm, and what Amish man really liked to cook? But she wasn't going to say either of those things. "I love visiting with you and talking. You know that."

He smiled. "You make me happy when you visit."

She sincerely hoped Mark would make him happy and visit soon too.

"Mark!"

Mark Byler turned as his assistant rushed up to him. "This just came in the morning mail. I saw it was from your grandfather and knew you'd want to take it with you."

Mark took the letter and slid it into his briefcase as he stepped into the elevator. Judge Patterson insisted on attorneys being on time, so he wasn't about to risk stopping to read the letter right now.

He made the short trip to the courthouse, found a parking space, and headed inside. The district attorney was right behind him and both were relieved to see that they'd arrived in plenty of time.

His client was brought in a few minutes later. Mark watched as the man's leg chain was secured to a leg of the table where they sat. He could literally hear his client's nervousness as the chain rattled faintly.

"Chill," he whispered. "Everything's going to be fine."

"I hope you're right."

"I'm always right." Mark figured it wasn't arrogance if it were true.

Mark focused on Dan's closing statement, noting on a yellow legal pad an adjustment to a point he'd make in his own closing statement. When Dan finally finished, Mark was ready.

He walked slowly to the jury box, taking his time, making eye contact with each of the men and women sitting in it, measuring his words.

His favorite law professor had always said that cases were won by careful, steady work, relentless study, investigation, and the slow, careful laying out of the defense in steps the often tired and over-whelmed jurors could understand.

"And so, ladies and gentlemen of the jury, that's why you should acquit my client," he said. He made a final eye contact with each of them, nodded, then walked back to his seat at the defendant's table.

"Man, that was good," Maurice whispered in his ear as he sat beside him.

Maybe so, but Mark couldn't help noticing the poor man still shook as he sat beside him. He'd sat there shaking throughout most of the trial. The guy was built like a linebacker, yet he trembled like the frailest client Mark had ever defended. He was accused of being in a gang and gunning down a rival. Mark hadn't believed it from the time he met the gentle giant.

He hoped the jury would believe in Maurice's innocence as well.

Two hours later the case went to the jury.

"This is gonna be a quick one," Dan said as they rode down in the courthouse elevator. He wore a hangdog expression like he always did while the jury was out. He shot a sharp look at Mark. "Want to bet on the verdict?"

Mark shook his head.

"I'm going to the coffee shop. No point in leaving," Dan said.

And since Dan was almost always right about how long the jury took to deliberate, Mark replied, "I'll join you."

"Your treat?"

"Sure." Mark had a good feeling about this one, but wasn't one to gloat.

Two women who were assistants to Judge Patterson got on the elevator. One smiled flirtatiously at him. He tried not to notice. It wasn't a good thing to get too friendly with the staff from the judge's office. Someone could yell conflict of interest.

Besides, he was happy with Tiffany Mitchell, his fiancée. Well, happy wasn't exactly the right word—more like content. Tiffany was a little high-maintenance, but she was beautiful, smart, and would make a great wife for an up-and-coming lawyer. Tiffany was a little wound up from all the wedding planning, but she hadn't become a bridezilla, and he'd felt a little distance between them lately.

They got out at the ground floor and headed for the coffee shop.

Dan checked his watch. "I figure we have time to split a BLT, if you're hungry."

"Sure." They ordered the sandwich and two coffees and found a table.

They'd just finished the BLT and Mark was thinking about

getting out his grandfather's letter when they got the phone calls to return to the courtroom.

Dan stood and tossed his paper napkin onto his plate. "Here we go."

The courtroom was buzzing with excitement. Reporters lined the first row of seats. Behind them were members of the families and behind them, the regular contingent of senior citizens who attended trials as a form of entertainment.

Officers brought Maurice to his seat and secured his restraints. The chains shook even more than they had that morning. "A short time out's good, right? I heard the shorter the deliberation, the better the verdict."

"I'm afraid that's not always true."

Maurice gave him a desperate look. "Lie to me, man. Tell me a jury coming back so quick means they found me innocent. Otherwise, I'm gonna pass out right here."

The bailiff called for all to rise as the judge walked in. He gave his traditional stern look at the assemblage and recited his admonition for the courtroom to remain calm when the verdict was announced.

"Have you reached a verdict?" the judge asked the jury.

"Yes, your Honor," the foreman said.

The bailiff took the square of paper from him and carried it to the judge. Mark stood with his client and waited for the judge to read the paper.

"Is this your decision?"

"Yes, your Honor."

"On the charge of first-degree murder," the judge read aloud, "not guilty."

"No! You killed my son!" a man shouted.

Mark turned and saw two officers wrestling the father of the victim to the ground. He screamed threats as they dragged him from the courtroom.

Maurice stood still for a moment, then threw his arms around Mark and hugged him so tightly Mark was afraid he was going to end up with cracked ribs.

Grinning, he extricated himself and the officer in charge of security went to work releasing Maurice from his leg chains.

"There's some paperwork and then you're free," Mark told Maurice, slapping him on his shoulder.

"Can't thank you enough, man."

"No problem. Now I don't want to see you again, right?"

"You won't. Like I said, I gave up that life years ago."

Mark grabbed his briefcase, accepted the grudging congratulations from Dan, and headed out of the courthouse. He paused briefly in his car to text the verdict to Lani, his paralegal and assistant.

A brass bell clanged the minute he walked into the law offices. It was the celebratory greeting for an attorney when he or she won a case. Mark thought it was kind of silly, but it was a tradition and law firms loved tradition. Especially staid, well-established firms like this one.

His boss came out of his office to clap him on the back and other attorneys joined him.

Mark finally extricated himself and went to see if his assistant had any messages for him. He took them into his office, scanned quickly, and then settled back in his chair. He was tired—a good kind of tired. Satisfied tired. There had been a lot of long days and long nights preparing for this and other cases.

"You look exhausted," Lani said.

"Gee, thanks."

"Think about taking some personal time soon. You've earned it."

He gave her a cool stare. She just laughed. Ten years older than he, she'd been with the firm for a long time and wasn't intimidated by any of the attorneys. He was lucky she chose to work with him. She knew what he wanted and produced it.

"Let's just say the rest of us could use the break," she said as she collected the stack of work. "I'll get these out right away."

Mark glanced at the clock on the wall and decided to quit for the day. For once he didn't have anything to take home and review, due mostly to Lani's usual good work of keeping his calendar clear for a day or so after a case expected to wrap. He'd been careful not to plan anything with Tiffany so he could go home, find something to eat, have a glass of wine if he wanted, and relax.

His condo was blessedly quiet and spotless. The cleaning service had been there that day. When he looked in his Sub-Zero refrigerator, he found a couple takeout containers that looked like they were growing science experiments. The inside of the freezer was an arctic wasteland. He sighed. It looked like he was ordering in one more night. Tomorrow he'd make himself shop for groceries. But tonight it wasn't going to happen.

He rooted through the takeout menus in a kitchen drawer and ordered his favorite baked spaghetti and Greek salad, then changed into sweats while he waited for delivery.

Later, he sat eating his solitary dinner on the coffee table in the elegantly decorated living room—done with the help of an expensive interior decorator—and watched ESPN.

Such was the life of a successful big-city attorney, he thought wryly.

Reaching into his briefcase, he pulled out the letter from his grandfather and ripped it open. "Dear Mark," he read. "I need to see you to talk about an important matter. Can you come to the farm?"

That was it. Two sentences. Well, one sentence and one question. His grandfather was a man of few words, but this was very terse even for him.

He frowned. Was his grandfather ill? He pulled out his cell phone and dialed, then frowned again when the call went to voicemail. The call was being recorded out in the phone shanty, but who knew when his grandfather would check the answering machine. Phone calls weren't a high priority in his grandfather's world, unlike Mark's own smartphone-driven life.

A couple hours later, Mark lay awake in bed, unable to sleep. He'd been in his line of work too long. His imagination ran wild with worry about the reason his grandfather wanted to see him.

He needed to go visit him right away.

About the Author

Barbara Cameron is a gifted storyteller and the author of many best-selling Amish novels. Harvest of Hope is her new three-book Amish series from Gilead Publishing.

Twice Blessed, Barbara's two-novella collection, won the 2016 Christian Retailing's Best award in the Amish fiction category. Two of her other novellas were finalists for the American Christian Fiction Writers (ACFW) awards. She is the first winner of the Romance Writers of America (RWA) Golden Heart Award. Three of her fiction stories were made into HBO/Cinemax movies.

Although Barbara is best known for her romantic and Amish fiction titles, she is also a prolific nonfiction author of titles including *101 Ways to Save Money on Your Wedding* and two editions of *The Everything Wedding Budget Book*.

Barbara is a former high school teacher and has also taught workshops and creative writing classes at national writing conferences as well as locally. She currently teaches English and business communication classes as an adjunct instructor for the online campus of a major university.

Barbara enjoys spending time with her family and her three "nutty" Chihuahuas. She lives in Jacksonville, Florida.